WISHES AND CHOICES

MYTHRAL'S WISH

D.B. Thomas

Published by St. Petersburg Press
St. Petersburg, FL
www.stpetersburgpress.com

Design and composition by St. Petersburg Press and Isa Crosta
Cover art by Justin Groom

Paperback ISBN: 978-1-964239-01-9
eBook ISBN: 978-1-964239-02-6

First Edition

WISHES
AND CHOICES

MYTHRAL'S WISH

PROLOGUE

I am an enigma trapped within a fur coat. You may address me as Cat. That's Cat with a capital C and no preceding article. If you would prefer an adjective in lieu of a noun, try Inscrutable. I define myself as such because, to me, time and space are choices—not limits. Within all space and time, I can go whenever and wherever I choose, merely by wishing it so.

Out of great sufferance and kindness on my part, I come to caution you, curious reader, about wishes and choices. Both have consequences: some good, some bad, some embarrassing, some terrible, and a few unbelievably fulfilling. Even more significant, I must warn you, every choice or action has a ripple effect. Some might call this the "butterfly effect," where small actions result in greater impacts later in time.

Before those of you with quick wit think to neutralize my warnings by suggesting you'll just avoid making choices, I have sad news. When faced with any choice—small, large, difficult, or impossible—doing nothing is itself a choice. Willful inaction, or avoidance, has consequences that ripple through time. And as you will see from my story, some ripples can impact the past. I probably should not have mentioned that so early in this tale. But since I have mentioned changing the past, let me digress briefly.

You may think time moves from the past to the present and then on to the future in a constant and orderly fashion. Wrong! The Time-Path we all travel is a complex, intertwining, overlapping, nearly infinite loop where time is nonlinear. Confused? Your math and science teachers probably would be as well. I mention this up front only to encourage you to keep an open mind when these concepts appear in the story. For proof, think about times when you've had the feeling that what you are experiencing has already happened to you, but it could not have. Or when you have the feeling something will happen in the future, and then it does. Finally, how often has a situation or person seemed familiar but the perspective is all wrong, like viewing it from a different angle? These occurrences prove time is multidimensional. The past and future can happen at the same moment, but in different dimensions. The overlapping Time-Path can bleed through at certain intersections, allowing for glimpses of the past and the future. Too much, too soon? Just keep that open mind.

Getting back to our topic of wishes and choices. My wish is to discover my origin. From whence I came and how, I cannot recall. My choice is to traverse as many worlds, universes, and stops along my Time-Path as possible in search of answers. My choices have had consequences and ripple effects, as my tale will tell. However, as my personal story would leave you unsatisfied by its lack of an acceptable ending, I have elected to tell you about the wishes and choices of three individuals: a good wizard, an evil wizard, and a young girl caught between them. All three seek to achieve their primary wish. To do so, they must face their own weaknesses and flaws while struggling with impossible choices. They will strive to overcome fate—known as the Law of Equilibrium—by free will choices. Again, I digress too much. These complex mechanics of the universe will be revealed later.

Our choices, especially the difficult and impossible ones, are the mileposts that mark our journey on the Time-Path. Sometimes the difficulty lies in a physical challenge or our appearance or capabilities. Can I run fast enough to make the team? Am I strong enough to stand up to that bully? Do my feelings about my looks hold me back?

However, moral dilemmas can bring to light who we are and what we value. Unlike some physical challenges, personal quandaries arise in all our lives to test our character and dare us to do the right thing. You may say, "The right thing isn't always clear." I'll agree, it certainly isn't always easy. I have some more bad news for you: The right thing is, more often than not, the harder choice. Doing the right thing requires integrity and courage.

Our story begins, as all really good tales do, long ago in a realm far, far away. That realm was devoid of advanced science and industry. Such things were not needed. The realm was infused with magic at its core. Like all diverse societies, they had the usual minor conflicts, and a few major ones. There was only this one realm. Until there wasn't.

Society's norms seldom were violated, at least not seriously. The values and principles of the vast majority, and the power of the Council of WISDOM, served to keep those with evil tendencies in check. Until they didn't.

Only a few could recall tales about the Wizard Wars—the ultimate battle of good versus evil, or so they thought at the time. After the Wizard Wars, good magic again was strong within the realm. Until it wasn't.

After many generations, the Council of WISDOM had grown older and complacent. The dark wizards, on the other hand, were younger, stronger, and very active. Dark magic was gaining the upper hand. The weak and innocent were being cruelly used. This, then, was how the one realm came to be split into three. The worst of the dark wizards would be exiled to Realm Three. Those without magic would be tucked away in safety and ignorance into Realm One. The eternal struggle between good and evil would continue in Realm Two, minus the worst offenders and the innocents.

Now, six years later, critical flaws in this Three-Realm solution threaten the Realms' undoing and the return of dark magic. Mythral and Kit must confront a series of difficult, sometimes impossible choices to save the Realms. One false step and evil wins.

I happened upon the Realms during my travels. I was fascinated by their evolving approach to managing magic and those who abuse it. I stayed a while and even became part of their story. Mythral's primary wish is to save the Realms from the rising threat that dark magic will plunge the Realms into chaos and a new world order where the mantra is "might makes right." The dark wizard MorKano's wish is to destroy Mythral and the Council of WISDOM, thereby taking control of the Realms. Kit, Mythral's new protégée, innocently wishes for an adventure and maybe a bit of romance. (Another lesson of note: Be careful what you wish; it might come true.)

You may well ask yourself how you would deal with the impossible choices our two heroes must face. Those among you possessing courage will make your own choices before reading on to discover their choices, consequences, and ripple effects.

I'll be popping in and out of the story as needed to help our heroes and to clarify for you some confusing facts about the structure and mechanics of the universe.

CHAPTER 1

THE END (OF MYTHRAL)
[Realm Two]

Abolt of dark magic singed the black curls on Mythral's head as he dove for a nook in the wall. The bulk of the flames passed down the corridor as Mythral squeezed his six-foot frame into the restricted space. The stench of burnt hair and the odor of expended magic overwhelmed the musty dead smell of the underground passageway.

In a straight-up battle of magic, even against more than one opponent, Mythral could not be bested. The secret that made him seem invincible was known only to two other people. Well, only one, now that Vivyen was dead.

However, in the now and here, he was caught off guard. MorKano's trap had been well laid and well planned. Mythral had "sensed" the dark wizard in front of him, but the wizard behind him had been well cloaked. Mythral had been saved by his uncanny ability to sense disturbances, such as dark magic, in the fundamental harmony of the universe.

Trusting his instincts and his enhanced sensing, he reacted automatically at the very second the evil spell was unleashed. However, now he was trapped between threats at both ends of this dark and dreary corridor.

You idiot, Mythral thought—not for the first time, but very possibly for the last—as he prepared for the next assaults.

Vivyen, his murdered love, and Perci, his friend and confidant, had been most insistent. "You need an apprentice," they said. Even Cat had weighed in on the subject. But he, the Great Mythral, always was too busy.

Except for a select few confidants, he preferred his own company.

Now he was alone in the Third Realm on a dangerous and unpredictable covert mission. His morbid humor often arose at such moments. Mythral thought, *If the worst happens, at least I won't have to admit they were right.*

The recent intelligence, even if obviously planted, about MorKano's conspiracy to undo the Three Realms was too urgent. It had to be investigated. If he survived this one, he vowed to act on that apprentice thing.

But now and here, in this battle, what choice remained? If he had brought along an apprentice, he could have chosen to trust him to deal with the threat from behind. Or at least provide cover or distraction.

A complex and dangerous Translocation Spell would give away one of his best-kept secrets, and he might not have the time to safely execute that Spell.

All these thoughts flashed in a split second as he confidently uttered the Entanglement Spell, *Gonathra*, that would occupy the wizard in front. His spells never were designed to kill, only to incapacitate his enemies. Mythral, always thinking ahead, wanted to keep at least one wizard conscious to answer questions, should he escape.

While the first wizard fought against Mythral's Entanglement Spell, Mythral prayed for time. There was still the adversary behind.

Dark wizards with powerful magic rarely worked together. This was no coincidental encounter. Mythral had been led to exactly where they wanted him. And, as was his habit, he had come alone, ignoring the counsel of others. This, too, the dark wizards had anticipated.

Just as Mythral had unleashed the forward spell, he did the only thing he could: He dove back towards the nook. There was no time for a protective counter spell to defend the rear. As he dove, a Boomerang Spell formed in Mythral's mind, to turn the rear wizard's attack back upon himself.

Too late! Mid-dive for the nook, he realized the opponent behind him had anticipated his actions.

These last thoughts quickly crossed his mind as his body went rigid with pain. Death was not far off.

This death was too slow. Mythral experienced the explosion and incineration of every cell in his body. His final moments of life were expiring. His body was suffering the fate of dark magic at its worst. His final thought, *Why is she not here?* confused him.

Mythral, likely the most powerful wizard of all time, was dying. His future was ending.

He was doomed by his overconfidence and his unwillingness to trust others with any significant task or decision. It wasn't even a brilliant or glorious death—just his being outsmarted and outmaneuvered in a dark and dingy corridor in MorKano's fortress.

Perhaps a few would wonder, "Whatever happened to the Great Mythral, Wizard of the Ages?"

And then, Mythral awoke from his vision of the future.

CHAPTER 2

SHE
[Realm One]

Kit's Diary, May 2: As I sit at my window, the rose-scented evening breezes from our garden are still pleasantly cool. The frogs are in fine voice with the late afternoon rain.

I have a comfortable home, a brother who's more positive than a nuisance, foster parents who care about me, a good school, and a reasonable number of books to read. My world is good, but I am not. I'll be fourteen at the end of the summer, and in all my years I've not had one real adventure or romance. Nothing worthy of making into a story like in the books and novels.

Long ago and far away. Isn't that how the stories start? Putting a foot outside your door and stepping onto a path. Isn't that how adventures begin? I've gone outside. I go into town. But nothing happens to me. The summer will end, school will start, and I'll still be just as boring.

Other people have adventures, so why not me? I'm smart. I am stronger than most girls and a lot of the boys, even at four feet, eleven and three-quarters inches. Boys find enough interest in me, at least enough to tease me. Why do I miss all the exciting things that happen? Like when Billy disappeared down the old well and no one found him 'til the next day.

Do you need friends before you can have adventures? You certainly need another someone to have a romance. I don't have any good friends, and the only boy I really know well is my brother. Why don't I have friends? I won't tolerate bullies and liars, but that accounts for only a part of my classmates. Everyone else has friends. Why not me? Is it that I like reading and learning about things, people, and the world, instead of gossiping and joining groups? I guess I hold back too much. Maybe I should try to join some groups.

So, where does all this leave me?

I have some good characteristics. I read a lot and learn quickly. I know immediately what is right and what is not—I think. I really can tell when people are lying to me. But I have no special talents or skills. No friends and no adventures in all my years. Unless you count getting lost in the woods. Wait. There was that large blue-gray cat that showed me the way home. He was very odd. He seemed to know I was lost. Does that count as an adventure? Why do I assume it was a he?

There certainly hasn't been any romance. Heck, by the time Juliet Capulet was my age, she had experienced romance, drama, marriage, and death. Not a good ending, but definitely a real adventure.

I keep this diary, but I'd be embarrassed if anyone read it, and not because of what is in it.

Am I deficient, incomplete, because I have no real parents? Or, did my parents abandon me because I'm flawed? There must be something wrong with me, and with my brother, too. Toro and I both avoid interacting with others our age, or any age, for that matter. That must be it. There is something wrong with the two of us, and our parents just couldn't face it. Or maybe they had problems as well, which is where Toro and I get ours from. Maybe it isn't our fault. Maybe it is. I wish I knew about our parents, good or bad. Why can't I remember my parents? My last birthday is perfectly clear. I remember the cake and my presents. The Greenes often have told us how happy they were when the orphanage said there were two new children needing fostering. Why can't I remember the orphanage? And it's not just me. Neither Toro nor I can remember anything before my last birthday.

I need a plan. I have the whole summer ahead. Before I turn fourteen, I need at least one good adventure. Tomorrow, and every day after, I'll step out my front door onto the road, and when I get to the woods, I'll take a new path away from things and places that are safe and comfortable. And I'll try to make my foster parents tell me what they know about my real parents. And maybe I'll ask about town records. Somebody must know something.

CHAPTER 3

A SENSE OF THINGS TO COME
[𝕽ealm 𝕿wo]

The secret cellar of Mythral's bookstore in Realm Two was frigid, and he was exhausted. His robes were soaked. He uncurled his long legs, working out the cramps as he went.

What he had just seen—rather, experienced—was his future. Sensing into the future was a gift very few wizards possessed and even fewer had mastered. Mythral also possessed the ability to tell when a thing or person was false or evil. With those gifts, the future, and sometimes the correctness or incorrectness of a future choice, would be revealed to him. Choices would ring true or false against the fundamental harmony of the universe.

Mythral's sudden withdrawal from this planned excursion into his future was an automatic defense of his mind and body to avoid death. What he had sensed was his reality, or to be more accurate and complex, a future that was happening simultaneously with his present but on a different part of the Time-Path loop. The nonlinear nature of time allowed for such bleed-throughs of the past and the future into the present moment. These bleed-throughs allowed for events such as premonitions, déjà vu, or recollections of past lives.

Death would have claimed him but for this automatic wake-up defense. That dream death would have caused his mind and body to die in the now and here. In simple terms, he would have died in his bed, in the present, from a Killing Spell uttered in his future. Only the Recall Before Death Spell had saved him in the now and here. Saving himself in the future was another matter entirely.

No one fully understood the specifics of "sensing," and the "Time-Path," or how they fit into the workings of the universe. Mythral, however, had unearthed books and lecture notes left behind in the old, now-forbidden Schools of Magic. These mostly forgotten relics remained after the Wizard Wars. Only a few individuals, such as Mythral's mentor Galapas, could recall any details of the schools and the wars.

Even at a young age, Mythral was the most skilled and strongest wizard Galapas had ever trained. Spellcasting had come easily to Mythral. Maybe too easily. He intuitively knew the right words for the needed spell. The proper choice at each critical moment. Yet, it had taken Mythral nearly three days of extreme effort and concentration to slip past the defenses and curses around that first School of Magic. He swore to Perci that the school was actively thwarting his efforts.

The schools' wealth of lost and forgotten knowledge had astounded Mythral. He immediately recognized the danger such knowledge and spells would generate in the hands of dark wizards. Thus, closing and cursing these schools clearly had been necessary for the realm's safety.

Such schools had marked the beginning of a downward spiral leading to a most horrific end-- the Wizard Wars. These wars pitted the worst of the dark wizards against the Council of WISDOM and all others who stood in their way. Those dark wizards sowed anarchy and chaos, by which they sought to control the realm.

The Council of WISDOM (which stood for Wizards in Service, Decency of Magic) had been created long ago as a roadblock to the dark uses of magic. In a world controlled by dark magic, power and might would rule the day.

Mythral shook his head to clear away his reminiscing. Too many steps on that path into the past would lead him to reflect on how he came to be alone. Vivyen would have rescued him from such a life, had she lived. Perci did what he could. And Cat was always a distraction and a source of intrigue. Beyond Perci and Cat, Mythral filled his days with duty to the Council and fighting dark magic. Often since Vivyen's death Perci would find Mythral in meditation. Mythral sought solace and calm by joining with the vastness of the universe. Not much of a life, when you think about it.

Mythral faced a real and deadly problem now. Or, more accurately, soon.

Most individuals' choices rarely altered the Time-Path. The Law of Equilibrium tended to assimilate unexpected changes. Free will was a complicating factor. The Time-Path, the flow of events, was designed to remain essentially unchanged as to "fundamental" events. Therefore, his chances of changing the future he had just witnessed were slim to none.

In his hurry to start this session, he had forgotten to warm up the hidden room in his bookshop cellar. People in Realm One were reputed to take "ice baths" or swim in freezing waters like polar bears. He could relate to that experience right now.

Before caring for his freezing body, he reviewed what he had sensed. Committing it to memory. The smallest detail might hold the key to altering this future. But his future must wait long enough for him to change out of his wet, icy robes.

Alter the future he must. Otherwise, a sad and painful demise awaited him. Mythral really did not want his epitaph to read, "He chose to go it alone, so he died alone."

This vision, just moments ago in his past, was his actual future. Of that, he had no doubt. But who was this missing "she" at the end of his vision, and why did that feel so important?

Years of experience had taught Mythral to feel the vibrational harmony of the universe. If things were true, they were harmonious with the rest of the universe. False visions, like false people, were discordant against the fundamental frequency of the universe.

This harmony was well known to most wizards, but it was not well understood, even by Mythral. His vision of the future rang true. His fate was all but sealed.

He wanted—no, he needed—to change that future. Yet doing so would be difficult and complex. The Law of Equilibrium prevented people like Mythral from playing with the Time-Path, even though he could sense the future.

The Law of Equilibrium would find clever ways of taking attempts to alter the Path's fundamental events and absorbing them into the existing Path. By doing so, fundamental events were preserved.

Certainly the demise of someone like Mythral would be one of those fundamental, and therefore unalterable, events. To skirt the Law of Equilibrium, Mythral needed to create what the forbidden texts called an Inherently Unbalancing Event. Texts from the old Schools of Magic reported such an event was a theoretical solution. It was a possibility that no one, to date, had proven in practice.

Once again, Mythral would have to be the one to break new ground, or else pay for his failure with an excruciatingly painful death in MorKano's trap.

CHAPTER 4

MORKANO'S PLANS
[Realm Three]

Valak is too slow. I might incinerate him out of frustration before I can pound this plan into his brain. But then, the slow ones are less of a threat to my power and plans.

Taking a deep breath to keep control, MorKano focused once more upon Valak. His eyes were drawn to the wall behind Valak, where a mirror reflected MorKano's dark eyes radiating power and determination. Even at six-two, only his dark hair and eyes were visible over Valak's head in the mirror.

Shifting his focus back to the task at hand, he took another deep breath and continued, "Mythral must pay for what he did to my brother, and this is the first step to ensure Mythral's ultimate humiliation and then death. So, pay close attention. We use the old, abandoned soap shop at the edge of town. Mythral will be expecting wizards and a trap, but he'll still enter. Once he is in the middle of the main floor, rescuing the bait, five of our wizards will attack from all four sides and from above. My spy will be carefully cloaked from Mythral and will observe how he manages to escape."

"I still don't get it. Why do all this if you expect Mythral to escape?" whined Valak.

Taking yet another deep calming breath, MorKano continued, "If they destroy Mythral, all the better. But Mythral is known to use some trick or spell to survive multiple attackers when no one else could. This trap is designed to find out how Mythral does it. Then I'll devise a better trap to defeat him."

"If Mythral knows it is a trap, why would he come?" persisted Valak.

"Because Mythral will risk anything for his pet assistant Percivale. And Mythral the Arrogant will assume he is in no real danger from any wizard in Realm Two. Earlier that same day, when we know Mythral is at the Council meeting, our wizards will entice this Perci by means of a false message from his former girlfriend, Jasmine. In the note she'll beg to see him immediately about a threat to himself and Mythral.

Once he enters the building, don't give him a chance to use any of Mythral's tricks. Stun him immediately and leave him tied up and gagged in the middle of the floor."

"Why not just kill him, to be safe, and leave his body for Mythral to find?" interrupted Valak.

"Two good reasons," MorKano answered. "First, Mythral might sense if Perci were dead, and that would ruin our trap. Second, with Perci needing to be rescued by Mythral, our wizards can escape once they break off the assault. Or, perhaps you'd like to tell them it is a suicide mission?"

"How do we get Mythral to show up?" asked Valak.

"They'll send a ransom note to Mythral's shop, demanding Mythral release two of our wizards from prison and bring them to the exchange location, alone, in one hour, or Perci dies. Which two wizards are freed does not matter, as Mythral will ignore that part. By limiting his reaction time, and with the threat to Perci, hopefully Mythral will not suspect anything more devious than this ransom. Have them use an unwitting third party to deliver the note and wait until Mythral receives it. Our spy will be watching and will alert everyone at the factory before Mythral even opens it."

"So you want these instructions sent through the gate to Realm Two by the usual method?" asked Valak.

"Yes. And tell our agents to send back a report immediately, even if it means having one of our wizards banished to Realm Three so he can bring me the information."

CHAPTER 5

PARADOX
[Realm Two]

While MorKano laid out this near-term Realm Two trap for Mythral, Mythral was seeking a method for escaping MorKano's as-yet unplanned long-term Realm Three death trap. Both men sought to shape or reshape the future.

The paradox between "free will" and "fixed fundamental events" on the Time-Path seemed unavoidable. However, the forbidden texts helped Mythral to accept, if not fully comprehend, their coexistence. The Time-Path was like a continuous loop without a true end or beginning, having endless gyrations, inter-weavings, and complexities.

Mythral got completely lost when the texts described the "multidimensional aspects" of the path. The gist was, with time and space being multidimensional, one could envision the future, the present, and the past as happening all at once. And not just that, but all in the same space—so to speak.

Mythral's early efforts to absorb these theories left him confused and with a head ready to explode. It was all unproven theory and not of much use--until now. Mythral had been ready to reject these texts when he realized the proof of the theory had always been there, staring him in the face. That which people referred to as premonitions, déjà vu, and unexplainable knowledge of past or future events was directly caused by this overlapping of time and space. Allowing for a bleed-through from one part of the Time-Path loop to another would explain it all.

But now was not the time to dwell upon old lectures and texts. What Mythral really needed was to get upstairs and find Perci. They needed to strategize possible options.

Perci, or more formally Percivale, had been with Mythral since before the Three Realms Spell. And, since the loss of his true love, Vivyen, Perci was the one person whom Mythral could trust completely.

From the latest vision, Mythral was confident his demise would not occur in the now and here. He was ordained to die in a very different place—MorKano's fortress—at some future time. Mythral was not scheduled to die today, or perhaps even tomorrow.

His strength returning, Mythral grabbed a warm cloak and headed for the worn stone spiral staircase. The heavy oak handrail sat atop wooden banisters ornately carved with magical creatures. He slowly began the winding climb from his Realm Two bookstore cellar up to the main floor, where he and Perci could review the details and options concerning his vision of the future.

A similar staircase on the opposite side of the back room of the main floor led upstairs to Mythral and Perci's sleeping rooms and other private areas.

In one alignment, these staircases exited into some ordinary-looking rooms. Upstairs were bedrooms having a view of the street below with the feel of a small English village in the Middle Ages of Realm One's history. The stairs downward led into a cellar. However, rotated 180 degrees, the staircases would exit into the concealed chambers. One of Perci's clever ideas.

Reaching the main floor, Mythral resigned himself. Certainly Cat, and likely Perci, would have much to say about his future demise. After they had finished chastising him for going alone into Realm Three, in the future, perhaps they might offer some helpful insights for the now and here.

CHAPTER 6
PERCIVALE
[Realm Two]

Before the casting of the Three Realms Spell, and her death, Vivyen and Mythral were among the few good wizards who actively sought out and opposed dark wizards. When there was just one realm, MorKano was recruiting young males to join his plan of overthrowing the Council of WISDOM. MorKano's recruitment method was simple: Join willingly or watch your family suffer.

One day it was an eleven-year-old Perci whose family was being tortured to coerce his allegiance to MorKano. MorKano's younger brother Durstin was the recruiter, along with two other dark wizards. They were so preoccupied with applying their enthusiastic recruitment tactics to Perci's parents that they failed to notice Mythral's arrival.

Before they recognized that the interloper was Mythral, they defaulted to attacking him. Mythral immediately shielded himself and assessed the situation. These dark wizards were extremely powerful. Mythral shouted to Perci, "Get your family to safety; I'll deal with these three." Turning his attention back to the assault, Mythral failed to notice that Perci had remained behind.

Perci could not bring himself to leave the battle. He had never seen powerful wizards in an all-out confrontation. This had to be the legendary Mythral. Only, something was wrong. Mythral was showing signs of fatigue and giving ground under the dark wizards' assault. It seemed to last forever, and at each moment Mythral appeared ready to fold. Perci felt compelled to help Mythral somehow, but his own magic was too weak. Entering this confrontation would be, at best, a distraction and, certainly, suicide. Yet he could delay no longer. Mythral looked nearly finished. Then a voice entered Perci's mind, quiet and strong. *I did not come here to see you die. Please just be patient and watch. It will all work out, and I'll explain later. Maybe.*

As Perci watched the one-sided battle, Mythral continued to retreat, and the dark wizards advanced. When it looked as if Mythral was spent, the three sent the last of their combined deadly magic at Mythral in one final burst, certain it would end the battle. When the smoke cleared, there was Mythral, looking as calm and fresh as if he'd just arrived. There was no fight left in the other three. They were drained and barely standing, while Mythral radiated power. Then Mythral flashed Perci that quirky little smile Perci would come to know. One minute later, the attackers were unconscious, entangled thoroughly, and ready for transport to prison.

That day six years ago, Perci joined Mythral in opposing the dark wizards. Having sensed Perci's willingness to sacrifice himself just to buy Mythral a bit of time, Mythral knew all he needed to know. Thus began their friendship. Though Perci lacked the strength of magic to become an apprentice, his quick mind and loyalty to Mythral were valuable assets. He and Perci saw eye to eye on all things magic, and not just because they were both six feet tall. Once you went beyond attitude and altitude, Perci's blond hair, fair skin, and gray-blue eyes starkly contrasted with Mythral's dark features. Perci easily comprehended the nuances of magic and understood the science of Realm One.

CHAPTER 7

THE WIZARD BEHIND THE CURTAIN
[Realm Two]

While waiting for Perci, Mythral had poured himself a cup of strong dark-roast coffee, an indulgence from Realm One. The coffee now was cold. He absentmindedly warmed it with magic while he reflected upon the Three Realms Spell and the abuses that necessitated it. "All that is necessary for the triumph of evil is for good men to do nothing."[1] Where had he heard that? Was it from Realm One or Realm Two?

Good men had acted. The spell to create the three separate realms had taken the power of two dozen of the strongest wizards to set the pieces in place. Mythral and the Council of WISDOM trusted that such a large number of strong cooperating wizards would be sufficient. No such group of dark wizards ever could cooperate to destroy the spell.

As an added benefit, only those wizards involved in casting the spell even knew of it. Everyone else just believed there always had been three realms. Individuals outside of the spellcasting had their memories replaced via a special sub-spell that backfilled the history for each realm and each individual.

This Spell of Separation was devised out of desperation during the Wizard Wars, but it never had been used. Discovering it while investigating the old Schools of Magic felt like more than just a coincidence. So, Mythral approached the Council with a similar solution: two realms out of one.

In this new realm, all those without magic would live safely removed from the dark wizards. Their memories would be altered and a backfill history created so they would not remember the magic or the other realm's existence. Each Realm would be populated only with physical items and knowledge consistent with the Backfill Spell.

In the original realm would be all the rest. There, the great majority of good wizards could focus upon confronting and defeating dark wizards without being distracted by concerns for the innocents who might be caught in the crossfire.

Mythral's plan was accepted by the Council, and all was in place for the Two Realms Spell. With mere days left before the casting, a Council member proposed an improvement. Why not have three realms instead of just two? Why not take the worst of those dark wizards and isolate them in a third realm? The Council would battle each evil wizard only a single time—"once and done" was the phrase proposed. So enticing was this enhancement that it immediately received nearly unanimous approval.

It was further decided to encourage a few good wizards to emigrate as well. Having some eyes and ears inside Realm Three was deemed prudent by the Council. To that effect, Realm Three was given enhanced scenery and heightened sensory experiences. Sights, sounds, smells and tastes all would be intensified. Any good wizard who felt strong or cunning enough to survive in Realm Three could escape society's norms and rules. There were several who accepted the challenge and went voluntarily. After the initial choices were made as to voluntary and involuntary exile to Realm Three, very little movement was required or desired. The number of dark wizards caught and banished after the Three Realms Spell had been surprisingly small.

All "official" movement between each pair of Realms (One and Two, Two and Three) was through a single gate between those Realms. Mythral, however, was not one to be limited by what others did not know or could not understand. Mythral had discovered in the Schools of Magic the old, and dangerous, spell for translocating.

Mythral could move between Realms without going through the gates. Without anyone knowing he had left or arrived, he might, and often did, appear anywhere. This had been useful on many occasions. However, he always was careful to conceal his movements when not using the gates. No one must suspect his use of a Translocation Spell.

All had gone smoothly as planned. Too smoothly for Mythral. Something was off. He knew it, but he could not name it. The Three Realms Spell, by all obvious appearances, was working well. However, problems were beginning to surface. Realm Three had become increasingly dangerous. Good wizards had vanished. Many of the voluntary Realm Three immigrants now were suspected of being MorKano supporters. Control of the gate between Realm Three and Realm Two might have been compromised by spies among those guarding it.

Evil had been left essentially unchecked in Realm Three. The lack of scrutiny created an opportunity seized by MorKano.

Mythral's twinges of doubt about the creation of this additional third realm had become more frequent. "Once and done." The theory that the worst of the dark wizards could be expelled "safely" and forgotten had seduced the Council.

Mythral had been distracted by grief over the loss of Vivyen the week prior to casting the Spell. Otherwise, he might have argued against creating three realms. Expelling the worst of the dark wizards into Realm Three and then ignoring them seemed just too easy a solution.

The right choice usually was the hard choice. Easy choices frequently turned out to be a trap, with a price paid later for taking the easy way out. Mythral was fond of demonstrating these truisms to Perci every time reality presented a new example.

Experiences, good and bad, had taught Mythral to listen very carefully to subconscious signals. However, on this occasion, the speedy and limited debate about casting the Spell to create three realms rather than two had found him totally distracted. No one had voiced any compelling reason against having that third realm.

Maybe he should have asked for an extension on the decision. It would have required only a day or so for Mythral and a few others capable of sensing into the future to explore the outcome of such a choice. "If only." A refrain Mythral had found himself uttering too often. This "ifinating," as his mentor had called it, had to stop.

Better than most, Mythral knew instincts or first impressions about things usually were right for a good and logical reason. The subconscious has access to all our prior experiences and knowledge. The mind quickly and efficiently processes all that information at the subconscious level. Everyone's brain does it. Some just do it faster and better than others. The real trick is to eliminate distractions and false motivations, and then to trust your instinct or first impression. Experience had taught Mythral to trust this extremely speedy subconscious analysis. Run that subconscious solution by his ability to read the correctness of a choice, and Mythral could come to a decision and act upon it in an instant. This ability to process data and sense correct solutions, combined with his powerful magic, made him the most powerful wizard of his time.

Mythral was unwilling to use a spell that would cause death. Instead he often combined science and magic to incapacitate his opponents.

The science unique to Realm One was a curious thing. If you thought about it logically and carefully, magic had created the non-magical Realm One and retrofitted it with a certain amount of basic scientific knowledge. Advancements from that point forward belonged to the normals of Realm One. Yet, all their science got its start from the magic Backfill Spell.

Mythral was especially proud of Vivyen's contribution of the Self-Fulfilling History Sub-Spell. Once the Three Realms came into existence, a history was created for Realm One. All that remained of magic in Realm One was fairy tales and folklore. That Backfill Spell took people, places, and actions from the original Realm and worked them into histories and myths for Realm One. The books in Mythral's Realm One Bookshop were fascinating examples. One fiction series about schools of magic and warring wizard factions was uncannily close to the Realm's own history.

Realm One, being left without any magic to speak of, continued to develop the science added by the Backfill Spell. Protected from potential abuse by wizards, Realm One's population of "normals" had no one to fear but themselves. And, Mythral reflected, they often had good reason for that fear.

However, in Realms Two and Three, the availability of magic to solve most problems had made science unnecessary. Consequently, very little scientific progress had been made in those Realms. Yet, the science of Realm One was compatible and consistent with Realms Two and Three.

Mythral's increasingly sleepless nights were haunted by thoughts of dark wizards in possession of Realm One weapons and science. Should any dark wizards ever obtain access to them, the damage they could do in Realm Two and Realm Three would be catastrophic.

The Council failed to appreciate that the gate between Realms One and Two was more important for protecting Realm Two from "science" than for protecting Realm One from magic! That Realm One science could pose a threat to Realms Two and Three was an unintended consequence of the Three Realms Spell.

CHAPTER 8

THE NEED FOR AN APPRENTICE?

[Realm Two]

While Mythral never had been near MorKano's fortress in Realm Three, he immediately recognized the location in his vision. When Perci finally did return, they reviewed what they knew.

A conspiracy was afoot to undo the Three Realms Spell. MorKano's forces and scheming were well known to be behind those efforts. How MorKano had learned about the Three Realms Spell was another mystery. Only those wizards casting the Spell would have known of its existence.

Had one of the casting wizards let something slip? Or, worse, had one of the casting wizards been a traitor from the beginning? That possibility would raise all sorts of potential problems.

What if MorKano had been aware of the Council of WISDOM's plans and placed a spy on the inside during the casting? Perci reminded Mythral that everyone on the Council of WISDOM had been vetted for many years, and surely Mythral, with his truth-reading ability, would have sensed any false wizard among them.

Mythral had been following up on information concerning the conspiracy during his near-death sensing in Realm Three. However, the specifics about that information and its source had not been part of the vision.

"Get an apprentice" were the first words out of Perci's mouth as Mythral ceased recounting his experience.

Just as Mythral had apprenticed to another great wizard, his late mentor Galapas, Mythral needed to share his knowledge and experience with the next generation. By training a skilled novice, Mythral would have someone to guard his back, or at least to warn him when danger approached from the rear.

Mythral never had been good at sharing, and he steadfastly resisted being bothered by an apprentice. However, he had kept his eye upon one particular family to see if they might provide a viable trainee.

A year earlier, he had created in Realm One a duplicate of his Realm Two Bookshop. With the shop as cover, Mythral had kept a close watch over Realm One and that family. Perhaps it was time to look in on them again.

Something in the past called his attention to this family, the Greenes. Perhaps it had been Cat who mentioned them. And, for one instant, his mind questioned whether the universe, or perhaps that darn Cat, had manipulated him in the direction of this family.

Two young siblings in foster care, a thirteen-year-old girl and her eleven-year-old brother, were the two he had been watching. Their life before foster care was hazy. That might have counted against them, but Mythral's own parents were unknown to him. Something about the two of them seemed familiar to him, as if he already knew them.

To many this might seem strange, but Mythral understood that time was not linear and such experiences of déjà vu were products of the nonlinear nature of the Time-Path. Thus, he might know them in the future, but he could feel that connection here in the past.

Besides familiarity, Mythral also sensed a strong suggestion of power and potential in these two. How and why such potential had been born into Realm One was a mystery. Perhaps traces of magic lingered among certain inhabitants; but its existence would be overlooked if the potential never was activated.

Mythral had procrastinated about bringing on an apprentice by arguing the boy had yet to come of age—generally thirteen or older, depending upon maturity. As much as he disliked the idea of training someone, his latest sensing had made the need apparent. Still, he resisted. The urgent threats of the moment demanded his full attention. Training would be a time commitment.

Why do choices always seem hard to make? Mythral reflected. *The girl might be the stronger of the two, and her age is right, but a girl apprentice is too complicated.*

In Realm Two, girls learned their magic skills from family or friends and at home. Before his well-entrenched, culturally-formed male bias kicked in, Mythral reflected on how society's traditions had left the girls in Realm Two dependent upon boys and men. The boys were better trained and more self-reliant.

No, there are too many potential pitfalls with girl apprentices. Besides, the consensus is they tend to be less dependable and less stable, although Vivyen clearly was an exception to the rule. A few female wizards have served on the Council. As Mythral reviewed the usual objections to girl apprentices, his innate sense of right and wrong pushed back against that common consensus.

He still did not understand how Vivyen had come to confront MorKano all alone, without Mythral there to support her. But he was digressing again on the subject of Vivyen. *No, the chances of another female being as exceptional as Vivyen are very remote,* he thought. *Strong magic often is found within members of the same family, but I know Vivyen's family history. There is no chance this girl and her brother could have descended from a relative of Vivyen's. I must wait for the boy, if at all possible. But how much time do I have? My demise has been foretold, but the timing is vague.*

Let me save you from any more of Mythral's internal debate. You humans really do like to waste time and energy struggling with choices where there is no viable alternative. Mythral needs an apprentice now, not a year from now. He needs the strongest, best choice, not second best. And yes, it was I who pointed him towards the girl. She is the best choice for several reasons. Some of which I cannot share with Mythral—or even with you, dear reader. After all, I don't know you well enough to trust you with my secrets.

The position of Mythral's apprentice is crucial to the future of the Realms, requiring intelligence, integrity, and honor. There is a great deal of science as well as magic to be understood. Strong intuition and imagination also could help said apprentice stay alive long enough to develop into a full wizard.

Mythral's apprentice will have access to more knowledge and power than any other wizard. Therefore, his apprentice will be at a greater risk than any other. Such knowledge and power have corrupted many wizards throughout history. Wizards' abuse of magic was the reason Mythral and the Council of WISDOM cast the Three Realms Spell.

Having decided to check in on his potential apprentice in Realm One, Mythral summoned the gate key, which allowed travel between Realms Two and One in the official way. He reserved his prized, secret

Translocation Spell for emergencies, lest its existence be suspected or deduced.

Only Mythral and Perci knew the key's location and how to use it. The key looked like a book and could not be "exposed" by magic. It responded to a cymatically generated wave or harmonic vibration. This relationship between a specific sound or vibration and a unique corresponding physical shape or pattern was established science in Realm One.

The gate key was a combination of science and magic, which reasonably ensured that no dark wizard could use it. First, Mythral drew or traced in the air a pattern that, in science, would have been created by certain cymatic vibrations.

Next, he used magic to activate the physical pattern and create a unique sound that corresponded with it. To the uninformed observer, he appeared to be summoning a tuning fork, which would generate the sound, and the book key would appear.

He put on the act so no one saw how he actually called the key with the magically activated cymatic waves. Once the book appeared and did its job, it changed into another object and hid in plain sight.

Mythral activated the gate and gained passage. When he arrived at his bookshop in Realm One, he found a very large, frowning, furry, four-footed feline waiting for him. Cat.

Mythral called him Cat because the blue-gray conundrum had refused to offer any other name. Cat, something of a mystery, possessed the ability to do active magic, which was rare among animals, and his background always had been closed off to Mythral, even through sensing.

Yet, Mythral trusted Cat. They had history. No other person or creature had projected the same sense of total harmony with the universe. When Mythral turned his sensing abilities upon Cat, the feline almost disappeared into the background frequency of the universe.

While Cat rarely involved himself in the events of the Realms, on occasion he had provided to Mythral invaluable advice and insights. Such assistance always seemed to come at a cost to Mythral's pride. On one very rare chatty occasion, Cat had implied he was four-dimensional and not bound by time.

Mythral was skeptical, although it would explain a lot. Mythral especially was curious about Cat's ability to move between Realms apparently at will.

Cat liked to toy with wizards and even with normals in Realm One.

Cat confronted Mythral in the back room of the bookshop. Faced with a large frown framed by a blue-gray ball of fur, Mythral began to greet Cat with some witticism. Mythral was particularly fond of making cat jokes, and Cat usually responded with an annoyingly smug look upon his face.

Today, Cat rudely preempted Mythral's forthcoming jest with a loud proclamation: "You need an apprentice this week! Choose, or I will!" Mythral wondered how Cat knew about his vision back in Realm Two.

Cat favored the girl, Kit, over the boy. Mythral still felt he must wait for her brother to mature enough, and he said so. Cat stared, shook his head, and stalked out of the room.

Even the best wizard has no business challenging my advice.

Someone needs to get an apprentice on board. I cannot leave it to Mythral. The fate of the Realms is at stake. Perhaps here I should mention the prophecy: "Mythral's choice will doom or save the Realms." Curiously, Mythral never speaks about the prophecy.

Not to worry. When necessary, I'll step in and give everyone a little push.

CHAPTER 9

AN APPRENTICE IS SOUGHT.

[Realm One]

Kit lived with her foster parents, the Greenes, and her younger brother, Toro, in a small house that was trim and well kept, despite its age. Its thick stone walls and sharply peaked roof had weathered many years of winter snows and summer storms rushing in from the Atlantic Ocean just to the east. Behind the house were the fields farmed by her foster family and generations before. A forest of tall, dark, old-growth trees lay to the south. The large expanse of ancient trees separated the house from the edge of the little town of Landow.

To the west and north of their farm were a few other small family farms, also owned by the same families for generations. Carrots, corn, and beans were the traditional crops. The town was just large enough to provide everything the family needed. Kit had not traveled beyond the town and the surrounding forest, seashore, and little farms.

She was very grateful to her foster parents. They took in both her and Toro when they were quite young, or so she was told. Her memories before her thirteenth birthday never had been clear. Kit, as well as Toro, did everything they could to help out around the house.

Kit's real name was Cinta Kilme. On the rare occasions she had been required to give her full name, someone always asked its origin. This was embarrassing, because she had no memory of her real parents. She had no idea why this name was chosen for her. To keep life simple, she went by "Kit."

While fully a teenager at thirteen, Kit didn't look or behave like most typical teenage girls. She didn't act bored or cool, as many of her classmates did. She was quick and smart. Although she was small and slender for her age, she was surprisingly strong and graceful. Her curly dark brown hair, sky-blue eyes, and the dimples in both cheeks reinforced the impression that she was still a child.

People tended to dismiss her because of her cute and diminutive appearance, which was a mistake she found useful or just fun on some occasions. Behind those eyes was a keen and inquisitive mind, excited by the new and unknown.

Kit wanted to learn about everything, so she spent most of her free time reading. When she wasn't exploring the woods around her or the nearby shore, she usually could be found on the window seat of her bedroom with her feet tucked under her while reading a book and oblivious to the world. Her favorite books were about adventures and mysteries, real and fictional. Romance never was the main theme of her books, yet it often was in the background.

While she dreamed of travel to exotic places, she accepted it was unlikely. Even less likely was finding true love in her little town or in her future.

Kit also spent time trying to encourage her younger brother, Toro. He was smart but also quiet and a little shy. His lack of interests and direction was a bit confusing and frustrating to someone like Kit. She hoped his newly discovered interest in helping their foster father repair equipment might bring him out more.

When he wasn't busy with the crops, her foster father repaired farm equipment and small appliances for people in the village and surrounding farms. Toro had surprised the entire family by how quickly he could visualize both the problems and the fixes for such items. His skill and inventiveness with tools and solutions surpassed even Mr. Greene's. Yet, he seemed uncomfortable around anyone outside the family. Kit had to be brave and strong enough for both herself and Toro at school and around others.

All her life, she had hated people who abused power. She couldn't explain why she was so triggered by bullies, but it always had been so. *Someday, the way I react to bullies is going to get me into a whole lot of trouble*, she often thought.

CHAPTER 10

CAT ATTACK
[Realm One]

Pardon the interruption, kind reader, but this magicked retelling of the story does not sufficiently explain my position. I try very hard not to interfere in the lives of others. However, being possessed of great knowledge and impeccable judgment, the universe seems to have imposed an obligation upon me to help good people avoid bad choices.

Yet good deeds can be dangerous, too. So far, I've not paid too dearly for violating my self-imposed promise not to meddle. I'll let the story continue, but you must understand I really had no choice but to act.

Just outside the gate in front of Kit's home, Cat was observing and reflecting upon Kit as his choice to be Mythral's apprentice. Cat rarely showed any impatience, let alone acted impatiently, but enough was enough. The future of the Three Realms could not, would not, wait for Mythral's procrastination to end.

Today, a morning in early May, was the first day of summer vacation for the students in the village. Kit was about to leave the tiny garden in front of her home, with its red, yellow, and white roses climbing the surrounding fence and the lilacs and azaleas in bloom. Her favorites were the azaleas with lavender colored blossoms.

All this Cat observed without being seen. He was deep in concentration and scheming. How to get this girl in front of Mythral? And, how to get Mythral to see her as the one?

Kit was on her way to the library in Landow, yet again, hoping to find even one book she hadn't already read too many times. Just as she opened the gate, a large blue-gray cat streaked past her and down the lane towards the woods. Two boys she recognized from the class ahead of her at school were chasing the cat and throwing stones.

Kit dashed into the lane and confronted the boys, despite their height and weight advantages. Kit instantly had formulated a plan to deal with these bullies.

As they began to go around her after the cat, Kit yelled at them, "Oh, good, you're headed the right way. Officer Jenkins was just asking where you two were. He went off in that direction. He looked awfully mad about something!"

The boys were cowards and possessed guilty consciences about past misdeeds. They pulled up short and looked at each other, shrugged, and then turned back the way they had come.

As they passed Kit, one said, "Thanks, Squirt," with an unpleasant and somewhat threatening tone.

Like most bullies and cowards, he probably had blamed the messenger, Kit. Strangely enough, on this occasion he was right.

Kit ran down the path after the cat, hoping it wasn't injured. She finally caught sight of a blue-gray blur and followed it deeper into the woods, out another path, and back towards the village. The cat stopped for a moment to inspect its right paw in front of a small bookstore on the very edge of the village.

Kit never had visited this store before. In fact, she didn't even remember it. It sat far back from the sidewalk and in the shadow of its neighboring hardware store to the left. Something Toro would notice. A coffee and bakery shop was to the left of the hardware store. Now that shop was something she had noticed, but she could not afford to go in.

She was sure that the bookshop must be new. Yet, the stone structure appeared to be old and tired and a little lonely, situated there at the end of the lane. It looked as if it had been standing there for many, many years. The name, "M. Hartly's Books," was painted in worn gold letters above the door. The window displayed stacks of books with fading covers.

A real bookshop in her town! How did she not know about it? She stared in wonder and delight at this new found treasure. When the cat nudged the front door open and slipped inside, Kit followed without conscious thought. She pondered the possibilities of so many "new" books in one place.

Once inside, Kit stopped and stared. It was as if she had walked into a treasure cave. Only this was better than gold and jewels! Stacks and stacks of books everywhere. The shelves were overflowing, and every surface displayed books of all sizes and kinds, covering more interesting topics than even Kit could have imagined. The disorganized heaps were covered with a thick layer of dust, but Kit didn't care. It took all of her self-control to keep from rummaging. She even forgot about the cat for a moment. Then she remembered why she was there and began to call the cat.

The cat materialized from behind a tall bookshelf at the back of the room and slowly approached her. He was followed by a tall, trim man with dark, wavy hair flecked with grey and startling dark blue eyes. Eyes that saw everything, even what she was thinking. Then she realized that the man was asking, "What are you doing in my bookshop?"

Before Kit could answer, the cat replied, "You're far too slow in such matters, so I have chosen to bring your new assistant to you. She loves books and is well-suited for the position with you. Now play nice."

Kit was surprised that the cat knew this about her, but then she realized that the cat was talking. For some reason, that itself did not shock her. Kit found herself at a loss for words. She managed to say, "You have a talking cat. What is its name?"

Mythral appeared to be trying his best, well sort of, to be polite. Clearly, he was not happy to have found Kit in his bookshop. He replied tartly, "I have no cat, but 'Cat' appears to have me—-at least at a disadvantage." This last comment sounded more like a riddle than an answer.

Before Kit could figure it out, Mythral said with an edge in his voice, "My name is M. Hartly, and I own this bookshop. This well-meaning, but impertinent creature who has brought you to my shop is called 'Cat'-—not because that is his name, but because he will provide no other. He likes it with a capital 'C' and no article in front."

Now things were getting really confusing, and Kit felt compelled to get a few things straight. "First," she said, "the cat, I mean 'Cat' did not bring me. I followed him here to be sure that he was not injured by some bullies back near my home.

"Second," Kit continued with a bit of frustration and anger creeping into her own voice, "animals do not give their names. They are named by people. Oh, and my name is Kit."

Mythral now was looking amused. "Let's call a truce. However, I can assure you that Cat never was in any danger from any bully. He was, in fact, toying with you and leading you here for his own purposes. As you see from my profession, I love a good story. So, pray tell me how this poor Cat was abused by a couple of normals."

There it was again Kit thought to herself. Another strange word or thing that seemed out of place. As did so much of M. Hartly's bookshop. What did he mean by "normals"? Moving quickly past this latest mystery, Kit proceeded to retell the events from a few minutes ago. As she did so, Mythral's expression changed from amused to laughter. Kit was quick to emphasize how large and heavy were the rocks being lobbed at Cat.

By the end of her story, Mythral had regained most of his composure and said, "I'd have given a great deal to have seen Cat running from those two bullies. You must retell this story to Perci."

"Who is Perci?" Kit inquired.

"A young friend of mine that you might meet one day."

Pausing to consider his words, Mythral continued, "Cat is quite unhappy with the way that I have been organizing things of late. He wants me to hire an assistant to help out here at the store. Cat clearly has selected you as that assistant. What do you say? Are you interested in helping out?"

Kit's attempts to process what this M. Hartly person was saying were all befuddled by the underlying premise that this Cat could think, talk, and offer advice. Yet, M. Hartly was standing there waiting for an answer. She realized that he just had offered her the chance of a lifetime! She could have access to all of these books and get paid for it. Kit's reply foreshadowed their future interactions together. She chose to answer his question with one of her own, "When do I start?"

CHAPTER 11

IT'S A GIRL!
[Realm One]

Mythral still had serious doubts about this girl being his apprentice. If he pursued this just long enough to prove she was unsuitable, only a small bit of time would be lost. Also, it would get Cat off his back. He told Kit the type of person he was looking for must have intelligence and problem-solving skills. He offered a simple puzzle he said any thoughtful person should be able to solve, even if but a young girl.

"You have four bags of gold coins. One contains real gold coins. The other three contain counterfeit coins."

Mythral pulled four bags, a set of weights, and a scale from somewhere—really, from nowhere. Kit suspected he was a magician and maybe a ventriloquist, which would explain the talking cat trick.

"The real coins are ten percent heavier than the false coins. The real coins each weigh one and one-tenth ounces. The false ones each weigh one ounce exactly. You cannot judge by feel; you may use a single set of scales. If you can use the scales only twice, how can you be certain which bag is filled with the real coins?"

Kit took no more than a minute to figure out you would weigh any two bags. If they were the same weight, then they both were filled with false coins. If one was heavier, then it contained the real gold. Assuming the first weighing showed the bags to be of equal weight, you then would put the next two bags on the scale. The real gold would weigh more.

Mythral smiled an annoying smile that said, "There is something you don't know." Then he said, "That's fine, but now tell me how to prove which bag has the real gold using the scale only once! And to make it interesting, let's say you have seven bags of gold coins, only one of which is real."

Mythral produced three more bags and told her he would give her thirty minutes to ponder the solution. Mythral extracted from Cat a firm promise not to give her the solution while he attended to some other matters.

Cat replied, "It's your funeral. Literally." Then Cat watched Kit pondering the riddle for several moments.

Kit asked Cat, "Please, at least tell me if it's possible."

Cat smiled and said, "I can reveal two hints. First, the riddle is not only possible, but quite simple when you know how. Second, when dealing with seemingly difficult problems, or difficult individuals, it often helps to think outside the bag."

With that, Cat strolled off to a comfortable spot on one of the counters and settled down to observe Kit's efforts. Kit kept repeating "outside the bag" while she randomly picked up different bags and continued to ponder the riddle.

Time was running out, and Kit kept asking herself, *What can I do, outside of the bags?* Slowly a possibility began to form in her mind about removing individual coins from their bags.

Mythral walked back in after thirty minutes, clearly expecting Kit to fail, and asked if she was ready to give up and go home. She did not look up. She shook her head "no" while still concentrating on the puzzle.

A smile spread across her face. "I think I have worked it out. I take one coin out of bag number one, two coins out of bag two, three coins out of bag three, four coins out of bag four, and so on. Then I place all the loose coins together on one side of the scales. On the other side, I set the weights initially to twenty-eight ounces, which is the number of coins I pulled from the bags. I add one-tenth of an ounce to the side with the weights, counting as I go, until the scales balance. The number of tenths of an ounce I add corresponds to the number of the bag of real gold coins."

With a slight lift of his eyebrows, Mythral turned to give Cat a suspicious look.

Cat was unfazed and merely said, "As I promised, I did not give her the solution."

Accepting the outcome of the test, Mythral asked to see her hands. He told her he liked to read palms to get a sense of people. The truth was their physical contact would allow him to sense Kit's future.

Kit noted with some concern the ever-increasing oddities surrounding Mr. Hartly and Cat. Yet, the temptation of so many books was too much. She offered her hands.

With that first contact, he detected effortlessly an immediate strong connection—something that never had happened before.

Their connection revealed to him an overwhelming vision of a future that included very dark scenes from MorKano's fortress, somehow related to his earlier sensed confrontation, which would end in Mythral's death in the near future. *Is this the 'she' from my vision?* was his immediate reaction.

Then an even stronger message entered his consciousness: a repeat of the prophecy "Mythral's choice shall doom or save the Realms" reverberating through his being. He thought, *This must be how a church bell feels when struck.*

Mythral and Kit recoiled simultaneously. The shock and horror on her face assured him Kit had seen the same thing. Mythral expected her to turn and run out the door the very next second. She did not. Mythral added another point in her favor to his informal scoring.

Kit had never before "felt" evil. The loathing she had for bullies wasn't even on the same scale. It was her worst nightmare multiplied. This had to be more of Mr. Hartly's testing her. What else could it be? She was determined not to show how deeply it had frightened her.

For his part, Mythral never had sensed such a strong and immediate connection, not even with Vivyen. Something was familiar about this girl. Yet, Mythral was sure he never had met her, at least not in his own past. Perhaps a trip into the future, via sensing, would resolve this riddle?

However, in the now and here, Mythral needed an apprentice with specific skills and talents. After the meeting with Kit and this easy, strong bond between them, Mythral recognized her as nearly the perfect candidate. If only she were not a girl.

Still, one had to look beyond an individual's limitations and hope for the positive exceptions and surprises in life. At least with a girl apprentice, Mythral knew their journey would be anything but boring. After all, to overcome the Law of Equilibrium during the future battle in MorKano's fortress, Mythral needed to do something drastically different.

Despite the obvious shock from their common vision, Kit could not resist the allure of so many "new" books. She agreed to become Mythral's assistant shopkeeper and to work the front, sorting old books, cleaning, and waiting on customers. At least, this was how Mythral chose to describe her position.

She accepted on one condition: someday Mr. Hartly must explain how he did that last trick of putting those weird thoughts into her mind. Mythral intended to study her further before explaining the job for which she really was being considered.

Kit suspected something extraordinary about Mr. Hartly. Certainly, a talking cat was strange, but that hand holding session was downright scary. Had he hypnotized her? Was it done with holograms? She feared she had stumbled into a very dangerous situation. The evil she felt in that room—more like an old building or castle—was overwhelming. Obviously, the whole thing was not real. This job offer was just what she needed. Even what she wanted.

Kit reminded herself, *I actually got what I wished for: an adventure. People occasionally get what they need, but getting what you want is rare.*

Today has been a very good day.

She loved any book that was well written or otherwise interesting, regardless of its condition. She could spend the rest of her life in a little bookshop like this one, happily reading and working in peace and quiet. She longed to experience life and adventures through these volumes. Books that spoke to her soul and her longing for adventure were most prized. She never dared to hope for so many exciting books at her fingertips.

A particular series about wizards and sorcery had been one of her favorites, and this shop had the same feel. She could almost feel the magic here.

CHAPTER 12

CLERK BY DAY
[Realm One]

Kit spent the rest of the day dusting the shop and organizing the books. One book in particular kept getting in her way. She already had filed it away in another part of the store. Yet here it was again, right in front of her. Were there two copies of the same book that had worn exactly alike? She went to check on the first copy.

It was not there. She put this copy into its proper place, exactly where she had put the first one. This time she tucked two pieces of paper inside, on pages eight and seventeen to mark it, for August Seventeenth, her birthday. She returned to dusting and arranging. An hour later, she came across the same book again, now in a new location.

This time there was no doubt. The slips of paper were right there inside, on pages eight and seventeen. Someone was playing a joke on her when her back was turned. Was Mr. Hartly up to more trickery? He did not seem the type for practical jokes. She suspected Cat. But was that even possible?

The next time it happened was just too much. Letting her frustration get the better of her, she said to the book, or to whomever was behind the little joke, "All right already! I give up. I will take this book home with me to read, but I have no time to deal with it right now. This shop is a real mess."

Later in the day, Cat showed Kit around the back of the shop. Of course, Cat did not reveal the secret of the spiral staircases and the hidden rooms.

In the middle of their tour, the realization dawned on Kit that Cat was talking and acting like someone who could think and reason. The accent was foreign. Maybe British? While it certainly must be some trick by Mr. Hartly, she could not begin to guess how he was doing it. Finally, Kit decided to risk looking like a fool. She asked Cat directly, "How is it that you can talk? And very intelligently, at that?"

"Well, well, you compliment and insult me all in the same breath. You and Mr. Hartly should get along famously," Cat said.

Before Kit could get out an uncertain apology, Cat continued, "I have my secrets, like Mr. Hartly, and someday if you prove yourself trustworthy, I might just share a few of them with you."

Kit pondered the implications of this conversation. If Mr. Hartly was a ventriloquist, how was Cat's mouth in sync with the words?

Cat continued the tour without allowing Kit to inquire further. He told her the bookshop was more of a hobby with Mr. Hartly, rather than a real business enterprise. Mr. Hartly really did not care if anyone bought a book or even came in to look around. He just liked owning the shop.

Kit completely understood how Mr. Hartly felt. She would have loved to own so many books. She imagined she would feel sad any time a customer bought one and took it home. After the little tour, she returned to sorting. She found odd titles about things she never had heard of and a lot of books about science and history. There was a book titled, *Gryphons: Myths and Facts*, complete with a chapter on gryphon etiquette.

Could this day get any better? I must be at home, fast asleep, having my best dream ever, kept repeating in Kit's head.

Later in the afternoon, Mr. Hartly popped in to check on Kit. When Cat had given her the tour, he was nowhere to be seen. There was no back door, and Mr. Hartly did not leave through the front door, as far as she knew. The oddities around here just kept on accumulating.

Mr. Hartly said he had another question he wanted Kit to ponder overnight and answer for him the next day.

"What is the real value of good deeds?"

As Mr. Hartly reminded her, good deeds could end up punishing the doer in some way, so the question was, why do them? "Assuming a deed is small and insignificant, what is the value of it to the recipient, to the doer, and to the world? Just some light thinking for you tonight." He spoke in a way that left Kit uncertain if he was being mean or playful.

"Why all these riddles and tricks?" Kit asked.

On his way out he replied, "Because I need to really know and understand the people with whom I work."

Kit turned to Cat, who had walked in during the conversation with Mr. Hartly. Kit looked at Cat and rolled her eyes. "At least I don't have school tomorrow. But why does he care what I think?"

Cat smiled and said, "Not every question has an answer, but it surely has a reason for being asked." Then Cat said, "Once you have exhausted the obvious lines of logic and reasoning on a question, try approaching it from an unexpected angle. Think outside the bag again."

CHAPTER 13

MORKANO'S TRAP
[Realms Two and Three]

MorKano's spy in Realm Two was becoming more confident as each step in the plan went off without a hitch. *Perci fell for the note supposedly from Jasmine. Five simultaneous spells subdued him without a fight once he entered the shop. Now this boy who knows nothing is knocking on Mythral's door with the ransom note in hand. No answer. Patience. Ah, here comes Mythral down the street. Even better. I have more time to return to the soap shop ahead of Mythral.*

Mythral read the ransom note in the day's fading light and immediately acted. A quick reconnaissance of his shop confirmed Perci was absent. Mythral headed straight for the soap shop. *I guess all the intelligent dark wizards are now in Realm Three. Only a true idiot would try something like this against me. And if they have injured Perci, they may not get expelled to Realm Three in one piece.*

The angry look on Mythral's face as he rushed through town cleared his way down the almost-empty rain-soaked streets. By the time he reached the soap shop, he was ready to explode—and might have blown up the shop but for Perci's being inside. Having no fear of any wizards in Realm Two, Mythral paused at the front door. Having considered all likely scenarios, he was ready for whatever awaited. To the participants, the confrontation seemed to take minutes, but it was over in seconds. Opening the door a crack, Mythral peered in and thought: *Perci is in the middle of the room and no one is in sight. The trap will spring as soon as I move into the room. I'll throw a protection shell over both of us and see what happens.* As he entered, dark magic came at Mythral from all four compass points and from above. The attackers were reasonably strong wizards. Given more time, they would wear down Mythral's defensive shell. Mythral had to choose one of his secret spells to escape this trap. He could translocate with Perci, or he could siphon off their magic until they were exhausted. Disclosing either of these old School of Magic spells to dark wizards would be dangerous. Looking around the room and remembering it was once a soap shop, Mythral went for the sleight-of-hand trick.

Those old barrels next to Perci contain glycerin for the soap. I'll take the water from the rain outside, mix it with the glycerin, and inject the mixture into my defensive shell. The heat from all that dark magic will vaporize the mixture into a dense fog.

Once the fog thickened sufficiently, Mythral translocated the two of them back to his shop. With Perci safe, Mythral considered going back and cleaning up. However, by the time he got there on foot, he doubted anyone would be still there.

He had used one part glycerin to two parts water, to be sure the fog was thick. Perhaps the attackers would assume Mythral and Perci had been incinerated by their combined firepower. If so, perhaps they might still be there. But Perci was his first concern. Mythral turned his attention to reviving Perci and learning his part in what happened.

While Mythral tended to Perci, the spy considered his failure and what MorKano would do to him. He had learned nothing of value. Somehow Mythral had created a smokescreen and disappeared. Of what use was that information?

Yet, when the report reached MorKano, he dismissed the messenger and found answers where he least expected them. *I must combine this report with other, less reliable reports about Mythral's escapes. Fog isn't reported in any other episode. Nor is there any spell that would cause fog to the point where Mythral's defensive shield met the attackers' fire. These other reports have some similarities. Something happens that does not appear to be normal magic, and it creates a distraction during which Mythral escapes.*

What was it my spy on the Council said? Mythral always is going on about how dangerous the science from Realm One would be in the other Realms. I need to learn all I can about science.

With that revelation, MorKano began planning his ultimate trap.

CHAPTER 14

BOOKWORM BY NIGHT
[Realm One]

Dinner that night with the family was like prior dinners except for Kit's news. She told them all about her day and her new job at the strange old bookshop. Well, not quite all. She omitted the talking cat part and a few other details that might cause Mrs. and Mr. Greene to worry. Despite the unusual events that she was relaying to them, her brother, Toro, was the only one who showed much interest.

Overnight she read, *Mythral: The Wizard and the Man*, the book that had kept popping up all day long. The book represented itself as the history of the wizard Mythral. She thought it was an interesting account of a fictional character.

While asleep, though, her brain sorted out that M. Hartly was an anagram for Mythral. That, plus all the strange events at the bookshop yesterday, fed her curiosity. Quite possibly M. Hartly fancied himself a wizard like Mythral and used magic tricks to create that image for himself.

Her dreams turned darker: A classic battle of evil versus good had Mythral at the center. He was alone and being overwhelmed by dark wizards. As the battle built to a climax she feared to watch, she woke.

Lying back in bed, she was exhausted by the nightmare. *Is this new job, my dream job, worth such disturbing visions? Maybe my dreams will get better. They have to. I really want to be around all those books.*

She pushed her thoughts back to the book about Mythral. According to the book, Mythral was—and continued to be—the greatest wizard who ever had lived. His learning had gone well beyond his mentor's teachings and knowledge. He had found a way to enter the old Schools of Magic that had been sealed with powerful and deadly curses after the Wizard Wars devastated the realm.

From those schools, Mythral had obtained vast amounts of forgotten magic, which he combined with science for maximum effect. For some reason not made clear in the book, other wizards were unfamiliar with science. The book implied, without explaining, that Mythral's secret knowledge and access to science had made him undefeated in magical combat. Mythral had a history of fighting against dark wizards and those who would abuse the power of magic.

The book made clear that after the wars, a common belief was the Schools of Magic curriculum had been one of the two primary causes of the Wizard Wars. The second cause was the use of schools to teach new wizards in lieu of the old mentor-apprentice system.

Without a mentor having daily oversight, many a new wizard had lost his way and his moral compass. The Wizard Wars were a long-running battle pitting the good wizards against dark wizards who believed strong magic gave them the right to impose their desires or will upon others. The book left no doubt about who eventually had won the wars. For mankind, history almost always reflected the views of the winner. However, the world described in the book bore little resemblance to the world Kit knew.

At breakfast in the morning, Kit was dumbfounded. Her foster parents had no memory of what Kit had told them the night before about the bookshop—as if they had heard almost nothing she had said. That she now had a part-time job during her summer vacation was all they seemed to recall. Even odder, when she tried to describe the day's events, this time including the talking cat, they seemed not to hear what she was saying.

However, her brother, who did remember, assumed she had made it all up. He just sat there and shook his head.

After breakfast, Kit walked the path through the woods back to the bookshop. Having finished reading the book on Mythral, she had it in hand. Would it now stay put on the proper shelf?

Her mind wandered to the events of yesterday and the story of Mythral in that book. She was deeply absorbed in her thoughts as she walked through the front door of Mr. Hartly's Bookshop for her second day of work.

She gasped.

Though she had spent hours dusting and rearranging the books in proper order the day before, everything had reverted to its previous state. Every bit of the dust had reappeared, and the books again were totally disarrayed.

She had designated one shelf for magical beasts, where side by side she had placed books on gryphons, dragons, charmbirds, shocker fish, and more. Those books were gone.

Would the surprises and tricks never end? This was all just too much! It felt like some elaborate hoax.

First a talking cat, then the book about Mythral always getting in her way, and now all her work in the shop undone!

For the life of her, she could not figure out who would do this. Surely, someone was setting her up with that book on Mythral. Then all the pranks with a talking cat! Like a magic trick, it all would make sense if she knew the secrets behind how it was done. The only thing she really could not begin to explain was the realistic, dark vision she had experienced when Mr. Hartly had touched her hands.

As she wandered about the shop, bewildered, her frustration and anger rose.

Adding bad timing to Kit's list of his faults, Mr. Hartly showed up while all of this was going through Kit's mind.

"Have you an answer to my question from yesterday?" he asked. "About good deeds?"

She barely resisted the urge to throw the book she was holding at

Mr. Hartly.

As she remembered what book was in her hands, something clicked. Something she had thought of in the middle of the night but then forgot.

M. Hartly was an acronym for Mythral. If M. Hartly really was Mythral, then everything in the book might be true. It was a crazy thought, that magic could be real, that the famous Mythral owned a bookshop in her little town, and that he would just happen to take an interest in her.

On the other hand, it made just as much sense as a talking cat and books and dust acting on their own!

CHAPTER 15

THE TRUTH COMES OUT.
[Realm One]

Rather than attack Mr. Hartly with the book in her hands, Kit channelled her anger into grilling him about the bookshop and the history of Mythral the Great Wizard.

"Are you Mythral?" It came out as an accusation more than a question.

Surprisingly, he did not immediately deny it.

Mr. Hartly retreated into a long thoughtful silence. When he finally emerged, he said, "I guess we will have to discuss the question of good deeds later. You are quite right. My real name is Mythral."

"The 'Mythral' in this book?" asked Kit.

"Book? What book?" As he flipped through the pages, a smile and a look of loneliness appeared on his face. "I did not know this was here." The words came out ever so softly. "Yes, I am he."

Kit felt a twinge of sympathy, but she could not contain her frustration. "How can you be? Tell me now what is going on with you, that talking cat, and this shop, or I'm leaving for good."

"The shop's antics are part of the magic spell protecting the shop. It always will look dusty and disorganized. Otherwise, strangers with no real business here might walk in and waste my time."

Kit listened, amazed, as Mr. Hartly, or Mythral, further explained that, in this world he called Realm One, the spell on the bookshop kept "normals" (non-magical folk) from even being aware the shop existed. In Realm Two, whatever or wherever that was, the spell kept people from wasting his time by coming in for a book.

Mythral was impressed that Kit had worked out so much on her own in such a short time. A very good sign of adequate intelligence. Even he had not known about this book concerning his life and achievements. The shop might have magically placed the book in her way all day. However, being suspicious by nature, Mythral had a strong hunch Cat had orchestrated everything.

Perci and Cat both desperately wanted Mythral to take on an apprentice. If not soon, it might well be too late. Mythral's fated death was approaching at an unknown pace.

When he studied the book about himself, Mythral discovered it was magicked by Vivyen and was fairly current. Fortunately, Vivyen seemed to have cast the spell to avoid disclosing sensitive details that would be helpful to his enemies. Details, like the old Schools of Magic, could be seen only by Mythral's closest allies. *So, did Kit read these sections?* Mythral wondered.

The book seemed to stay several years behind. There were no details concerning Vivyen's death. At this point, Mythral related to Kit the story of his true love, Vivyen. She had mysteriously died fighting his worst enemy, MorKano. That was just one week prior to something called the Three Realms Spell. Vivyen had left the shop in Realm Two one afternoon without saying much. He just had finished his portion of the Three Realms Spell with help from Vivyen and Perci.

Mythral had been deep in thought, reviewing the details of the new Spell. Vivyen was more skilled with magic and stronger at it than most of the Council of WISDOM. Yet, ingrained prejudices meant only a few of the oldest and most respected female wizards were permitted on the Council. For that outdated reason, Vivyen had no acknowledged role in the casting of the Spell.

It was a touchy subject, with her helping behind the scenes to perfect Mythral's sub-spells within the larger Spell but not being allowed to participate directly. Because of that sensitivity, Mythral had not questioned her as she left. A fateful decision he always would regret.

Late that afternoon, Vivyen had found herself fighting the worst of the dark wizards, MorKano. A few bystanders in the sketchy part of town saw the fight. They said Vivyen had held her own until the very end, but she perished under MorKano's final spell.

Mythral always had rejected vengeance as an end unto itself. He had vowed to reconsider that position. Mythral and others on the Council of WISDOM searched for MorKano immediately after Vivyen's death, with no success.

The realm was not endless, but it was vast. The outer areas were sparsely populated and wild. The Council might have located MorKano with a spell. Why try? The Three Realms Spell would send him and his known cohorts into the new Realm Three. That Spell was less than a week away.

The witnesses' physical description and the type of magic used clearly spoke MorKano's name. There were few wizards other than Mythral who could hope to best Vivyen in a fair battle of magic.

Why MorKano would want to harm Vivyen was a mystery. Certainly MorKano, if he knew about it, would have had a strong interest in stopping the Three Realms Spell. Once cast, the Spell would exile the likes of MorKano to Realm Three. Never would they return to what would then become Realm Two.

But why would he pick Vivyen as his target? She had no direct role in casting the Spell. The loss certainly would be a blow to Mythral, but more effective would have been for MorKano to attack others on the Council of WISDOM. MorKano was more than a match for any of them, except Mythral.

Mythral's reputation for being able to withstand any force of magic and still successfully battle his opponents kept him safe from most attempts by dark wizards. Very few knew the secrets behind his success at magical confrontations.

If only the Council or I had acted sooner, she still would be alive. Mythral still blamed himself for not persuading the Council of WISDOM sooner to separate the Realms. The Three Realms Spell was intended to stop abuses of magical power. With known abusers removed from the rest of the magical community, good magicians would have a better chance at a peaceful and safe existence in Realm Two.

To put the temptation of abuse even further out of reach, all non-magical entities would be safely tucked away into Realm One to be visited only by Mythral and a few individuals with special approval. If the Spell had been completed only a few days earlier, MorKano would have been banished before the fatal showdown with Vivyen ever could have taken place.

As Mythral looked down at Vivyen's book in his hands, he wondered how he had not known it was in his shop. Then again, there were several thousand volumes, and they changed seemingly at will. This random shifting of books was due to some quirk in the spell that created the bookshop. He never had gotten around to fixing it. He had grown accustomed to occasional surprises.

CHAPTER 16
TELL, DON'T ASK.
[Realm One]

Kit would be safe enough in Realm One, but not in Realm Two for now. That was what Mythral had said.

"That might clear things up if I knew what Realm One and Realm Two are. Or *where* they are."

"There is no way to explain all at once," Mythral began. "So, let me begin with the immediate details: your duties as my apprentice, and my expectations. Then we can go into the background. Finally, I'll tell you about my impending death and my hopes of altering it.

"After you accept magic as real, only the theory and structure of the universe's interaction with magic will be hard to comprehend—and harder still to believe.

"I am going to give you a short and very incomplete overview. Don't analyze it yet. Don't attempt to apply reason or logic. Just let your subconscious play with it, and I'll fill in pieces as we go."

"Okay," Kit injected into Mythral's lecture. "So, you want to start my training with telling me some basic stuff I will not understand and won't believe. Sure, why not?"

Mythral caught Kit flat-footed with his reply. "You are absolutely right. It would seem to make no sense whatsoever. Yet maybe it allows me to gauge just how much you are willing to trust that I know what I am doing. Without developing that trust, there is likely no hope for me or for the Realms. So, while I can appreciate sarcasm and satire as part of an intelligent conversation, this is not the time or place."

Kit stifled the impulse to roll her eyes.

"Despite what Cat told you," he continued, "you were not lured here to be my shop assistant but to help me save the Realms by becoming my apprentice. I have foreseen my death in a dark wizard's fortress in Realm Three, where I got myself trapped in a corridor between two powerful dark wizards and underestimated them. I foolishly went alone, which is where you come in: to change that outcome.

"Your new duties are to study magic with me and with an associate of mine. You will meet Perci later. Cat you already know. Cat knows more than he will share. He explains even less. You can place absolute faith in whatever he does share, unless he is playing with you. Good luck in distinguishing one from the other.

"Back to where I tried to start this discussion, with a brief overview of magic and the universe. Think of the universe as a figure-eight racetrack. The actual universe is endless, convoluted, four dimensional with time as the fourth dimension, and crosses itself an infinite number of times.

"This track we'll call the Time-Path. Let's put three cars on that track at different points. Pick any car, and that is the present time. The car ahead of it on the Time-Path is in the future. The car behind is in the past. The Time-Path is so long that someone in the present car cannot see the future car or the past car. Yet all three cars exist, let's say, 'simultaneously,' rather than 'at the same time' to avoid extra confusion.

"Where this Time-Path crosses itself, a bleed-through from the past or future can occur in the present. But this is not a collision of the cars, because they each are at a different point in the fourth dimension of time.

"Let's take a break. I'll finish today's explanations when we come back."

During their break, Kit said little. She had plenty of questions, but inside her head they all sounded as if she thought Mythral was quite insane. So, she chose to think and not speak. When Mythral indicated he was ready to continue, she put down her cinnamon tea and decided to listen without interrupting. Again, she was fearful of how her thoughts might come out.

In the interest of full disclosure and fairness, Mythral explained, his needs should be clearly articulated.

"Before you agree to become my apprentice, you must understand not only the duties but the potential risks. How I know about the future on that Time-Path, I'll cover later. What I know is that in the near future I will die in a trap laid by the worst of the dark wizards, MorKano.

"The Law of Equilibrium makes changing the events on the Time-Path, past or future, virtually impossible. That topic will consume a whole day if you make it that far. My only hope of altering that future, according to Perci and Cat, is to train an apprentice and use him or her to unbalance that future."

Breaking her self-promise to listen and not speak, Kit commented, "I can see how doing something different now would alter how things work out. I don't see how my becoming your apprentice is connected."

"I am looking for ways to prevent my demise that would not put you at risk. However, at some point in the future you might find yourself facing such dangers and even death. That vision when I took your hand could be your future. Sleep on this tonight. No significant decision should be made without serious reflection.

"On the other hand, trusting first impressions and instincts is wise and proper, too, if you need to act immediately, as long as the reaction is not tainted by emotional biases or prejudices."

Kit was sorely tempted to call out Mythral on his inconsistent positions: putting off important decisions, trusting unbiased first impressions. Too much input. All she could do was nod her head and head for home.

If she could believe all Mythral had said, then the hand holding episode began to make sense. The overwhelming evil and darkness she experienced must be connected to Mythral's future and her part in it. That was something she did not want to face in her future—even if she could make herself do it.

She had lots of doubts and fears that night. She worried about leaving her younger brother behind and alone. She had concluded she was not the one for apprenticeship with Mythral until one final question entered her mind. What would happen to Mythral, the Realms, and her family if she said "no?" She had not considered this point. Kit spent hours that night awake, contemplating its importance. As she realized that Mythral's answer to this final question would make the choice for her, she finally found that sleep came easily.

She would have to wait until she could ask Mythral her question. Her answer would depend upon his, and there was nothing more to think about until then.

C H A P T E R   17

LET THE GAMES BEGIN
[Realm One]

On Kit's return to the bookshop the next morning, Cat, as usual, was pretending to nap among the books on an upper shelf. While not showing any obvious interest in their conversation, Kit suspected Cat was there to listen in on her decision.

"I'd decided last night to decline your offer of an apprenticeship, even if it meant giving up access to all these amazing books. After considering everything you said and the evil I experienced firsthand, I decided to pass." Off to the side, she noticed a definite movement in Cat's ears. "I'm not sure I have what it might take to do the job and to be responsible for the outcome.

"Currently my life is pretty good for me and my family. My younger brother relies upon me. What would happen to him if I left or died?"

To herself she added, *Why should I risk it all for magic and power I never knew existed before? Why risk everything for a problem created by others without my consent and even without my knowledge?*

"That was my conclusion, until I thought of something. A small detail you omitted when we spoke. The final question that arose in my mind, for which you gave no answer. A critical issue surely you had considered but about which you said nothing to me.

"What happens if I say "no?" Is there another person, a runner-up, next in line for the apprentice position? If not, what happens in the future, if you die, as in your vision? What if evil wins in the future? What would happen to me, my brother, and my foster parents then?"

The "why me?" she had been asking herself the night before had been replaced by a much more important question that was actually relevant to the problem at hand. Kit asked Mythral again, "Is there anyone you might find that could serve as your apprentice instead of me?"

Understanding and concern resonated in Mythral's voice. "I, and others, have been searching for some years. Only you and Toro appear to be suitable. Your brother is too young. For Toro to be my apprentice, I'd have to wait a couple of years. That is time I may not have.

"Even if another suitable candidate could be found, even one with some training already, the connection when we touched hands tells me you are the one. If that strong, unexplained bond between us is not in our past, then it must be in our future.

"That one fact makes me certain you are the right choice. It is quite logical and simple. The first touch and connection prove we have some very close and definite interaction at some point on the Time-Path. We both know it is not in the past. Our future together must happen prior to the events in my vision of death. Based upon the Law of Equilibrium, which I promise to cover later, our future together must happen, to justify what we have experienced now and here.

"Your discovery of the one true compelling argument for accepting the offer was probably the Law of Equilibrium at work, assuring you become my apprentice now and here. That allows the future to remain consistent."

Cat's thoughts on the subject were similar. *If not her, then whom? The future of all Realms cannot be left to chance. Or to MorKano's schemes.*

Mythral confessed, "I held back much in yesterday's discussion. I threw an awful lot at you. After you had the night to reflect, I planned on covering all this before you gave a final answer. In my defense, I did not want your decision to be based solely upon guilt or duty to the needs of others.

"I had hoped you would feel the positive aspects of the offer, a life of magic and wonder, would outweigh the risk. Even if that life might be quite short."

Kit admitted, "I guessed at the answers late last night. Well, actually, early this morning. I wanted to be certain I wasn't missing something else. Now I have a new question.

"Explain to me why I cannot reject a vision of some future that has yet to happen, just because I had the vision. What you seem to be saying is I cannot escape fate, so what difference does it make what I do now?"

Mythral answered, "You are wise beyond your years to ask such a question. Go grab a large cup of hot tea and a bottle of aspirin and find a comfortable chair. As I attempted to explain yesterday, time is not linear. The past, present, and future do not have to occur in the order you would call normal. But that is the easy half. You also must understand how free will can coexist with certain fundamental fixed events in the past and the future. Go get that tea and aspirin, and we will begin."

CHAPTER 18

THE LAW OF EQUILIBRIUM
[Realm One]

As Mythral waited for Kit to return and settle in for their discussion of the Law of Equilibrium, he reflected on his specific problem. *How much time do I have, days or months, before MorKano's trap ensnares me?*

I know the 'where' and 'why.' Just not the 'when.' And I have no real clues. However, I have some measure of time before that confrontation in Realm Three could happen. As long as I avoid going to Realm Three, there can be no confrontation. Do I have enough time to train Kit? And, for the life of me, literally, I can't see how inserting her into my future can overcome the Law of Equilibrium.

How best to explain to Kit the Law of Equilibrium and the nonlinear nature of time? As Mythral contemplated this key question, Kit returned and settled herself in a large, old, overstuffed armchair that had faded to a soft blue. Mythral noticed the upholstery matched her eyes. *What will those eyes have seen a year from now?* Mythral wondered as he began.

"Things might seem to happen one after the other from an individual's limited perspective. Most would agree time has a natural order, where the past precedes the present, and the future follows. But then, as with many commonly held beliefs, they often are wrong.

"Past, present, and future coexist in the Time-Space Continuum," Mythral stated. "As explained by the forbidden texts from the old Schools of Magic, time is not linear. Time is more of a multidimensional flow that wraps or 'folds' the past, present, and future all together and, thereby, explains the existence of déjà vu, premonitions, and certain 'impossible knowledge' that cannot be explained by an individual's history."

"Hold it! Stop." Kit nearly shouted at Mythral. "Are you telling me the mystics and fortune tellers actually know the future? That I didn't waste my two dollars last year at the fair?"

"Yes and no," Mythral replied. "Does that help?"

"Of course not. Saying yes and no to a question does not explain anything."

"Well then, I suggest you let me finish, and things may, I hope, become clearer.

"The Time-Path should be thought of as a loop without a true ending or beginning and no outside or inside. Your science books would liken it to a Mobius curve, but in at least four dimensions. In actuality, it is a complex overlapping, interweaving loop, but for simplicity's sake let's think of it as a circle. If you mark one point on that Time-Path loop and assume a directional flow, say clockwise, then everything behind that point is the past and everything in front of that point is the future. At some point while moving around that loop, what is in your future becomes your past. However, our curve is very long.

"Now we add the conflicting idea of 'free will' to the concept of a Time-Path where all points in time exist simultaneously. So how can we have free will to change our actions when the past and future already exist? Does the universe 'anticipate' a free will choice from the beginning of time, or does it restrict free will to conform with an existing string of events and outcomes? Any upfront guesses?" Mythral stared at Kit with his all-knowing smile as he awaited her reply.

Feeling mentally agile and alert after the aspirin and tea, Kit thought she might just outmaneuver Mythral with her response. "You tell me how it matters, and I'll answer your question. If we are going to end up doing what the Time-Path says we have done or will do anyway, what is the point?"

"That sounds like one of Cat's answers. Twist my question into a new question and send it back at the asker. Not bad for an apprentice. But it will not work."

Again, apologies to readers for the interruption. But as Mythral is often long-winded on this science stuff and my good name has again been misused, I thought you could use a break. Mythral has only read about nonlinear Time-Paths, whereas I have actually traveled them. I'll make it simple. Wherever and whenever you are on your Time-Path, you can go in only one of three directions. One direction is often called forward or the future. The opposite direction is backwards or the past. Or, as overlooked even by Mythral, you can step from one part of the Time-Path onto a different part, at an intersection. Such crossings are rare, and usually you only get a glimpse or vision of the part intersecting your path.

That is really all you need to know. The interplay of free will and the Law of Equilibrium consumes much of Mythral's mental energies. I prefer just to get on with living and not worry about why it works out the way it does. I'll turn you back over to Mythral's lecture, but to show you he is not the only one who can blow your mind with this stuff, think on this: In my travels, I once met a woman who was headed in the opposite direction of everyone else on her Time-Path! She said her past was yet to be lived and would be a surprise, while her future was set

and clear in her memory. Very confusing and very
dangerous. Imagine a large concert crowd leaving
the venue and you are the only person trying to go
in. If you figure out how she can live anything close
to a normal life, please let me know. Ah well, back to
Mythral. I hope you are seated comfortably.

"I'm going to explain two more points, and then you can decide for
yourself if it matters and answer my first question," Mythral continued.
"Does free will exist as an integral part of the Law of Equilibrium, or are
we misled into thinking we have free will?

"First point, which is not new: This twisting, looping, convoluted
Time-Path is so complex and multidimensional that it crosses and
intersects itself at countless points, allowing for 'bleed-through' at these
points of intersection. How much, and for how long, depends on the
nature of that junction. When this happens, you might glimpse some
future event. Or you might see a past event from a different perspective,
and that past could seem different from what you remember."

Kit made the connection. "Like when you took my hand that first day
in the bookshop. I was seeing the future, our future, that hasn't happened
yet. It was so full of evil and darkness. Is that destined for me no matter
what?"

"Let me cover point number two before we speculate. In order to have
continuity, not chaos, on this Time-Path, we have the Law of Equilibrium,
which keeps events from being significantly changed by free will. The Law
absorbs or mitigates the impacts of any significant deviation from the
events on the Path, such that all fundamental events remain unaffected.

"You may ask, what if some significant public figure were never born?
What if some minor diversion kept that person's parents from meeting?
All sorts of disruptions could occur. In Realm One you have many books

and movies based upon just such a premise."

"I know what you mean. In the movie 'Groundhog Day,' Phil kept trying to change his future, but he kept waking up to the same day. He spent weeks, maybe longer, trying to break the cycle. The only thing that worked was changing himself in a radical way. Or maybe it was falling in love. Or maybe both! But that was pure fiction."

Mythral continued, "I would have said 'The Adjustment Bureau,' but you get the idea. The Law of Equilibrium acts to neutralize any significant aberrations and keep the Time-Path essentially stable, allowing the past, present, and future to coexist."

Then Kit fulfilled Mythral's initial prediction. "If I understand what you're saying, it seems impossible. Maybe I misunderstood some part of it."

"The fact that you find it unbelievable is a strong indication that you heard me correctly," he said. "Just give your mind some time to toy with the concepts."

"But, the way you have explained it, free will is a myth. Or, it is insignificant. What is going to happen or what has already happened in the future isn't going to change. So why give it any thought?"

"Exactly. I should just sit back and let my death in MorKano's trap happen. I haven't yet explained everything. Some degree of adjustment to the Time-Path is possible without chaos. It's called an Inherently Unbalanced Event. If free will can manufacture an event more significant than the Law's ability to adjust or absorb it, then, in theory, such an event would create an alternate universe with its own unique Time-Path. And that is my only hope.

"We will come back to free will and Inherently Unbalanced Events in a couple of days. Tomorrow we start on real training, with real magic."

Chapter 19

DEADLY SCHEMES
[*Realm Three*]

MorKano's trap to test Mythral's unusual talent for escaping or defeating multiple attackers had yet to produce anything useful. Still, he had some of the smartest wizards under his control investigating this thing called science. He had devised a daring plot to attack Mythral where he'd least expect it: in the home of Nate, a wizard with almost unlimited powers and no desire to use them. Nate was an anomaly. And, worse, when he did get involved, dark wizards disappeared.

I suppose Valak will have to do. He's talented enough to carry out my plans, but he is slow to comprehend nuance. MorKano's thoughts were interrupted by Valak proving MorKano's point.

"Why not eliminate Ergotimos now and take the gemstones we need? Why wait until Mythral is already here in Realm Three?"

"Focus," MorKano said while suppressing the implied "*you fool.*" Once Ergotimos' murder is known, it will raise questions and suspicions. If the gemstones are discovered missing, Gemma might start asking questions. All she does is facet gemstones and infuse them with her magic or the magic of others. If she'd just given me the gemstones when I asked, her friend would not need to die."

"Why not take them directly from Gemma?" Valak persisted.

"As a worker of gemstones, Gemma has a cave full of power infused stones to protect her. I could break through, but that would be noisy, and she might alert Nate. They are quite close.

"No," MorKano continued. "Ergotimos is a weak wizard who uses the stones only to augment his powers for digging clay and running his pottery equipment. He has what we need, and he'll be easy to kill quietly. We'll need at least five gemstones for my plan. However, take all you find when the time comes.

"Now don't interrupt. You need to memorize these steps, in order. Miss one or mix up the order, and you'll disappear like all the other dark wizards who entered Nate's valley. They say Mythral can sense dark magic near him, and Nate knows immediately when it enters his valley. We have to be clever about the attack. Once we know Mythral will spend a night in Nate's home, we'll implement the plan. I'll preset each stone with what you need and color code them for ease.

"Step one: Before entering Nate's valley, use the Power Removal Spell, and then use a yellow gemstone to cloak yourself in neutral magic. There must be no remnants of dark magic about you.

"Step two: Make your way to Nate's home and find Mythral's bedroom. Use the green stone to restore your powers and attack Mythral immediately. Use all the red gems, into which I'll pour power to kill Mythral quickly. You'll have to finish and move to step three before Nate knows you are in his house.

"Step three: Use the Power Removal Spell and a yellow neutral magic stone to cloak yourself, and get out! Once out of Nate's valley, use the last green stone to restore your powers and report back here." *If you are still alive*, MorKano added silently.

"Just three easy steps. We'll go over them until they sink in."

Unbeknownst to MorKano, by plotting Mythral's death at a point in the Time-Path other than predicted in Mythral's sensing, he was attempting an Inherently Unbalancing Event and would very likely fail because of the Law of Equilibrium.

CHAPTER 20

CONFLICT AVOIDANCE: 101
[Realm One]

The next day Mythral started Kit on mental communications. Wizards who were not related by blood or marriage rarely bothered trying the technique. Mythral's mentor had insisted upon training him extensively in the use of mental communications, which Mythral and Perci used routinely. Mythral explained to Kit, just as his own mentor had done, that the method had special advantages. "Consider the benefits of being able to convey thoughts and even images instantly without having to use language.

"The spoken word very often can lead to misunderstandings, given differing assumptions and definitions," he said, shifting into lecture mode.

"On top of that, you have the listener's degree of concentration and the speaker's inflections, the two primary factors in misunderstandings. Even special words or phrases might affect clarity. All communication failure can be avoided when parties express themselves mentally instead of vocally."

"Is it something I can turn on and off?" asked Kit. "I'm quite sure most of the time I don't want to hear what people are thinking."

"Not to worry. It takes trust, concentration, and cooperation. A rare combination between individuals these days. It gets much easier with practice, and I intend for you and Perci to do so every day until you can do it without any effort.

"However, at the beginning you will need to center yourself, eliminate distractions, and learn to listen with an open mind. Start by sitting upright in any chair or in any comfortable seated position. Most wizards these days do not trust one another enough to open their minds. With vulnerability comes risk."

As Mythral had warned, Kit did, in fact, have difficulty at first hearing Mythral over all the chatter in her mind. Her frustration erupted. "I cannot do this. The noise in my head will not stop. The more I try to quiet my thoughts, the louder they become. Words and images just keep popping in and out. We might as well move on to something else."

"Not yet," said Mythral. "This is an essential step for any attempt at magic. Imagine, at the moment of releasing a Blinding Spell, your mind conjures an image of a pizza. It might still work. But instead of blinding your opponent, you might just hit him in the face with a pizza.

"Your initial failure was expected. You needed to fail so you could appreciate the importance of what we're doing. Two techniques I'd like you to practice. The first is deep breathing, and the second is focusing on a single object or image.

"Deep breathing is an excellent exercise for the mind and body. Besides calming and harmonizing your mind, body, and energies, it provides crucial oxygen to your systems. I'll give you a book covering several styles of deep breathing. To start, just slowly take in as much air as you can. Fill your lungs completely. Hold that for as long as you comfortably can, and then expel all the air, emptying the lungs completely.

"Simple. Yet very effective. Over time, your intake will increase dramatically, as will the time you can hold your breath. You should do this as often as you can throughout the day.

"The second technique is much harder, and we will not spend much time on it until you master your breathing. It is extremely difficult to cease all thoughts or to think of *nothing*. So, first you learn to focus upon a single object to the exclusion of all other thoughts. This single focus is just a little less impossible than holding nothing in your thoughts."

"But what shall I focus upon?" inquired a skeptical Kit. She'd never minded homework, but this seemed awfully boring.

"The 'what' is entirely unimportant," was Mythral's ever so helpful reply. "It can be a word, a flower, a scent or even a sound. Many find focusing on their breathing as an easy way to begin. That way your mind and body have a single focus."

Much to their common surprise, two days later, Kit began to hear Mythral very clearly. Once again, Mythral was pleasantly shocked by Kit's accomplishment. Their daily exercises in breathing and focus had gone well, but this breakthrough was unexpected. Kit demonstrated proficiency with each new subject. Even more unexpected was how easily they connected. Mythral was so impressed with her accomplishment that afternoon, he decided to broach a related topic for intellectual discussion.

"I want you to keep practicing this communication skill with Perci daily; soon you'll be going into Realm Two. You also will need to learn how to block those whom you do not trust from using your open mind to attack or distract you at a key moment."

"You want my mind open to you but closed to others. Just how do I do that?" *This is getting way too complicated,* Kit thought.

"We'll work on that fine point later," Mythral deferred before he continued.

"I mentioned before about differing assumptions and miscommunication. I cannot emphasize the following enough, and I'll express it to you both vocally and mentally, to be sure the message is clear and unambiguous."

Immediately, the following was being shouted inside of Kit's head: *Perhaps the most common reason for conflicts, including wars and interpersonal adversity, is the failure of the parties to recognize they have differing underlying assumptions!*

"Whoa, no need to shout," Kit vocalized and then, remembering the lesson, responded mentally to Mythral.

Sorry, he replied mentally. *Most people require more volume during the initial phase. You are clearly an exception to many rules. Did you notice how much clearer and more expressive that mental statement was?*

Not really, Kit answered. *The volume was so loud, subtle distinctions were drowned out.*

Mythral continued, *People have disagreements all the time when the underlying assumptions held by each are different. One person might believe murder is always wrong. A second person might believe killing is justified in self defense. Another person might believe killing is justified to defend property or honor.*

Mythral was in his lecturing mode, and Kit's question went unasked.

If these people are having a discussion about a wrongful killing and they do not share a common definition and context for "wrongful," they are likely to experience much confusion and have serious disagreements without even understanding why.

If their differences were fully understood, they might well agree or at least agree to disagree. Even better, if they fully understood one another, one person would stand a much better chance of convincing another of his point of view.

Therefore, you, Perci, and I must beware of differing assumptions. The use of mental communications often can bypass such problems by conveying thoughts as well as emotions and related images.

Switching to vocal speech out of concern for Kit's long day, Mythral continued, "Let me pose a riddle to illustrate how one concept might mean so many different things to different people.

"The riddle goes like this. What is: greater than everything, less than a true Void, possessed by the poor, needed by the rich, and deadly if consumed?

"I'll give you a few minutes to think."

After several minutes of studious concentration by Kit, Mythral injected, "These types of riddles are so obvious once you know the answer. The point is to understand what we so easily overlook.

"Okay, that is enough time spent. The answer is *nothing*," Mythral announced with a twinkle in his eyes and a bit of a smile.

Frustrated, Kit snapped back at Mythral, "Well how does a riddle with *no* answer explain anything?"

"I did not say there was *no* answer. The answer to each part of the riddle is the word or concept of 'nothing.' What is greater than everything?–-nothing. What is less than a true void?–-nothing. What is it that the poor have?–-nothing. What is it that the rich need?-—nothing. What is it that if you eat it, you will die?-—nothing? "While this one answer may not be entirely correct for all people in all situations, it does illustrate the problem. 'Nothing' means different things to different people.

"We must not underestimate the frequency with which such misunderstandings occur or the harm they can cause. You and I must be vigilant to avoid such misunderstandings. Which is partly why we are going to spend so much of your training efforts on mental communications."

CHAPTER 21

SCIENCE OR MAGIC?

[Realm One]

At the start of their lesson the next day, Mythral got a ping from Realm Two, letting him know he was needed. This was a method of communication Perci and he used between Realms, Mythral explained to Kit before she could ask. "One ping means when convenient. Two pings for sooner. Three pings for as soon as possible. Nonstop pinging for right now."

Kit asked, "What is the magic behind this method of communicating? And, why not use a pleasant sound?"

Mythral gave her a smile that said he knew an inside joke. "What do they teach in your school? This method of communicating between Realms is just pure science. It is called 'entangled particles' and has been known for years in your Realm."

"That's hardly fair," Kit replied. "My teacher has mentioned these particles; she could not have known about other Realms or magic."

Conceding her point, Mythral continued, "Perci came up with a useful way to employ them for communicating between Realms. Essentially, two particles are connected by laws of physics such that, regardless of distance, time, or possibly even other dimensions, when one particle is flipped one way, the entangled particle, wherever and whenever it may be, flips correspondingly.

"After that, all you need is one device to do the flipping and another to acknowledge the flip and then create a 'ping.' You can use either science or magic for the device here in Realm One, but in Realm Two magic is the best solution.

"One rule you must follow very carefully is never take unfamiliar objects, especially those employing science, into Realm Two. I have warned the Council about this danger.

"Magic and science coexisted before the Three Realms Spell, and they remain quite compatible. However, the scientific advances in Realm One are dangerous enough in the hands of normals. If wizards were to have access to that science and combine it with their magic, the results could be devastating.

"Have I mentioned 'inverted sayings or phrases' to you?" Mythral asked Kit.

"Not yet."

"You may have some difficulty at first with the way things are expressed in Realm Two. It is not clear in every case why, but some expressions in Realm One are inverted from what they were before the Three Realms Spell.

"'Outside in' is one such example. With magic, the inner working of a thing could be examined by a spell that put the outside on the inside, and the inside on the outside. The original could have been said either way, but historically it always has been 'outside in.'

"However, with magic gone from Realm One, that way of saying it makes no real sense. Without magic, you cannot harmlessly invert insides and outsides. You can, however, physically remove the insides of things to view them. You might even be able to put them back, if you know what you are doing. Therefore, in Realm One, the saying had to be adjusted to 'inside out.'

"Your expression in Realm One is 'live and learn,' the theory being the longer you live, the more you learn. This is not true for every person. The proper expression in Realm Two is 'learn and live.'"

"What's the difference?" asked a puzzled Kit.

Mythral barely paused. "If you don't learn a few essentials, then you will not live much longer. Learning is essential to continued living, but living does not ensure future learning. In Realm Two and Realm Three, this includes learning about magic and how to defend yourself.

"One final example is the phrase 'here and now.' If you say that in Realm Two, you will get some strange looks. The proper saying there is in the 'now and here.' As you will see, time is a much more important factor than location in almost everything."

Mythral called for the gate key so he could move from Realm One to Realm Two.

As he did so, Kit was full of more questions. She asked one after another, until Mythral held up his hands to stop her.

Mythral told Kit, "If anyone else had been present, I would have disguised my use of harmonic vibration and pretended to use a verbal spell on a book. I also would have made sure any third party present saw the title of the book very clearly, because the title changes after each use.

"By using such distractions, I prevent leaking valuable information to my adversaries and substitute false information that will waste their time and efforts. Even if an observer is not an adversary, knowledge can be given only to those who need to know it and who, hopefully, can protect it.

"We will pick up your lesson in the morning. I must see what Perci needs."

"Might I come with you?" Kit asked, excited by the prospect of an adventure.

"Perhaps next time," he replied. "You are due home soon, and I do not know how long I'll be away."

CHAPTER 22

FREE WILL: FACT OR FICTION?
[Realm One]

The next day Mythral started in on the theories that had given Kit sleepless nights and pounding headaches. "Given what I said earlier about the Law of Equilibrium, you might well ask if free will exists," he said. "And, if it does exist, can it really change the future? The answers are 'yes' and 'maybe.'"

In his tutorial voice Mythral continued. "Originally, there was only one realm inhabited by all: those with strong magic, weak magic, and no magic. The abuse of magic used on the weak or magic-less became so prevalent that the Council of WISDOM was formed to deal with such abuses.

"The Council's failure to fully control dark wizards and their abuses resulted in a decision to create three realms so the non-magical beings, so-called normals, could be isolated from those who might abuse them, and the worst of the dark wizards could be exiled from society.

"We can speak of this more at a later time, but those are the basics behind the Three Realms Spell, which is a fundamental piece of the present Time-Path."

Clearly Kit—and you, readers—are in for another
of Mythral's lectures, and I'd like to spare you
the extraneous details. But this time there is an
important point to his discussion, so be patient with
him. I, on the other paw, am off to give a lecture on
the Time-Travel Paradox to a room full of inquisitive

students. I am curious so see how they react to me
as their lecturer. Probably better than most adults
would. Now, if you will patiently listen to the rest of
Mythral's oration, I just might share my Time-Travel
Paradox speech with you later.

Kit shifted uncomfortably in her chair and wondered *Am I a normal or a wizard? I'm from Realm One, but Mythral says I have magic.*

Mythral lectured on. "And while it is impossible to be certain from inside our current Time-Path, quite probably, the Three Realms Spell was a free will exercise that may have resulted in an Inherently Unbalancing Event.

"According to some of the forbidden texts, an Inherently Unbalancing Event also could be created by a successful Time Inversion Spell, which might result in very significant changes. A Time Inversion Spell was rumored to have been successfully performed, in desperation, when I was just a boy.

"Only one of the participants survived, if he is to be believed, and he went quite mad. The other, found dead, had sustained injuries from dark magic.

The surviving wizard claimed a Void was coming that would destroy the universe. It had been sensed by several of the best wizards of that time. The one who returned alive said they did not know how to travel forward in time, so they went backwards until they reached the future. They, too, knew the Time-Path was a continuous loop.

"There in the future, they helped stop the Void from coming. The only other thing anyone could make out of his ravings was a chant he kept repeating: 'Mythral's choice will doom or save the Realms.'"

"That prophecy has haunted me ever since I first learned of it.

"This brings us to my personal dilemma regarding free will. Most significant choices, even if inconsistent with the future, are absorbed into the current Time-Path. On this current Time-Path, I have sensed my own death in the near future."

The pieces fell into place, and Kit bolted upright, standing and tense. "That is what I saw the day you took my hand. I was seeing your death and all the evil and darkness that followed throughout the Realms. Yet it was different from what you have described, and I was there. Does that mean we will fail?"

Ignoring that very important but unanswerable question, and sensing Kit might be getting tired of his long-winded lectures, Mythral said, "To put it briefly, any routine attempt by me to alter my future most likely would be absorbed and adjusted. A key event, such as my demise, would remain the future outcome. The actual method or timing of my death might be shifted a bit by extraordinary efforts. But, if I cannot find an Inherently Unbalancing Event, my death is unavoidable. I, therefore, must believe in free will and in the possibility of a free-will choice radical enough to create an alternate Time-Path."

Kit finally managed to ask, "What would it take to create this alternate Time-Path?"

"That's what you and I are going to discover—if we are very, very lucky. If we can create this alternate Time-Path, we must make sure it is a good path, or at least a better path."

That was a bridge too far, for Kit. "How in the world do you judge a good path from a bad path before you create it?" She'd momentarily forgotten questions led to answers, and Mythral's were often in the form of a lecture.

"The universe vibrates at a certain fundamental frequency. According to present-day science, this has something to do with the creation of the universe and background radiation.

"While contrast and conflict are natural elements within a universe, the universe prefers a harmonious vibration, and that fundamental vibration can be felt during sensing. Have you ever heard a specific musical note or chord that resonated in your body? It just feels natural and pleasant. Contrast that with a discordant noise, like fingernails on a chalkboard. The feel of harmonious vibrations allows you to identify 'better' outcomes. Good versus evil in a simple test.

"In the present, when applied to people, this ability to sense inconsistencies with fundamental harmonious vibrations is known as truth-reading a person. I do it without even knowing I am doing it."

"Can I do this truth-reading?" Kit asked, letting the possibilities play across her thoughts.

"You did it when we first held hands," Mythral informed her. You sensed our future, and you knew immediately how bad that future would be.

"I must caution you on a significant limitation for truth-reading someone. When the person you are reading does not know he is lying, if he truly believes what he is saying, then you will not sense any discord with the universe.

"A less obvious limitation has to do with the confusion caused by differing underlying assumptions. Fortunately, we've already covered that subject."

CHAPTER 23

KIT'S FIRST DARK WIZARD
[Realm One
and 𝕽𝖊𝖆𝖑𝖒 𝕿𝖜𝖔]

Another "ping" from Realm Two interrupted their morning's training. To Kit's surprise and delight, Mythral allowed her to come with him to Realm Two. They went to the secret cellar where Mythral could safely show Kit just how he operated the gate key. On the stairs going down, Kit was impressed. "You mean these stairs have two different exits, depending how you rotate them?"

"Yes. That was Perci's idea. Hide things in plain sight. Should anyone make it this far into my shop, all they would find is a normal staircase and cellar."

Mythral activated the gate key and Kit "arrived" just where she had been. She looked perplexed. She felt as if they had moved, but her surroundings looked exactly the same. Aware of Kit's confusion, Mythral immediately began explaining as he led them up the stairs towards the front of the bookshop.

"The Gate Spell that we just used is a permanent and carefully crafted point-to-point spell, used to move from one location to another. You felt little or nothing, because it was designed to be smooth. Your surroundings look exactly the same because, essentially, they are. My bookshop in Realm One structurally is the same as this one in Realm Two. Although the books you will find here in Realm Two," Mythral indicated with a sweep of his arm, "are different. They still are dusty and disorganized for the same reason."

Kit gazed around the shop at the strange assortment of books of all colors and shapes. Some appeared to move a bit. Some changed in appearance. Still others made strange, muffled sounds.

As she was taking it all in, Mythral interrupted her thoughts and headed towards the back of the shop. "I'll be back in a flash. Try not to give away the shop or talk to strangers." Realizing by her facial expression Kit had missed the joke, Mythral added, "Just kidding. No one actually buys books in this Realm. I just like to collect them."

"Fine. I'll see if I can amuse myself somehow," Kit replied automatically. She was completely distracted by her surroundings. There were many books on magic and almost none on science. At least, there were no books on what one would call current science.

She came across an unusual volume titled *Tattle Tales*. As she soon discovered, when you opened the *Tattle Tales* book, it screamed aloud the secrets or embarrassments of the one who had opened it, until it was closed. Worse, the voice sounded like her least favorite teacher.

Kit's shame, as announced by the book, was she secretly wondered what she and her brother had done that was bad enough to make their parents abandon them. Would they ever return? Had that possibility kept their foster parents from adopting them, or was it something much worse?

At just about this time, Cat came in the front door and explained the book she held, saying, "Mythral sometimes uses that book as a clever form of interrogation."

Kit asked Cat, "How did you get to Realm Two from Realm One? When Mythral used the gate key, I did not see you."

Cat smiled at her on his way to the back rooms and said again, "Mythral is not the only one with secrets."

While Kit continued looking through the many strange volumes, a sinister-looking individual approached from the street and looked in the window. Upon spotting Kit, he came into the shop and asked to speak with

Mythral. She said she would let Mythral know. As she started towards the back of the shop, the stranger seemed surprised to hear Mythral actually was in the bookstore.

"Wait a moment. I have a few more questions." He stated this more as a command than a request. After some seemingly routine questions about certain books on magic, none of which Kit could answer, he asked if Mythral had any extremely rare books on magic.

Kit, like Mythral, could assess a situation very quickly and commit to a course of action based upon her instincts. She handed the stranger *Tattle Tales* and stepped back. He looked at it with suspicion and then opened it. The book screamed out, "TREACHERY AND MURDER!"

The stranger immediately dropped the book and turned to glare at Kit. How dare this mere girl trick him? He began casting an evil sounding spell. Kit was scared, but she was unable to do much. Mythral had not yet shown her how to deal with magical attacks.

After releasing his spell, the stranger gasped in disbelief. The spell had failed. Menacingly moving towards Kit and producing a wicked-looking knife, he exclaimed, "There is more than one way to skin a cat—or an insignificant little girl."

At that moment, Cat nonchalantly walked out of the back rooms. After announcing his opinion, "Such an awful phrase never, ever should be used," Cat issued a series of meows that felt powerful and rhythmic. The result was a spell that sent the stranger flying out the front door and into the roadway. The door opened just barely in time for his outward passage, and more than a few bumps and bruises were delivered along the way.

At this point, Cat explained about the Protection Against Magic Spell, which Mythral had placed on the bookshop in Realm Two. In that way, Perci could deal with any threats safely, even when Mythral was not around. Only Mythral and Perci could perform magic inside the shop.

As could Vivyen.

Before Kit could point out the obvious problem with what Cat had just done and said, Cat noted, "You will discover I am an exception to all rules.

"I call that my Catapult Spell. You may use it to eject someone from a room or building. It is a very simple one that even a novice can perform. Most wizards' normal defenses would render such a simple spell useless. That is, unless they cannot perform magic. Then they have no defense."

If you readers will pardon yet another short interruption. I rarely use magic. In fact, I was born without the ability to perform magic. By chance I arrived in the world of elves during my travels, and they unlocked that potential in me. However, that is an entirely different story for some other time. In the now and here, as the Realm Two expression goes, that bit of magic to expel the dark wizard was a spur-of-the-moment invention. Although I did impress myself with naming it the Catapult Spell.

Cat taught Kit the words to the Spell and then promptly walked out the front door, which opened for him, magically. When Mythral returned from the back rooms, he was dressed in long black wizardly robes. Kit was astonished. She never had seen anything like them, except in books and movies. There was an extra shimmer to his robes that Kit could not describe in words.

"This is the usual attire for serious wizards in Realm Two and Realm Three," Mythral explained. "If you become proficient in magic, you will be given robes of your own to wear during your official visits to the two Realms with magic."

CHAPTER 24

AUTOCORRECT FOR NOVICES
[Realm Two]

"I have some urgent matters to attend to," Mythral said on his way towards the door. "You are not to leave the bookshop."

"Wait!" Kit practically shouted. "There was an evil stranger in the shop. He was asking about you and old magic books. When I tricked him with the *Tattle Tales* book, he attacked me with a spell and then a knife."

"Are you hurt?" Mythral asked. "Where is he? What happened?"

Kit felt a sudden, dramatically intense buildup of power emanating from Mythral, and she rushed to explain. "I'm fine. Just a bit scared. I had no idea what to do. Cat showed up just as he pulled the knife and sent him flying out the door."

Mythral was silent for a moment. "Never before has one of them dared to enter my bookshop. Something serious must be afoot. Stay inside the shop. I want you to start learning basic magic.

"When learning new spells, it is okay to speak a magic spell for practice, as long as you do not put any force into the spell. That way, you can practice the words and the proper pronunciations without actually casting. It would not matter inside my shop, because only Perci and I can do magic inside. However, it is best to do things properly from the start. Bad habits can be hard to correct. When I return, I'll adjust the spell on the shop so you, too, can do magic."

"How do I defend myself if he returns?"

"Not to worry. I am going to lock the door, magically, until Perci or I return. While you are waiting, you might as well begin with some basic spells. See that red and gold striped book there on the top shelf, seventh in from the left?" Mythral asked as he pointed. "Work with that until Perci or I return."

With those words, Mythral was out the door and on his way before Kit could ask anything further about the book and what she was meant to do with it. As she approached the bookcase, she thought, *That shelf is just too high for me. What I really need is a Levitation Spell*. After finding a chair to stand upon, she pulled the book down.

She was not quite sure what to make of the title, *Remedial Spelling*. Inside the front cover, in letters that seemed to rise off the page, was a warning. "This book is the property of the First School of Magic and is not to be removed from school grounds."

As Kit opened the book to the first spell, her shock caused her to say her thoughts aloud. "It's a Levitation Spell. What a coincidence."

"Not at all," said the book, which so startled Kit she dropped it immediately onto the old, dark wood floor. The book responded with a loud, "Careful there! We books have feelings too, especially along our spines. Even you novice wizards should know better how to treat a book. Especially a book trying to help you with your studies."

After retrieving the book from the floor, Kit explained, "I'm very sorry. I'm just not used to talking books."

"Well, where have you been all your ... Wait! Where am I? This is not my school. Now you really have done it. You are absolutely prohibited from removing me from my school grounds!"

Kit seized the opportunity to explain, "Schools of Magic are no more. They were closed and sealed. Mythral must have removed you from your school to preserve you. Possibly, to give you to his new apprentice, whom I happen to be."

After a few moments of silence, the book said, "I'll want a word later with this Mythral fellow, but for now let's begin your Remedial Spelling.

First, the Levitation Spell is no coincidence; you asked for it, mentally, so that is what we will cover first. I'll give you the Spell, and you repeat it several times before we try it with magical force."

Kit thought to herself, *Magic, different Realms, talking cats, wizards, dark wizards ... so, why not a talking beginner's guide to Spells?* After several attempts with improper wording and then mangled pronunciations, Kit got a bit frustrated by the book's constant corrections of minute details. She complained.

The book explained, "There is nothing I can do about that, dear. Until you get the spell exactly right, I am required by my autocorrect feature to tell you what you did wrong. Wording and pronunciation are critical. Make a mistake, and you can do a great deal of harm. If you think this is nitpicky, just wait until you try a potions spell."

"Well," said Kit, "if I have to work this hard at getting it exactly right, why don't we work on something really useful? I want a spell to defend myself against dark wizards."

"I am sure you do," said the book, "but I am authorized to teach only basic spells. After all, you have to learn to levitate before you can learn to fly. Unless otherwise instructed, always emphasize the second syllable. Again, the spell to levitate, or fly in air, is *Renia-Vi-Gwelu*. Now you try it."

Kit decided any magical spell was better than none, and she continued working with the book until she finally perfected the Levitation Spell.

For the next spell, Kit insisted upon practicing the Catapult Spell that Cat had taught her. "It is really quite simple," lectured the book. "You just put the emphasis on the second syllable: *Nasta Ed*. It means 'thrust out' when translated from elvish."

"Wait a minute," Kit inserted before the book could continue. "What about elves? No one has mentioned elves."

"Where did you grow up? Of course there were elves. Long, long ago. Where do you think the language of spells comes from? Mind you, I've seen some disrespectful students in my day, spelling without using the elvish. That can be risky if you don't understand how spells really work."

"What happened to the elves? Why is it risky, not using elvish?"

"My, you do ask a lot of questions. I'm not a history book, so I cannot say what happened to the elves. Spells I can explain. Simple spells are just words with power behind them. The right words, plus enough power, make magic. Complex spells invoking complicated actions or concepts require enormous concentration to get right. Words are just the conduit for focusing that power and concentration to the desired end. In theory, any words, or none at all, would work. You just need the mental focus and the power. However, few wizards can do magic without words. Even fewer have the mental focus to do the complex spells. Now let's see if you have what it takes to perform first-year-level magic."

After perfecting her delivery of the first two spells, Kit allowed the book to choose the next spell. Then they began working on creating a light source. The Light Globe Spell, *Calad Coron*, was easy compared to the Levitation Spell. After mastering this spell, Kit decided to take a break. She wandered around the shop a bit.

CHAPTER 25

YET ANOTHER WIZARD
[Realm Two]

Kit lost herself completely in the overwhelming sensory experience of this incredible bookshop. Many of the books were in languages she did not recognize, but they fascinated her nonetheless. Some looked quite beautiful from the outside but contained dark and evil-looking pictures. One, with a nearly rotted-away cover, revealed the most wonderful fragrance when opened. There was an endless stream of surprises, good and bad, as she wandered among this hoard of treasures.

Because of her total preoccupation, Kit was surprised when another stranger walked in. That door was supposed to be locked.

This one was quite handsome. He was tall and blond and appeared to be a bit older than she was. However, she now understood the old saying about not judging a book by its cover.

Instead of looking at the books, he stared directly at her, with a strange expression on his face. Then he began moving towards her. Kit's brain worked very much like Mythral's. It immediately and subconsciously processed and cross-checked facts against what was stored in her head, and she reacted.

She forgot she could not do magic in the bookshop. Overwhelmed by her new surroundings, her recent encounter with a dark wizard, and the fact that both Mythral and Cat were out, she spoke the Catapult Spell, *Nasta Ed*. In her haste, she failed to emphasize the second syllable. It went all askew. Either her concentration or verbalization must have been off. It was her very first attempt at casting a spell.

Instead of catapulting the stranger out the door, the Spell knocked

98

a bookcase over onto him. Then the Spell itself exited through the door. As he levitated the bookcase off of himself, Kit focused properly and sent the Spell directly at him. Nothing happened. While she was preparing to try again, Kit noticed the stranger waving something white.

Laughing so hard he fell over, the stranger managed to say, "Truce!" While this interloper continued his laughter on the floor, the logic dawned on Kit. Only a wizard performing magic could evade that Spell. He had entered despite the locked door. He performed magic inside the bookshop.

Only two wizards could do that. She had just attacked Mythral's best friend Perci. Kit was mortified. Perci extracted himself from the mess on the floor, levitating the books and the fallen bookcase back to their original positions.

Brushing himself off and chuckling the whole while, Perci said to Kit, "We are going to have to teach you some more potent spells if you are going to attack every wizard you meet. I am Perci, and I assume you are Cinta Kilme."

"Yes. But I go by Kit. I am so sorry I attacked you! I hope I didn't hurt you." Kit felt her face flush as they spoke.

With a mix of awe and surprise, Perci said, "I was not aware Mythral had taught you any real magic. I certainly did not expect him to have allowed you to use magic inside the bookshop."

"He didn't teach me that Spell. Cat did."

"Well, your pronunciation and delivery were reasonably done for someone new to magic. Have you been practicing all day?"

"Practicing, yes, but on many spells. Mythral told me to work with this *Remedial Spelling* book." She held it out for Perci to see and he reached for it. As their fingers overlapped in the exchange, a definite spark passed between them, like strong, well-charged static electricity, but much more pleasant. Both were surprised by it, and the book fell to the ground. Again. It began to complain loudly about its treatment.

"If everyone here is going to keep throwing me on the floor, why bother picking me up in the first place? Is this that Mythral wizard you said had removed me from my school? I demand an explanation."

Perci, who obviously was used to talking objects, seemed oblivious to the book's ranting as he continued to look at Kit. His face was unreadable. His silence began to make her just a bit uncomfortable, so she offered an apology. "I am sorry for the shock on top of the attack. It must have been static electricity."

Perci, recovering from his internal thoughts, responded, "No need to apologize for either. Your attack reminded me not to make assumptions. I assumed safety inside the bookshop. A magical attack should not be possible. It was a good lesson. That spark was something new. Perhaps it was a bit of residual magic passing between us."

Mythral returned soon thereafter. He was at a loss for an explanation as to Kit's ability to perform magic in the shop. He was almost as amazed that she had successfully cast her first spell. Only Perci and Mythral (and, long ago, Vivyen) were allowed to perform magic inside the bookshop. Kit, like Cat, appeared to be an exception -- somehow. Giving up for the moment on this latest riddle, Mythral assigned Perci to continue Kit's training.

CHAPTER 26

LEARNING TO LIVE
[Realm Two]

Under Perci's close supervision, Kit's training was constant and rigorous. She had much to read and practice. She soon learned she had extra time in Realm Two. Mythral had secretly added a component to the Three Realms Spell. Time in Realm One ran slower than in Realm Two by a factor of pi squared. So, eight hours away from home in Realm One gave Kit over three days of training in Realm Two. Mythral's purpose in adding this component was to block anyone from successfully using a Translocation Spell to enter Realm One—if anyone besides him ever rediscovered the Spell.

After a few months in Realm Two, Kit showed ease and speed in learning to use magic. Physically, she had grown stronger and about an inch taller. At her height, every bit counted.

Kit learned early that, contrary to popular fiction, wizards, at least the good ones, rarely needed wands or much in the way of hand gestures. These were crutches relied upon by lesser wizards to focus their efforts.

The really good wizards did not even speak the spell aloud. As Perci reminded her often, "To do a spell without words, wands, or hands requires much greater concentration, which, in turn, requires extra practice, which leads to greater skill. Perfect concentration produces the strongest spell. Therefore, to be really powerful, we learn to perform spells mentally with our entire focus upon them. Hand gestures may be used to add flair or emphasis. However, they must never substitute for, or distract from, your full concentration."

Kit noted a commonality between the telepathy she was learning and spellcasting without vocalization. In both cases, the mental method was much harder and required much greater focus and concentration. However, once mastered and properly performed, mental delivery was much richer, stronger, and more focused.

The Light Globe Spell was easy but unimpressive when spoken. However, Kit found the Spell, cast mentally, could produce a sphere of light with added texture and movement within. Even colors could be rendered with vibrancy and great variation.

Perci constantly was supplementing Kit's basic lessons with his own insights. "If you develop a primary focus and train yourself, you can achieve deep levels of concentration very quickly."

"You are going to have to explain that one better," said Kit, at a complete loss.

"You want to quiet your mind and your body. We quiet the body with deep breathing. Mythral already has taught you that technique," said Perci.

"Yes. He said it would calm the mind and body. So why do I need a different focal point?" challenged Kit.

"You do like to interrupt explanations with questions that are about to be answered. Have a bit of patience," Perci chastised her. "Once you are meditating, the technique of deep breathing helps focus your mind and body. What I am proposing is a way to drop in to a deep level of meditation quickly. In an emergency situation, you may need to tap your deepest sources of power quickly.

"If you are caught by surprise and need to survive, you might not have time to center and slowly tap into your power resources.

"By selecting something like an object, sound, or fragrance as a point of focus, you can train your mind and body to enter a deeper state immediately. Like learning to play a sport or dance, the term 'muscle memory' is used in Realm One. With practice, your body knows what to do, instantly and unconsciously, when triggered by this focus point.

Think about it. Once developed, this technique allows you to quickly and deeply center yourself."

"I'll give it some thought," Kit said, but the answer had entered her thoughts even as Perci spoke. Lavender. Its color, scent, and even its taste had always resonated deeply with her. She did not know why.

These details for spellcasting, deep centering and tapping into power, and the constant lectures on morals and integrity all had one purpose: to prepare Kit to back up Mythral in his upcoming battle with evil. Kit now understood what the Realm Two inverted expression "learn and live" meant. If she did not learn all Perci and Mythral had to teach her, she might not survive that meeting with evil.

CHAPTER 27

LEARN MORE, LIVE LONGER.
[Realm Two]

Mythral's reflection on Kit's progress caught Perci off his guard that morning. "I think ignorance is the reason she is learning with such speed and is so confident in her magic. Being from Realm One, she doesn't know enough to be nervous or hesitant about such power."

Emotionally and physically, Kit's magic was smoother, stronger, more confident and certain than any but the most skilled of wizards. Even Mythral at her age did not possess such confidence and skill.

Her look had changed during these months in Realm Two with Perci. She was tying her long, curly hair back, out of the way, and her clothing, better-fitting to enable freedom of movement, revealed her developing form. Yet, after months of productive study and great enthusiasm from Kit, Perci sensed her spirits were sagging.

Their present training was a spell that fell between a Blocking Spell, *Tafnen Balan*, and a Boomerang Spell, *Adertha Balan*. Perci called it the Right-Angle Spell. Kit was to channel the incoming Spell to the side, left or right. In a more complex version, she could split the Spell to go in both directions and in front. *Thane Balan* was a handy Spell when enemies were on your sides as well as in front. Perci noticed her execution was lackluster and slower than usual. He needed to understand what was bothering Kit.

After much coaxing, Kit finally unburdened herself to Perci. "I'm just feeling so lost in Mythral's world. In Realm One, I understood my life and my purpose there. Although I now realize there wasn't much to it, I had a life to lead back in Realm One. More important, it was a life I knew and was content to live.

"Now I spend so little time in Realm One, it is almost irrelevant to my life here in Realm Two. Even when I'm back there, all I think about is Realm Two. However, here in Realm Two, all I do is study and train." Quickly Kit emphasized how much she enjoyed learning, the confidence it had given her, but the meaning of it all was down the road somewhere, at some time in the future.

"Every step I take is on Mythral's path to his future meeting with his sensed death. I spend most of my time in Mythral's bookshop, living in Realms created by Mythral. Studying under Mythral. Learning what Mythral has learned previously.

"I feel like a cog designed and built solely to fit into a machine designed and built solely to fulfill Mythral's quest to alter his future. As exciting and wonderful as the experience has been, I no longer feel I matter as an individual—only as a part of Mythral's path."

Perci was surprised and overwhelmed by Kit's confession. Kit noted a sadness in his gray-blue eyes as he looked away. She immediately regretted having so fully shared with Perci her present sense of loss of self. She fully expected a lecture on how important she was to Mythral. How much good she and her new life here in Realm Two would bring to the Realms if she and Mythral were successful. However, Perci's response stunned her.

"I guess I am in the same boat as you. My life is and always will be about serving and helping Mythral. However, I don't feel the way you do. So just now, I was asking myself what the difference might be.

"You must realize that every person has his or her own story. Some are bigger stories and encompass more people, like Mythral's, which impacts all three realms and everyone in them.

"My story, on the other hand, is much smaller. It certainly impacts Mythral and you, and a few others. If Mythral were to die in the future, my story would keep going. I likely would look for some way to keep making a positive impact, and I might work with some other wizard."

"Okay," said Kit. "I see how we, or our lives, are alike. Why are you better at accepting it?"

Perci continued, "My story may intersect with Mythral's a lot, but it remains my story. Just as your story remains yours. You are the protagonist in your own story. You must own it. Live for yourself, not for Mythral or some other larger-than-life character.

"When your story intersects with another's, don't let yourself get lost inside their story. Stay firmly at the center of your own. Be the main character. Live your values. Be satisfied with what you are doing and why you are doing it."

Perci's advice made sense to Kit. She had gotten lost inside Mythral's completely overwhelming story. She thought about one of her favorite characters, a very smart and courageous young wizard attending a wizarding school. That character had been just one of several strong and capable characters in a much bigger story. Yet, that character never lost herself in the plot. Kit said, "I need to think about all of this. Do you mind if we take a break?"

Perci nodded his consent. As she walked away, she looked back at Perci putting away their latest training materials and sensed another truth. Her confession and their subsequent conversation showed her just how much she had come to trust and respect Perci. He was kind and understanding. His patience with her training had been unbelievable. And now, he had become a confidant, a good friend, and perhaps even a bit more.

CHAPTER 28

TORO

[Realm One]

The pep talk from Perci was a critical turning point. Kit settled with greater ease and confidence into her role as Mythral's apprentice and as a young girl with her own future and her own story. Her focus was laser sharp. She no longer was beset by self-doubt and concerns about how she fit into the lives of others. She understood that their lives might, and did, intersect with hers. But if she focused upon her own story and doing what she knew to be right, she'd have done her part.

Fortunately, the months spent training with Perci in Realm Two translated into mere days in Realm One. This was part of the Three Realms Spell. She had heard his words but couldn't grasp their meaning—something about offsetting the fourth dimension, time, in the Time-Space Continuum between the two Realms. Apparently, if one did not know how much to offset, one could not use magic to make the jump safely. There was no telling where (or when) you might end up! The established gate that Mythral controlled was the only safe option.

So, what seemed like days of training in Realm Two turned out to have been no more than a long summer day of work at her new job. Mythral said the ratio was something about pi squared, or about nine days in Realm Two for every one day that passed in Realm One.

The changes in Kit's confidence and appearance were unnoticed by her family in Realm One. Only her little brother, Toro, commented. He was curious, and she needed someone in Realm One with whom to share. Toro became her confidant. Kit felt he should know what she was doing and why. If she failed to return home one day, at least he would understand. At first, Toro refused to believe any part of her story. His disbelief was suddenly suspended once she levitated him off her bed and spun him around a few times.

From that moment, Toro eagerly awaited Kit's daily reports about life in Realm Two. He wanted to know when he could meet Perci and Cat. Mythral he was more cautious about. "When can I go to Realm Two? When can I meet Cat? Can I start learning magic?" Toro constantly badgered her during their evening talks.

Kit understood Toro's yearning for magic. Maybe she should have emphasized the danger more, but she did not want to scare him unnecessarily. At eleven years of age, Toro was too immature to train, Mythral had said. Yet, as soon as Toro heard about Realm Two, magic was the single thing that excited him. He enjoyed fixing equipment and things, but about magic he was passionate. Magic was another, more exciting way to make things work.

Her response was the same as always. "Once the crisis with Mythral and MorKano is past, I'll ask Mythral about including you. He did once say you would be a good choice for an apprentice when you were a bit older. The timing just might work out."

Rarely would her answer stop Toro's string of questions about all things Realm Two. "Where does magic come from? Is it internal or external to the wizard? What makes a wizard strong or weak? Do dragons eat people?" Toro asked.

Kit patiently replied, "I am not positive about the answers to your first three questions. I believe magic exists just like air, all around and inside of us. A wizard must tap into his magic and nature's magic. I don't really understand how. I guess what makes a strong wizard is the ability to plumb the available magic and then channel it for a purpose.

"Your last question, about dragons eating people, is disgusting. I don't know, and I don't want to. Boys! It's time for you to go to your room and sleep. I need to think a while longer."

CHAPTER 29

PRACTICE, PRACTICE, PRACTICE.

[Realm Two]

While Kit was in Realm Two, her time passed quickly. She always had loved to read and learn, and magic was exciting and empowering. What could be better? Even Perci was more than she could have dared hope for in an instructor.

Perci was one of the smartest people she ever had met. His mind might be sharper even than Mythral's. However, his magic lacked the power and force of Mythral's. Mythral was one of the few wizards that had been given more than his fair share of intelligence and inherently strong magic.

MorKano, the darkest of the dark wizards, was another. Mythral rarely discussed MorKano and his vision of dying in MorKano's trap. Only one time did he explain to Kit their past indirect history. "When I first met Perci, he and his family were being attacked by a dark wizard, Durstin, who was MorKano's brother. The two were building an army of dark wizards by recruiting willing and unwilling volunteers. I discovered them torturing Perci's family in order to force Perci into swearing allegiance to the brothers. It ended badly for Durstin, whom I sent to prison. He later died trying to escape. That day Perci showed a degree of courage and strength unusual in an eleven-year-old."

"I didn't know any of that. When did all of this happen?" asked Kit.

"Shortly before the Three Realms Spell, about six years ago. So, given the pi-squared time offset with Realm One, it would have been around your thirteenth birthday."

Perci's weaker magic was balanced by his agile mind. Through

Mythral, Perci had access to knowledge and spells long forgotten and left to rot in the forbidden Schools of Magic. Perci was the one wizard in all of Realms Two and Three who had access to Mythral's knowledge of science from Realm One.

Mythral often talked about how combining the science of Realm One with the magic of the other Realms could produce destructive outcomes. He or the Council of WISDOM would be hard-pressed to stop such a combination.

Realm One's science must never fall into the hands of any dark wizard. For many reasons, Mythral had shown only Perci and Kit his secret to winning, with little effort, any battle against strong wizards. His secret was to siphon magic into an alternate world, not merely to deflect it. A very special application of science and magic.

Perci and Kit had practiced together for many long hours and, lately, Perci trusted her more, even becoming the willing target of Kit's spells. Perhaps it was more than just his level of trust in her. The more they practiced, the closer their bond grew. He explained to Kit she needed real experiences. "Without them, you will have lingering doubts at crucial moments," he told her.

Perci taught her how to immobilize another person or an entire room full of people with the basic Stunning Spell, *Dar-Rinc.* (Mythral insisted upon using only nonlethal magic.) She did well with Blocking and Deflecting Spells, which seemed almost second nature to her. Perci marveled at her reaction time—as fast as Mythral on most spells. Kit was slower at the Distraction and Befuddlement Spells. They took a lot more concentration to get right. They still went wrong occasionally. Although Kit had some success with them sometimes, after one erroneous Befuddlement Spell, *Glavrol Nauth*, it had been necessary for Mythral to restore Perci's clarity. Now they practiced such spells only when Mythral was on hand.

Despite her inquiries, Perci absolutely refused to teach Kit anything that could intentionally kill or injure. Mythral and Perci knew a great deal about such spells because of their access to the forbidden texts—perhaps even more than the dark wizards knew. However, Mythral cautiously had retained only a few textbooks, dangerous as they were, from the old schools. Further, he cast his strongest spells over their sections in these old school libraries to prevent anyone from discovering them in the future.

Kit's repeated trips back to Realm One turned out to be a good thing. These trips back gave her time to reflect on what she was doing and why. This was not just fun and games. She was being trained for a dangerous mission to save Mythral. Doing so, hopefully, would save all the Realms and everyone in them, including her brother and foster parents. If she and Mythral failed, her family would soon face evil wizards who would abuse and torture normals. Could she really do what was necessary when the time came?

Practice time with Perci is all well and good, but I never have faced a real threat. I never have stared into the eyes of a wizard who wants me dead. Would I panic? Would I react fast enough to save myself, or to save Mythral? That dark wizard my first day in Realm Two hardly counts. Right? I was in no real danger while in Mythral's bookshop, although that knife looked deadly.

Most nights at home in her own bedroom found Kit staring out of her second-floor window at the forest and fields. This night, initially, her thoughts reflected her doubts. Later, they devolved into the *Why me?* questions and concerns. Then they took a turn into: *What did I get myself into?* Eventually, Kit recalled the first night after Mythral asked her to be his apprentice. All the same "ifinating" had wandered through her mind then, too. She originally had decided to decline his offer, until she posed the questions Mythral had not. *If I don't accept, who would become Mythral's apprentice? If I decline, who would risk his or her life beside*

Mythral to save him and the Realms? Is there no one else better suited for such an enormously dangerous and difficult task? Has Mythral made a mistake in choosing me?

If Toro were awake and in her room at the right moment, she would pose her questions to him. Yet, his answers were of no use. He only saw the excitement and thrill of magic. The dangers and risk of failure never occurred to him. But speaking the doubts aloud to Toro helped her to face them.

Understanding Mythral as she now did, Kit finally knew the answers to all these questions. She had guessed the answers on that first night of contemplation. She had continued to accept the responsibilities he had imposed on her. Months later, and after much learning, she no longer needed to guess.

Kit, there at Mythral's side, was the one hope they had to avoid his impending death. Thereby preventing dark magic from getting completely out of control in Realm Three, then in Realm Two, and eventually in Realm One. Thinking through all the risks and doubts had kept Kit humble and focused. Her Realm One time forced her to keep her magic mastery in perspective, weighed against the risk. "Overconfidence can be a killer," Mythral would say. Kit knew he meant it about himself and his vision of the future. She was wise enough to take it to heart for herself, too.

CHAPTER 30

QUESTION: WHEN DOES TWO PLUS TWO NOT EQUAL FOUR?
[Realm One]

Answer: When jumping back and forth between two Realms running on different clocks.

During one of Kit's returns to her home in Realm One, this odd time-offset presented a serious complication. In Realm One, summer was ending, and school, the ordinary Realm One type of school, would begin soon. How could she continue her training with Perci and Mythral in Realm Two if they expected her to be in school all day in Realm One? Then she realized the next day, August Seventeenth, was her birthday. She would turn fourteen.

Maybe fourteen by the calendar, she thought. She already felt much older, like a person in her twenties. All the training and responsibilities of becoming Mythral's apprentice had aged her.

Yes, she had been very busy in Realm Two, but how could she forget her fourteenth birthday? As a matter of fact, no one else appeared to have remembered it. Kit spent several hours trying to fall asleep on her birthday eve. Her mind could not shake the doubts swirling around in her head. The whole summer had gone by, and she had accomplished nothing in Realm One to show for it.

Realm Two achievements were different. Her training with Mythral was critical to the survival of the Realms and crucial for the survival of her brother, foster parents and everyone else in Realm One.

Yes, yes, she reminded herself. *There really is no choice in the matter.*

There was no other path she could live with, literally or figuratively. *But, what about my life as a fourteen-year-old girl? What about boyfriends, or at least a friend who is a boy? What about school activities, dances, sports?* she wondered.

Even if those options were available to her during her next year at school, how could she enjoy them? The time for experiencing her early teens seemed to have passed her by that summer. Some of Mythral's lectures on accepting responsibility for making the right choices were making more and more sense as she lived them.

Her thoughts would not quiet this evening. *Has all of this really been my own choice? Did Mythral manipulate me because he needed me?*

I made that decision before the beginning of summer. All alone in my bedroom, that second night after meeting Mythral. I had decided to turn down his offer. Then something changed my mind. What caused me to do a 180? Was Mythral influencing me somehow? Did he really need me, specifically? Or am I just his most convenient option?

Then she remembered Mythral's lectures on personal integrity. Naming what had changed her mind that night was easy.

Her initial decision to reject Mythral's offer, to preserve her safe and simple life, had just felt wrong. The decision to accept responsibility for being the best person for the apprenticeship felt correct. Yet, she failed to realize what she was sacrificing--her present and future. But, would that sacrifice have altered her sense of what was right? Apparently, she had possessed an innate ability to sense right from wrong even before she began training with Mythral. And now, this evening, she was doubting it all yet again. Mythral would call this another lesson in personal ethics.

Mythral could spend hours describing weak people who found the most ingenious ways to justify choices they felt were easier but knew to be wrong. Often, their efforts were simply to avoid making any choice. His list included: blaming others for one's actions or failure to act; procrastinating; ifinating; and asking "Why me?" They would carry on until it was too late to act. Frequently, they deceived themselves as to facts or as to their own true motives. She just had gone through nearly the entire list of excuses because of her birthday tomorrow. "How weak can you get?" she asked aloud.

"You have to tell me more before I can answer," was Toro's reply from her doorway.

Kit said, "I wish you'd shown up earlier. I wasted the evening talking to myself and getting the same answers." Kit told Toro her doubts. Not because he could help, but to hear herself talk. By the time Toro left for bed, Kit was aware of two things: Toro had not mentioned her birthday; and she would continue to do the right thing.

One thing she was certain about in her whole life was the decision to help Mythral survive his deadly encounter in MorKano's fortress. Not just because the future of the Realms depended upon it, but because of this inexplicable connection to Mythral that made her now "want" to do it. All doubts were gone. She, Kit, was the right person, in the right time, and in the right place. She would make a difference, no matter the cost!

CHAPTER 31

LET THEM EAT CAKE.
[Realm One]

A chorus of "Happy Birthday" at breakfast pleasantly surprised Kit the next morning. Two gifts awaited her at her chair. One of them, ostensibly, was from her brother. Her foster parents had bought and wrapped it, she assumed. Both gifts were books, and good ones at that.

One book was about moral dilemmas and the choices people make and why. The second was about traveling away from home, filled with recommendations such as paying attention to the places, people, and things around you to get the most from your travels.

The more she reflected upon the book selections, the more suspicious she became. She sensed Mythral's hand in this somehow. After some casual questioning, she once again was surprised to learn the books were Toro's idea. Upon intense cross-examination, Toro admitted the actual idea had come from Cat at the bookshop. At his statement, their foster parents rolled their eyes and said the gifts had been a good idea, wherever it came from. Toro said the man in the shop, a Mr. Hartly, was nice and helpful, claiming to know just what Kit would like to have. Toro was winking at Kit when he mentioned Cat and Mr. Hartly. Toro knew full well who they were.

Kit thanked her family for their wishes and gifts. After breakfast, she indulged in a small piece of the white cake with her favorite butter cream frosting and lavender decorations. Happy with the start of her birthday, Kit headed to the bookshop.

Upon her entrance, Mythral and Perci greeted her with another birthday cake. *This birthday is getting better and better,* she reflected. After the customary birthday wishes, Perci said, "Let's cut this thing. Mythral's lemon-lavender cake with butter cream frosting is one of my favorites."

Coincidence? Kit wondered. *I decided on lavender as my focus point just days ago, and it appears in a cake.*

Mythral, lost in thought, said, "It was Vivyen's specialty. I learned the recipe from her." As they each took a large slice and dug in, Kit noticed the sprinkles on top were extra-large and unlike anything she had tasted before.

Kit was about to ask about the sprinkles when Cat strolled in and announced, "It seems my invitation to this party must have gotten lost!" Cat wished Kit a happy birthday and then told Kit he had a very special gift for her: the gift of wisdom.

Kit was at a loss for how best to reply. It sounded like another book, but Cat had brought nothing with him. Noticing Kit's searching look, Cat announced after a dramatic pause, "A gift of wisdom is useless, and may even be a burden, if the recipient is not yet ready for it."

In her thoughts, Kit started to wonder if this "non-present" gift was just a clever way to impress people at a party without actually bringing a gift. In the past, Kit's increasing ability to sense, as Mythral did, had been useless when focused upon Cat.

Now when she looked at Cat, alarm bells echoed in her head. It was as if Cat could read her thoughts. She needed to ask Mythral about that. Out of the corner of her eye, she noticed Mythral had stopped eating his cake. He actually took a step back from Cat. Mythral also sensed a strong disruption in the universe. It was emanating from Cat.

"I always have appreciated Mythral's lavender cakes," said Cat. "However, the best part is my favorite mix of liver and tuna nibbles on top." Kit involuntarily choked on her mouthful of nibbles. Cat smiled and headed out the door, saying, to no one in particular, "You humans are far too easy. I really must find more challenging prey."

Mythral and Perci knew Cat was playing with Kit. The look on Kit's face put a stop to their eating. They were laughing too hard. After Mythral and Perci finally controlled their laughter, Perci again wished Kit a happy fourteenth birthday. Not one to let a harmless statement go unchallenged, Mythral said, "While that may be Kit's technically correct chronological age in Realm One, she is, in fact, quite older than fourteen.

"Because of the time differential between Realms One and Two, Kit is closer to fifteen. And then there is the level of maturity that comes with the burdens she has undertaken. Her training and lessons would age anyone. Kit's personal and emotional development is far beyond that of a fifteen-year-old.

"I guess I really should apologize to you," Mythral continued, "for the time difference between Realm One and Realm Two, which will make counting your years quite impossible. As I have explained, it was a necessary element of the Three Realms Spell, just in case any other wizard learned to translocate."

"No problem," Kit said without conviction. "I'll just go through life never knowing how old I am, or when to celebrate an anniversary. That's assuming I survive to my next birthday."

> Once again, gentle reader, I apologize for my interruption. A few things must be set straight. First, the family's gifts to Kit were entirely my idea. To give her a gift would never have occurred to Mythral. Male humans, even wizardly ones, are often ignorant of such norms. Second, I don't eat cake. It is far too sweet. But I do thoroughly enjoy playing with the brains and emotions of humans. Finally, my gift of wisdom was real, as you'll see later in my story. Wisdom is useless if it arrives too early. And before you feel too sorry for Kit, yours truly will never know

his age as measured by some calendar. Jumping around on the Time-Path makes counting linear days impossible.

CHAPTER 32
OUT AND ABOUT IN REALM TWO
[𝔎𝔢𝔞𝔩𝔪 𝔗𝔴𝔬]

Two days later, Mythral unexpectedly dropped into the training area in his Realm Two bookshop and announced Kit was about to get her first outing beyond the bookshop's walls. Mythral handed her a package, which contained a full set of black robes in her size. The sky-blue trim was the exact color of her eyes.

"Are you promoting me?" Kit asked, hardly containing her hope and excitement.

Mythral had failed to lay any foundation for this gift of robes, and he quickly dashed Kit's hopes. "Not yet. An apprentice typically wears these robes. You'll need to wear them so you blend in during our excursion in Realm Two. Your jeans and casual shirts from Realm One would call too much attention to our actions."

The bookshop in Realm Two was located on the outskirts of one of the few towns where people had chosen to live in a community. Crops' growth could be spurred with magic, but food could not be created out of thin air. So those who did not wish to grow food, magically or otherwise, found it more convenient to live in or near towns. This town of Fairhaven, one of the larger ones, hosted the Council of WISDOM whenever they met.

As Mythral and Kit ambled towards the center of Fairhaven, Kit was surprised by how little seemed strange. Yes, there was the constant use of magic for even the smallest of tasks; the exchange of spells or information apparently was part of the bartering system used in the local economy.

The look and feel of the town were something Kit easily could envision as having existed in Realm One—way back in the Middle Ages, that is. She had read much about that period in her local library, and this place felt like that. A few, only men, wore robes.

When Kit expressed her observations to Mythral, he replied, "You have a good eye for details. When the Three Realms Spell was cast and the normals were exiled to Realm One, removing most scientific advances from the other two Realms was essential. Indeed, resetting Realm Two and Realm Three in a period that had few precursors to scientific advances was advisable.

"As I have often said, combining science from Realm One with magic could be disastrous in the wrong hands. The backfill story for Realm One did have this period in common with Realm Two and Realm Three. What else do you see?"

As Kit continued to observe the activities of the town while they walked, she noticed how everyone around was reacting to Mythral. As a test, she stepped away from Mythral for a few moments and pretended to look at something in a shop window.

As she returned to Mythral's side, she mentioned her newest observation. "Everyone we pass reacts to you in one of two ways. Some stare in awe and wonder. Others want to avoid you and being seen by you. I get the distinct impression those who wish to avoid you are trying to make themselves as small as possible or to hide behind something or someone. Why is the town reacting to you in such extremely different ways?"

"There are many powerful wizards on the Council of WISDOM, and stories about my power may well cause people to react. Yet, these extremes have less to do with my power and more to do with my reputation for, and many stories about, my belief in personal integrity.

"A person who seeks to do the right thing, no matter the personal cost, who refuses to compromise values, who rejects rationalizations and convenient false justifications—that person causes a strong reaction from others."

"You really mean 'you' when you say 'a person,'" commented Kit.

"Not just me. The response is to everyone who exhibits personal integrity. You'll experience it firsthand soon enough," said Mythral. "All we can do is live by example and hope it inspires others. We must pity those who are too damaged or weak. No matter how they try, they cannot run from the truth of right and wrong. Yet while they cannot run away, they live in fear of having to face it."

After several hours of strolling around the town, Mythral was satisfied. Kit appeared comfortable in Realm Two with the sights, the people, and the slight variations in language. Kit had only one concern. She asked Mythral about a raven-haired girl who kept staring at them.

Without hesitating, Mythral replied, "Jasmine is the girl watching you. Be careful with her. She was Perci's girlfriend a while back, and it did not end well."

Kit resisted further inquiry. Mythral and Kit returned to the bookshop. Over the next week, Mythral and Kit had regular outings in Realm Two. After the second one, Mythral disguised himself and let Kit move through the town on her own. Jasmine always appeared, though she kept her distance.

While an individual wizard, especially a female on her own, was always at risk for having some misadventure in Realm Two, Kit's outings were uneventful. Mythral's scrutiny of Kit's bearing and attitude revealed much. She now radiated confidence and strength, and people sensed it. Even though Mythral was nowhere to be seen, they treated her with respect and deference. The few female wizards who had served on the Council of WISDOM would have been easily overlooked on the streets of Fairhaven. They would not have received the level of respect being shown to Kit.

Just as she was leaving the Realm One Bookshop for home that evening, Cat happened to be coming into the shop. *Here is someone I can ask about Jasmine.*

"Cat. How are you this fine evening, and may I ask you a question?"

"While I could stop you from asking, I won't. So, ask you may, but answers are another matter and come with a cost, as Mythral may have told you. Do you still have a question?"

"I think you sort of like me. After all, you recommended me to Mythral. So, yes, I'll ask. What can you tell me about Perci and Jasmine?"

"As to liking you, we'll wait and see how you do with the challenges ahead. However, this question of Jasmine is clearly going to distract you from your studies, so I'll give you the basics. For the rest, you need to ask Perci. Jasmine and Perci were together for a while. She had an agenda for the use of magic that was inconsistent with Perci's. She used her magic upon Perci, and their relationship ended badly."

CHAPTER 33

THE MISADVENTURES OF KIT AND PERCI

[Realm One and Realm Two]

When Kit entered the bookshop in Realm One, Perci surprised her. He'd made a rare visit to Realm One. For training, Kit usually traveled to Realm Two by herself. Mythral had shown her how to use the gate key.

Perci explained, "I could not take a chance that you might delay your arrival in Realm Two for any reason. Mythral has an assignment for us in Realm Two. It might be a bit dicey, given the location that we need to visit. Mythral does not want me to go alone."

"It sounds important and dangerous. Why isn't Mythral taking charge?" said Kit.

Barely acknowledging Kit's interjection, Perci continued, "Mythral is off in Realm Three to do some scouting and make contact with Nate. Mythral says you'll meet Nate later, so don't ask now. Since I've never been to Realm Three, there's not much I can tell you.

"However, there is a wizard, who should be trustworthy and claims to have important information for Mythral. That wizard has sent word that he needs to meet with Mythral this afternoon, or it may be too late."

Perci and Kit were to take the meeting. Mythral left strict instructions that if anything looked or felt wrong, they were to forget about the meeting and leave immediately. After they transported to Realm Two, Kit changed into her robes before they headed out to Fairhaven's rougher side of town.

Perci continued to fill in some of the details as they made their way to the meeting. "The wizard we are to meet is Antenor, a member of the Council of WISDOM. He insists on meeting with Mythral away from his home. The place chosen is a tavern patronized by a wide cross-section of the community. Antenor had suggested Mythral come in disguise.

"I have met Antenor, so we will spot him easily in the tavern. Because I am well known as Mythral's assistant, I will do the explaining. You must tone down your confidence and power. Try to look like a novice who is tagging along. Your real job is to watch my back while I find out what Antenor wants to pass on." Kit's abilities to sense and truth-read were growing quickly and soon might equal Mythral's.

While Perci preferred casual attire, he was recognized as Mythral's assistant. A certain level of respect, or fear, was accorded, such that nothing untoward happened on their way to the meeting. They reached the Black Cat Tavern. The Black Cat was a very old, weathered stone building with two large chimneys, one on either end of the dark slate roof. The windows were clouded and smudged with soot from the two enormous fireplaces inside. Its rundown appearance was ominous and far from welcoming.

Just before they entered the tavern, Perci mentally issued some final instructions to Kit. *Keep your eyes down and your sensing at full strength. A novice, especially a female novice, would be uncomfortable in a room full of wizards who are not her mentor. If you see or sense anything amiss, alert me using this mental connection we've practiced.*

The inside of the tavern looked much like the outside. It was dark, crowded, smoky, and filled with an assortment of rough-looking patrons. All eyes turned to this odd pair with a mix of contempt and suspicion. A young male and a female novice should not be in a place such as this.

Entering the room, Perci spotted Antenor in a far corner booth. Antenor, who obviously had been watching the door for someone who might be Mythral in disguise, clearly was not happy to see Perci.

As Perci and Kit made their way to Antenor's corner table, Kit broke in on Perci's concentration with a warning. *I sense dark wizards, two I think, off to our right. Their thoughts are well shielded, but I know they are there.*

Perci replied in Kit's head, *If they are here for Mythral, and now us, it is too late to back out. Let's play this through. No one will expect you to be a powerful wizard. If they attack, they are in for a major surprise. Have both a Blocking Spell and an Entanglement Spell ready. Depending on what Antenor has to say, Mythral might need to question those dark wizards as well.*

As they sat down at the table with this unremarkable, fidgeting, middle-aged wizard, Antenor's nervousness was obvious in his voice and in his string of questions. "Is he in the room somewhere? Why did he send you? Doesn't Mythral trust me?"

Perci explained, "Mythral could not make the meeting on this day. He sent me in his place. As Mythral's confidant in all matters, you can safely pass your information through me to him."

As Antenor appeared to be considering his options in the matter, Kit's voice intruded again into Perci's head. *There is something wrong about Antenor. It isn't clear that he is lying, but something just isn't right. And by the way, those two dark wizards are approaching us. What's the plan, "boss"?*

Perci took almost no time in mentally replying, *I have no doubt you are faster than they, even without the element of surprise. If they make any move at a spell, stun them first. I'll be ready to handle Antenor in case he is in on this.*

No sooner were the words out of Perci's mind and into Kit's than she sensed a disturbance in the harmony of the universe. The dark wizards were readying a spell. Before they realized Kit was the real threat here, she had acted. Not trusting fully her telepathic casting, she whispered, "*Dar-Rinc, Gonathra,*" first stunning them and then entangling them. Now the only problem was getting them back to Mythral for interrogation.

The room was full of wizards who were not sure what had just happened. To them, it appeared some novice girl had lost her head and attacked two wizards for no reason. Realizing the confusion in the room, and seeing no danger coming from Antenor, Perci turned to address the crowd gathering around Kit and the two entangled wizards.

"Some of you will recognize me as Mythral's assistant." Thinking quickly, in case Antenor's involvement needed to be minimized, he added, "Mythral sent me to lure these two dark wizards into showing themselves. Indeed, it is possible Mythral himself is here among us in disguise."

At this last suggestion, the crowd backed away from Kit and the two dark wizards. Clearly, Mythral's presence was a much better explanation for what they just had witnessed. Instead of this female novice taking down two dark wizards, it had been Mythral.

Perci continued, "I have no desire to levitate this pair through the streets of Fairhaven. If one of you would kindly loan us the use of a cart and donkey, Mythral would be most grateful."

While the crowd slowly was processing Perci's words, he turned back to Antenor to suggest moving the meeting to another location. Antenor was gone. In dealing with the crowd, neither Perci nor Kit had noticed his departure. They looked at each other, and Perci shrugged and mentally told Kit, *No hope for it now. I suspect Mythral will be able to locate Antenor when he returns. I suggest we take these two wizards back to the bookshop.*

The return trip garnered many outright stares and gasps. By appearance, here was this lad and a female novice leading a donkey, pulling an old cart stuffed with what looked like two unconscious dark wizards— quite powerful ones, as it turned out. They had to be stunned twice more before they arrived back at the Realm Two bookshop. Of course, once inside, the dark wizards' magic was useless. The Entanglement Spell was sufficient to hold them until Mythral's return.

CHAPTER 34

THE INTERROGATION OF EVIL
[Realm Two]

Mythral returned and chose to use a common interrogation ploy on the two very uncooperative wizards. There was little trust among dark wizards, and MorKano was feared even by his most loyal followers. Mythral began the interrogation by asking them to tell all. Naturally, they refused. Their fear of MorKano exceeded anything they expected from Mythral. Mythral turned to Perci and asked how long they had been in the shop. Perci replied, "About two hours."

Mythral said, "That is not long enough. Wait two more hours, and then release them through the front door. Make sure someone sees them leave, with you waving goodbye and smiling!" The look of shock on Perci's and Kit's faces prompted Mythral to explain.

Secretly Mythral wanted this opening to enlighten the two dark wizards. "Everyone knows I am not going to do horrible things to get these two to talk, so why waste time? The best I could do is have them sent to Realm Three, but that would take time and evidence and would only add to MorKano's followers in Realm Three. No. Why dirty my hands and waste my time when MorKano and his agents will get rid of these two for me?"

Kit said, "Why should MorKano punish them for not cooperating?"

Mythral wondered if Kit was playing along or just had not thought it through. Either way, she gave him the opening he wanted. "MorKano will have heard by now that these two have been captured and brought to my shop. He naturally will assume I have interrogated them. MorKano will assume I used spells strong enough to learn what they know. However, such mind opening spells usually damage the suspect.

"So given those assumptions, what will MorKano think when these two walk out the front door with our thanks? Simple: If he is in a hurry, he'll have them executed quickly as a warning to anyone else getting themselves caught or cooperating with me. If he can get them back to Realm Three and take his time, MorKano will use them as a teaching example, quite public and lengthy."

"And what should we do if they decide to talk?" said Kit.

"Should they decide on a different path and want to cooperate before the two hours are up, come and get me. Otherwise, push them out the door with happy faces and any other parting gifts you can think of—maybe a book or two."

Less than one hour after these instructions, Perci showed up in Mythral's private chambers with the news that the prisoners were ready to talk, on one condition. While these two wizards were quite strong, they also proved to be unusually intelligent. Mythral's ploy in threatening to release them was obvious, but still quite effective. Dark wizards, being the paranoid group they were, knew exactly how MorKano would respond to any perceived betrayal.

They were willing to share important information with Mythral on one, make that two conditions.

First, they insisted on being charged for attacking Perci and Kit and for "refusing" to cooperate. The Council of WISDOM could take its time, but eventually it would decide to expel them to Realm Three. This way, they had a fighting chance. MorKano might believe they did not betray him.

The other condition was obvious. Mythral, Perci, and Kit must keep the betrayal a secret. After all, to do otherwise would render useless most of what they intended to share with Mythral. They tried to demand Perci and Kit leave the room. They were especially concerned about this mere girl and her reliability to uphold their agreement. Mythral rejected their demands, pointing out, to their embarrassment, that this "mere" girl had bested both of them in straight battle.

Very little initially was volunteered by the two. They made clear MorKano had a way back to Realm Two that he used sparingly. Mythral surmised he was using a disguise and an agent within Realm Three gate security to get past the protection spells. Mythral hoped MorKano had not discovered how to translocate as Mythral did. That would be disastrous indeed.

While Mythral and Kit truth-read the two dark wizards, Mythral began the interrogation in earnest. With Mythral's penetrating questions and careful wording, the two were given no wiggle room. They had to confess all, or else violate the agreement with Mythral. They did try a lie early on, which Mythral and Kit detected easily. After Mythral threatened to end the agreement if they lied again, all went smoothly.

What was learned from the two dark wizards was very disturbing, but also very limited. They had met with MorKano on only two occasions since he was expelled to Realm Three. However, their prior association with MorKano confirmed the worst about him. MorKano used torture as his first and preferred method of interrogation.

After hearing the first two examples of his torture, Mythral moved on, to spare Perci and Kit's having to listen to talk of dismemberment and various psychological attacks. MorKano particularly enjoyed hurting the victim's family to utterly demoralize the interrogatee. Even when he got what he wanted early, MorKano took pleasure in continuing the pain and suffering for as long as it might hold his attention.

From the answers given, Mythral assumed MorKano and his followers were aware of the Three Realms and the Spell that created them. Implicit also was MorKano's scheme to undo the Spell, though he needed someone on the Council of WISDOM for his plan to work.

The two dark wizards had been instructed recently to follow Antenor whenever he was not at home or with the Council. They were to report on his contacts and his actions. His arrival at the Black Cat Tavern on this particular day had forced them to get closer than usual. Their decision to act against Perci and Kit was out of fear of angering MorKano.

Constituting the sum of their insights into MorKano, the interview lasted only about an hour and a half. As agreed, Mythral had Perci and Kit bind and stun the two for transport to the Council of WISDOM and then a holding cell. There the two were to be processed, given a hearing, and eventually expelled to Realm Three.

As Perci and Kit handled the transport to the Council of WISDOM, Mythral reflected upon what had been gleaned from the interview. Clearly, Realm Two no longer was safe from the evils that were exported to Realm Three. The system had broken down, and, worse, the evil in Realm Three had been left unchecked for a long time. If MorKano could execute his plan to undo the Three Realms Spell, then they'd be back to a single realm. Normals would be mixed in with the good wizards and the worst of the dark wizards, resulting in chaos even Mythral had no hope of controlling or fixing.

CHAPTER 35

THE TESTING BEGINS.
[Realm Two]

After the successful outings into Realm Two, followed by a few more weeks of intensified training, Mythral decided Kit should experience Realm Three on a controlled and relatively safe trip. He did not want Realm Three to be overwhelming when Kit eventually joined him to undo his impending death in MorKano's fortress. So far, Kit's knowledge, speed, and reaction time had been more than adequate. In fact, she was second only to Mythral.

However, she had been tested only once in a truly dangerous situation. While the confrontation at the tavern went quite well, Kit had the advantage of surprise, which might be lost for any future confrontations. Taking her into the impending battle without a reasonable expectation that she would survive was not his plan. Even if they failed to change his fated death, Kit must survive. Mythral was not certain of the source of his conviction. Was it purely emotional? He had such a strong yet unexplained connection to Kit.

Mythral decided to conduct some final testing of Kit's readiness before taking her into Realm Three and eventually into battle. After explaining his decision and reasons to Kit, Mythral told Kit, "You should take the remainder of today and all of tomorrow to rest and center yourself. These tests are unlike anything you have experienced, and they can be dangerous to you and to others. The reality of the danger is critical to the tests."

How in the world does he expect me to relax and rest after hearing that? Kit wondered to herself.

Two days later, Mythral began the testing. Magic was as much about intellect as it was about power, Mythral told Kit. "So, tell me how you would resolve this problem. Assume you cannot truth-read the subjects.

Are any of our readers willing to be put to the tests? As I suggested at the beginning of my tale, decide what you would do if you were Kit before you read the outcome. Do this for each of the three tests and compare how you fared.

"You are in a room with no doors or windows, and you can't get out by using magic or physical force. The room is shrinking slowly. Each minute, the walls will move closer to you by half the distance. Any attempt to use force or magic to escape will cause the room to shrink even faster. The release lever that allows you to exit the room is inside one of two holes in the wall. But the holes are mouths that can speak, and they have very sharp teeth.

"Like the bags-of-gold riddle I gave you on your first day in the bookshop, you get to ask only one question.

"You can escape only by pulling a lever inside one of the mouths. If you reach into the wrong mouth, you will lose an arm. The test will end, but you will have failed.

"If you reach into the correct mouth and pull the release lever, you will be set free.

"Choose your one question carefully. And, by the way, one mouth always will lie to you. The other mouth always will tell you the truth. You do not know which is which. You have ten minutes to solve the problem. Are you ready?"

Kit said, "I guess. Will I really have my arm bitten off by the wrong mouth?" Before getting an answer from Mythral, she found herself inside the room Mythral had just described. The walls began to close in upon her.

Will Mythral really let me lose an arm if I make the wrong choice? Could he, would he, heal me if I did? Her thoughts were swirling out of control.

Immediately she calmed herself, as Perci constantly had reminded her to do in dangerous situations. Overreacting was a recipe for disaster. If she failed, she could not change the outcome. Solving the puzzle was all she could do now and here.

What was the one question that would lead to her escape? She had been tested often enough by Mythral and Perci to know that the answers never were obvious. Or, they were just the opposite—too obvious to be spotted. What was the hint Cat had given her to solve the bags-of-gold riddle? "Think outside the bag."

Clearly, just picking one mouth and asking which one contained the release would not work. If she had two questions, she could ask one a test question and find out if it lied or if it told the truth.

She stopped pondering briefly to look inside the mouths to see whether anything was visible. As she approached, the first mouth called out for her to reach inside: "It is me you want."

The second mouth immediately shouted out, "Don't trust that open sore. It will do nothing but lie to you."

The first mouth said, "Like you could believe anything that gaping pit would say."

Kit backed off to get some silence. Reason and logic told her the statements were consistent, regardless of which was the lying mouth and which was the truth-speaking mouth. She stilled her thoughts again, even as the walls closed within eight inches of her shoulders. If she could not use magic, she must use logic. What else was there?

Sensing? If sensing isn't deemed magic, per se, then perhaps I can sense the right choice, thought Kit. She sent herself quickly into a light trance. Not too deep, because she needed to be aware of her surroundings and the changes occurring. She began to project into the future and sense a positive outcome to her dilemma.

Mythral's voice cut into her thoughts. *Extra points for thinking of a solution I had not anticipated. I'll give you two minutes more, but you cannot use sensing. You must solve the riddle with reason and logic.* Then all was quiet again.

Once more, Kit had no choice but to still her racing thoughts and focus upon the riddle. *How do I approach this from outside the bag—or box?* she asked herself.

Whether from her brief and interrupted sensing, or from somewhere deep in her subconscious, a thought arose, seeming totally unrelated to her current dilemma. She focused upon it, nonetheless.

A negative multiplied by a negative creates a positive. She recognized the statement from a math class in Realm One. It had caught her attention at the time, but there was a companion statement that said a negative multiplied by a positive creates a negative. She became irritated with herself for being distracted initially by such thoughts.

Then she recalled how Mythral and Perci always were saying the subconscious could access everything you ever have known, seen, or heard, and a clear and calm mind could process that information at the subconscious level to find a solution almost instantaneously.

So, if these math concepts were the solution, what did they mean? What did she know about this problem?

Lying was a negative in the harmony of the universe, and telling the truth was a positive.

If two lies make a truth and I ask the lying mouth to lie to me, I'll get the truth. No, that will not work. If I'm asking the truthful mouth to tell me a lie, then I'll get a lie. This math stuff does feel like the answer somehow, but how?

Kit's focus was distracted by the walls that now were only a few inches from her shoulders and moving closer. If she did not figure this out soon, she would have to make a blind guess and hope either she was lucky or Mythral wasn't serious about that arm.

My chances are 50-50. Focus, she told herself yet again. *When I don't know to which mouth I am speaking, how do I phrase one question to one mouth, if two lies equal the truth, while a lie about the truth and the truth about a lie both produce a lie?*

As Kit cleared her mind, for what was certainly the last effort at a solution, another idea arose. She quickly examined it from all angles. It seemed to work. She was startled out of her concentration by the walls touching one of her shoulders as she rocked ever so slightly. She squeezed forward to the two mouths. Before they could scream at her, she asked her question. She got her answer.

Kit shoved her left hand into the mouth on the left. She did not have time to be certain of her reasoning, but she felt certain that the other mouth was not the one to choose.

Abruptly the room dissolved. Grabbing her left arm with her right hand, she found both arms intact and a smiling Mythral in front of her. "You figured out the riddle. How did you get there? Most people take a very long time, if ever, to work this out."

"What do you mean a very long time? Any longer and those walls would have made me into a pancake. How could someone else take more time?"

"Mathematically, if objects get closer together by half the distance that separates them each time, they never will actually meet. You had all the time you needed, you just didn't know it. So, back to my question, how did you come up with the right question to ask?"

"Perhaps I cheated," Kit replied. "People in Realm Two probably never have had a class where they learned a negative times another negative makes a positive, and a positive multiplied by a negative creates a negative."

Mythral reflected upon her disclosure and said, "While that may be true in math, it does not by itself answer the riddle."

"Well," Kit said, "I added that theory to my experience of looking at these riddles of yours sideways, or upside down, or at least backwards. I realized I could ask either mouth what the other would say. Asking a liar to report the truth, and getting a false answer, is the same as asking a truth-teller to report the lie, and getting the same false answer."

Mythral was somewhat surprised and said, "I never have seen anyone reason through the problem quite like that. Your reaction to the element of surprise also was part of the test. You did extremely well for having no time to reflect or prepare for the test. Very well done. Now, get some rest, because your next test requires a very clear head."

CHAPTER 36

A MORAL DILEMMA

[𝔎𝔢𝔞𝔩𝔪 𝔗𝔴𝔬]

The next day, Kit was drained. She had spent most of the night worrying about this next test—until she realized there was nothing that she could do. She didn't know what the test might be. She only knew she would need a clear head.

Mythral began to explain the test. He said, "In this next test, you face a complex set of facts and no time to think. You'll find yourself in the middle of an impossible situation. You must decide what to do immediately and then do it.

"I'll give you a few pieces of information in advance, because you will not know how you got into this situation or why. You will be surrounded by attacking dark wizards on three sides. They are after you; they have cornered you in this room. You are in a closed room with many innocent people, including children. You must assume this is real and lives are at stake, possibly even the Three Realms.

"If you siphon their attack into another universe, the Siphoning Spell will become known to those dark wizards. Then MorKano will know. That one secret will allow dark magic to conquer good magic."

"Not an option, then," said Kit. "So, finish telling me what I can't do. I know I'm not getting any clues about what I should do."

Mythral continued, "If you use a normal Deflection Spell, you can save yourself, but many innocents will die. If you do nothing, you will die, and very likely so will the innocents. Your power to protect yourself from the attacking wizards will last only for a minute or two. If you try to shield the innocents in the room, your power to block will last only

138

seconds. The choices are yours. If you fight back, ignoring everything and everyone else, you stand a chance."

The next instant, Kit was in precisely the impossible situation Mythral just had described. The room had no doors or windows, and nine strangers were behind her. The three dark wizards in front of her promptly attacked. Instinctively, Kit threw a Protection Spell around herself and the nine non-combatants huddled in a corner. With seconds left before she exhausted her magic, what could she do? She immediately eliminated the use of Mythral's secret Siphoning Spell. Better for everyone in the room to die than to give that power to the forces of evil.

Mythral's comments on personal integrity flashed briefly in her mind. *If I use a Deflecting Spell and fight back, I just might survive, but the others will die. I need a better solution. Surely, Mythral did not design a test where I have no choice other than to let innocents die. I must act now, or we all die.*

What about attacking? Can I successfully attack these three wizards? Not likely in the few remaining seconds, with my power steadily ebbing away. If I try that, the innocents surely will die. What other options are there?

Just one, she suddenly realized. It presented a great risk to her, but it could save all or most of the innocents. The wizards were attacking because she was in the room. She needed to leave this place, and fast. A dangerous Translocation Spell was the only option.

Although she never before had attempted it and only had read about it when Perci wasn't paying close attention, she threw a Flash Bang Spell, *Bregol-Glam-Calad*, at the wizards in front, then performed the highly dangerous Translocation Spell, *Pathu Athrada*. She found herself back in Mythral's bookshop. Not until much later would Kit reflect on how she'd performed the dangerous Translocation Spell mentally and survived.

The test immediately ended with her standing, yet again, in front of Mythral. Her whole body felt like it might turn itself inside out at any moment. She was glad she'd skipped breakfast. Mythral's face was distorted. The rage and anger in his voice knocked her back a step. "What in the name of all magic were you thinking? That Spell could have killed you. And should have! Where and when did you ever learn it? Have you ever used it before?"

As Mythral's wrath burned itself out, he grew quiet. "That test was designed to teach you there is not always a good solution. Sometimes you have to accept the pain and suffering of others, even if you did not cause it. You just keep moving forward to hopefully a better outcome. You should have defended yourself. You must learn to live with the cost of difficult choices. Otherwise, I fear at the critical moment you will hesitate, and we both will die."

"That may have been your answer to the dilemma, but I saw another solution," Kit said, her anger smoldering. She had found a workaround for the dilemma and executed it safely. With just a tinge of attitude seeping into her words, she answered some of Mythral's questions. "I have read about that Spell, and I knew you had used it successfully, in emergencies. This definitely was an emergency, and I could not willfully choose to let the innocents die if another option, even a very risky one, was available."

Mythral calmed further. "I created that situation. No one actually would have died."

Kit interrupted, "How was I supposed to know that? You said I was to assume it was real and people would die if I did not act."

He was completely deflated by her final arguments. Mythral relented, but not without a final warning. "Yes, so I did. However, you performed the Translocation Spell, and that really should have ended you. Long ago many wizards died or were horribly scrambled in the attempt at that Spell. The old schools and the Council banned its use.

"I am amazed at how your talents and skills have progressed. However, you must promise me you never will perform that Spell again unless you have absolutely no other choice."

Kit nodded her consent. The adrenaline had waned, and her body was barely under control. A nod was all she could manage.

Mythral continued, "You already know not to do the 'wrong' thing for a supposedly 'right' reason. This test was designed to teach you impossible situations may call for a 'wrong' choice over a 'worse' one. Life and its choices are not always fair or simple."

"And what about finding a way to avoid both the wrong and the worst choices?" inquired Kit with strength returning to her voice.

"I guess, in hindsight, you did choose a bad option over a disastrous one," Mythral said, giving voice to his inner thoughts. "You chose to reveal the Translocation Spell to dark wizards over disclosing the Siphoning Spell or the death of innocents."

"Actually," Kit said, "I used a Flash Bang Spell immediately before the Translocation Spell, which upped the risk but kept the dark wizards from knowing how I escaped. I hoped they would react to my absence and ignore the innocents remaining in the room."

CHAPTER 37

WHAT WERE YOU THINKING?!
[Realm Two]

Mythral turned and walked away. He looked like a semi-inflated hot air balloon, half on and half off the ground.

Not long after, Perci entered the room—more accurately, flew in—and immediately began a verbal assault upon Kit.

"What were you thinking? The Translocation Spell is the most dangerous and unpredictable spell I ever have seen. Mythral nearly took my head off, believing I had taught it to you."

After repeating himself a few more times, Perci's steam ran out, as he finally noticed how haggard and unsteady Kit looked. He asked in a much more compassionate tone, "Are you okay? I forgot how awful it is the first time coming out of that Spell. Mythral says you get used to it. I have translocated only twice, and I hope never to do so again."

Kit's face recovered from Perci's initial assault. "Did Mythral get this angry when you did it the first time?"

"No. He had no reason to. I tried it only at his suggestion and with him closely monitoring me. He was ready to take over if I made a mistake, which I did the first time. Had Mythral not been there in the Spell alongside me, there is no telling how many pieces I might have splintered into. The same outcome was more likely than not for you. How in the world did you learn the Spell?"

"I read it in one of Mythral's forbidden texts when you two were busy with other things. I never expected to use it. I just read it to try to understand how it works. I practiced the phrasing with autocorrect and no magic behind the Spell.

"At first, autocorrect refused to help, but when I said I would try the Spell with or without her help, she gave in. It's a good thing she did, because my initial pronunciation and intonation were way off. I never would have used the Translocation Spell if I had another option. Mythral's test was designed to take away all other options."

All of Mythral's tests were designed for realism, Perci explained. "With a willing subject, or victim, if you prefer, the spell makes him or her feel as if everything about the situation is real. Mythral never would have set up the test in this way had he known you might try to use that Spell."

Now they were talking like friends again. Kit asked, "Is Mythral ever going to forgive me? Have I lost his trust?"

Perci's face softened even more as he explained to Kit, "Mythral blew up because he was angry with himself. To me, he was berating himself over how he should have been more directly involved with your training.

"In his mind, this was all his fault for not knowing how ready you were for advanced spells and for not working with you on the dangerous and important spells.

"In fact, I detected a bit of admiration in his voice when he explained to me what you had done. He was angry, but he was also proud of you for managing that spell without mortally injuring yourself.

"However, from now on, you must agree not to attempt any dangerous spells without one of us helping. At least on the early attempts. If you really want to know something, other than a killing Spell, please ask." Kit readily agreed.

CHAPTER 38

BEFORE THE FINAL TEST
[Realm Two]

The second test was over. Had she passed or merely survived? She still wasn't sure. The third was ahead. Maybe. Despite Perci's assurance, Kit wasn't convinced Mythral's anger was at himself.

Mythral returned. "Since you still are alive and appear to be in one cohesive and properly functioning piece, I guess you might as well tackle the final test—the day after tomorrow. Go home to Realm One and rest for two nights. You need to focus and center yourself for the next test.

"This final test is not given often. To fail is expected. However, failure often teaches us more than success. As my apprentice, you will be entrusted with great power and knowledge. Can you be trusted to wield such power and employ such knowledge? That is what the final test will show.

"The test, pass or fail, will change you forever. If you have any doubts, now is the time to reconsider this path."

"Well, that revelation will help me rest and relax," Kit said. Her nerves were still raw from the day's events. Her words sounded like sarcasm as she prepared to leave for Realm One and home.

During her walk home from the bookshop in Realm One, Kit could not help but reflect upon her situation. *How many nights have I slept poorly, if at all, since this testing began? Yet, I must find a way to sleep and, as Mythral advised, to center myself for this final test. What can be so hard that it changes you regardless of the outcome?*

Kit was so lost in thought she didn't see Cat sitting in the middle of the road. Her last-minute avoidance of his tail found her sprawled on the ground.

"Your lessons are going well, I see, for that was an excellent choice," said Cat. "Stepping on my tail would be even worse than failing the final test. No one ever has survived stepping on my tail!"

With minor scrapes and bruises, Kit picked herself up. "Care to explain that statement in more de-tail?" she asked. Her joke fell upon deaf furry ears. She got no reaction.

Breaking the silence, Kit implored Cat to tell her something about the final test. Or, at least how she could get any rest until then.

Cat studied his right paw and claws and remained quiet while Kit was pleading. Finally, he had enough. "Stop already. Why do you think I have chosen now to sit in your path? I promised you the gift of wisdom at your birthday party. You might remember ... it was the one to which I was not invited. Listen very carefully, young lady, because I will say this only once. The final test is the simplest of all three and the most revealing."

Cat then listed four things the test would reveal about Kit:

"First, do you know what is right and what is wrong? Second, can you separate objective logic and reasoning from prejudices and rationalizations? Third, when your sense of right and wrong is in opposition to your objective logic and reasoning, which will you choose? Finally, will you be able to live with yourself and the choice you have made?

"My words will not help you to rest or sleep. They will, however, give you something productive to think about when you cannot sleep." Without waiting, Cat walked past her towards the bookshop. Kit was left with her thoughts now focused, rather than chaotic and disjointed. She walked home to her brother and foster parents.

Upon entering the house, Kit was stunned by the contrast between her life with Mythral and her life at home. Her foster mother had conscripted Toro to peel the carrots for dinner—a chore that once had belonged to Kit. Her foster father sat at the kitchen table, which was not yet set for dinner. He was tinkering with some piece of equipment that seemed to be getting the better of him, until Toro glanced over and offered a suggestion. This was life in Realm One.

To her foster parents, Kit merely had been at work for the day. Kit was struck by the disconnection between her apparent ordinary Realm One life as a teenage girl and her extraordinary Realm Two life as Mythral's apprentice. Thanks to that time offset between Realm One and Realm Two, school would not start for three more days.

No one had a clue that she had performed a highly dangerous Translocation Spell. Probably only three living wizards even knew about that Spell. Nor did her family know she quickly was becoming one of the strongest wizards in all the Realms.

As she took another step towards her room, she stopped again as the realization hit her. *Except Toro, no one in Realm One knows about wizards, magic, and other Realms. To them, I am just an ordinary teenage girl living a carefree life.*

Kit forgot these realizations quickly. She settled onto the window seat in her room. She pondered Cat's words about the ultimate test. The first part seemed simple enough. Her sense of right and wrong always had been strong. She always had found it difficult to compromise what she knew to be right for what might be convenient, even as to minor issues.

She could not think of a time when she had compromised. She might have held her tongue and not called someone out, but she never had given in to the pressure of peers or society. No, part one was the least of her problems. As best she could tell, she possessed what Mythral had defined as personal integrity.

Part two seemed only slightly harder. After many lessons with Mythral and Perci, she was aware of certain limitations. Identities are shaped by biases and prejudices we pick up along the way. Often when Kit would justify to Mythral a mistake in logic or reasoning with an excuse by saying, "I relied upon a false assumption or bias I picked up somewhere," Mythral would respond, "Well, put it back where you found it!"

Acquired biases wreak havoc on objective logic and reasoning. "If it isn't broken, why try to fix it?" This bias towards the status quo often came from people who wanted to avoid the risks or effort of considering improvements. Most people are averse to change.

These days, she could not listen to an argument, or even a friendly discussion, without noticing an underlying bias or prejudice in virtually every point or observation. Now that she knew what to listen for, she found it everywhere. She wondered how people ever agreed upon anything. If you got enough people together with similar biases or prejudices, you would have a group that could act. Hopefully not as a mob.

Her training also had covered the rationalization trap—the "why me?" laments and the "what if?" questions—which lured the weak away from the need to take responsibility and to act. The seduction of delaying choice and action with procrastination, or as Mythral called it, "ifinating."

She had fallen for these traps before she met Mythral. Now her life was so full and active with good and exciting things that she seldom rationalized anything. If this final test were to tempt her to rationalize and thereby fail, she was ready. What more could she do?

The third part was clear enough. On one hand, there was a choice you knew instinctively to be right. Yet, objective logic and reasoning, not subjective rationalization, told you something different must be done. Which would you choose?

This sounded like another impossible dilemma where logic said you could not follow your instincts without doing greater harm in the long run. It was like the second test. *My instinctive reaction was to save everyone by using Mythral's Siphoning Spell. Objective logic and reasoning revealed that saving everyone that way would, in the long run, doom those same individuals and the rest of the Realms to a fate worse than death. So, based upon test two, truly objective logic and reasoning should be allowed to temper an instinctive 'right' choice.*

Somehow I found a third choice that combined logic and instinct. But, if there was no third choice, what then? At this point, Kit's head was beginning to ache, and no clear answer was in sight. So, she decided to move on to part four.

Cat had implied part four was the hardest. Yet, it seemed to be merely the aftermath of going through the test. As Mythral's first two tests had instructed her, choices had consequences. Often those choices might be limited, and the consequences could range from bad to worse. Sometimes there just were not any good consequences. So, what could be so hard or spiritually damaging about making such a choice in this third test?

While the implications here were frightening, she could not think of anything more to do in preparation. She would do her best in the situation presented. She must accept the consequences along with the challenge.

After such a careful analysis, Kit expected to sleep more easily. She did not. Every time she fell asleep, a large red letter F chased her. It aimed for her forehead time and time again. Kit found herself screaming "why?" each time as she ducked out of its path. Exhausted by its relentless pursuit, Kit stumbled, and the letter hit its target. When it stuck to her forehead, the answer came to her. "Failed due to overconfidence."

The next day provided some distractions with routine activities around the house and yard. After dinner she huddled with Toro in her room, hoping a review of Cat's advice might add clarity. It did not. In her dreams that night the large red F always won.

CHAPTER 39

THE FINAL TEST
[Realm Two]

After another night of little to no sleep, Kit stood before Mythral. "If this truly is necessary, let's get on with it."

"As you wish," replied Mythral. "But, be warned, this test will be extremely difficult for you personally."

"If I lose any more sleep," Kit interjected, "I'll have no hope of passing this final test. I'm exhausted already."

Mythral explained, "This time, the risks are real. The people will die or live based upon your choices. The only way the test can provide a true and honest result is if the consequences are real.

"It is very, very simple. You will be in a room with one other person. Behind that person is the gate to Realm Three and MorKano. Once that person enters the gate, he intends to share with MorKano all the secrets he managed to get out of you."

Kit exclaimed, "No way am I sharing your secrets with some stranger. This scenario is no longer believable."

Ignoring the look of disbelief on Kit's face and the beginnings of a protest, he pushed forward. "I am about to instruct you in the deadliest of Killing Spells. This one Spell is the only thing that will penetrate the protection surrounding this individual. To be effective, the Spell must be delivered with all your power and focus, or it will fail. Fail, and all my secrets will become MorKano's.

"You will have mere seconds to act before that person can escape through the portal. Now listen closely to the Spell and then repeat it back without any force of magic behind it." In a daze, Kit did so, and Mythral said, "Good. Ready?" Before she could object, Kit was in that room. She saw the gate at the opposite end. Then she focused upon the foreground and the person who, having all of Mythral's secrets, was positioned just before that gate. The person Mythral was asking her to kill in order to save the Realms was Toro!

Immediately she thought, *It's a trick. Some dark wizard is impersonating my brother so I will hesitate and allow him to escape. Focus.*

With the greatest of effort, Kit forced logic into the equation. Whether real or not, the person being presented to her as Toro was merely a distraction. The choice remained the same: one life against the survival of the Three Realms. Logically, the choice could go only one way.

As if on cue, her brother's voice came from across the room, pleading with her. "I had no choice, MorKano made me steal your memories. Please don't kill me. I did nothing wrong. It is all his fault."

Toro turned and ran for the gate. A wave of anxiety washed over Kit. Still uncommitted to a course, she brought the Killing Spell to the forefront of her mind. How could knowingly killing her brother, when he was guiltless of intentional wrongdoing, ever be right? Why was she being forced to decide? Why?

Because she had chosen this path, and this test. If she delayed any longer, she would have failed because of "ifinating" for too many seconds.

In the second test, Kit successfully had considered two conflicting (and each unacceptable) choices of logic versus moral rightness, and somehow, she had found a third option. Could she do that again? Mythral had been very clear that no such option existed here.

Either she killed Toro immediately, or he would escape with the stolen secrets and hand them over to MorKano. Mythral's last words before he instructed her in the Killing Spell made clear she must be totally committed to the act of killing her brother, or the Spell would not penetrate his protection. Could she ever do such a horribly wrong thing? Even when logic demanded it for the greater good?

When Toro was only one step away from the portal, and with the Killing Spell ready to unleash, Kit stopped. She did not know whether she could survive and be of future use to Mythral if she executed her brother. She did, however, think of a way to reconcile morality and objective logic—one with which she could live. Just as Toro was entering the portal, she called out for Mythral to end the test, or she would translocate herself to Realm Three and intercept her brother there.

As the test ended, Kit found herself standing yet again in front of Mythral. She began to rush through her explanation: "I will explain on the way, but we must translocate to Realm Three. There we can intercept Toro as he leaves the gate and heads to MorKano's fortress.

"Now that I have allowed him to escape, this remains the only chance for the Realms. And if we cannot intercept him, then I, with or without your help, will battle MorKano before he can use that information or share it with others. I let Toro escape. I let this happen. I will fix it or die trying!"

Mythral assured her: "Toro is safe. The test was a simulation. We need not rush to confront MorKano. That will occur all too soon. The test is designed to make the test subject believe the threat and the consequences are real."

Kit finally calmed down enough to process what Mythral had said. Then she realized what she had done or, rather, failed to do. "For the greater good, I should have stopped my brother at any cost. Intercepting him in Realm Three before he could reach MorKano was just a farfetched hope—a rationalization I used to justify not killing him.

"Objective logic and reasoning should have been sufficient to overcome my innate belief that killing for any reason other than self defense was wrong. I could not manage it, and I failed."

As she began her apologies to Mythral, he held up his hand to stop her. "Actually, you passed. You chose to live with the consequences of doing what you knew to be right, and to take responsibility for that choice. Nearly everyone else chooses to act for the 'greater good,' using that justification later if their choice proves to be wrong. You surprised me. No one ever has emerged from the test with a clear idea of how to fix what happened.

"When my mentor had my mother stand in as the person I must kill, I refused to kill and accepted the outcome. However, I did not know how to translocate at that time. Yet, you are right. I should have followed her through the gate and attempted to stop her or confront the person to whom she delivered the secrets. You found a better answer to the test than I."

So, did you take the tests? Were you frozen by indecision? Remember my warning. Inaction is itself a choice with consequences and ripples. The test isn't about choosing to put the good of many over the good of one. Nor about self-sacrifice. Mythral's tests were meant to enlighten Kit about herself. Sometimes we must make a choice and take an action when there are only bad or terrible options. The lesson is in how you face that situation. As long as you are true to yourself and your values, no outcome is failure.

CHAPTER 40

FAILURE IS ONE POINT OF VIEW.
[Realm Two]

"A word of caution about the final test," said Mythral. "There is no single answer to such situations. What I deem to be the right choice is merely my opinion based upon my biases. Since you never can un-kill someone, I choose to avoid that option at all costs. However, someday I might have a different answer.

"If I could have gotten my hands on MorKano shortly after I learned of Vivyen's murder, I strongly suspect killing him would have been my only option. I'd like to believe I am stronger than that, but I'll never know. There are so many things we never truly can know until we actually face them."

The complexity of Mythral's back and forth positions on killing had Kit somewhat confused. She asked, "Are you saying killing is always wrong, but in a given situation at a given moment, one might be driven to it by passion, weakness, or both?"

"The answer to your question depends not only on the facts you have presupposed, but also upon the persons involved. So, the useless answer is, it depends. When we live together in a society, we agree willingly, and sometimes unwillingly, to be bound by the laws and morals of that society. This social contract between individual and society will give one answer to that question.

"Society's answer always has been 'it depends.' Some people live outside of society, as in Realm Three, or choose to live at a standard that exceeds society's minimum. Remind me to discuss this with you further tomorrow, on our way to Realm Three." Mythral chose to ignore the look on Kit's face at the mention of traveling to Realm Three.

"Those who do not settle for society's answers must find their own. I have my answer, or my standard, in this situation. You exceeded it today. However, someday you may decide upon a different answer for yourself."

More confused than ever, Kit interjected, "It sounds as if you are telling me we each decide for ourselves what is right and what is wrong. At least, as long as we meet society's minimum standards."

Mythral continued, "When history is written about what was done in the past, those writing it, the winners, or at least the survivors, are the ones to pronounce judgment. Which confirms that history is not a source for answering the question, 'Is it ever right to kill?'

"There is, perhaps, a partial answer to the question. As is universally agreed, at some point the defense of self and others requires killing an attacker. However, some would refuse to kill, even to prevent being killed."

"That is far too vague," said Kit. "What if the person who must die for the greater good is innocent? Toro, for example. How much harm or danger justifies deadly force?"

"All valid questions," said Mythral. "Let me know when you have the answers.

"With your testing complete, I hereby declare you a full wizard. Your apprentice days are over, but not your training. And just in time. Our trip to Realm Three is tomorrow. Please come early in the morning. Also, please dress appropriately. Wear your robes."

CHAPTER 41

REALM THREE
[Realm Two and Realm Three]

"We will be visiting a couple of my friends in Realm Three," were Mythral's first words the next morning. No mention was made of yesterday's test. "Our primary purpose is to enlist Nate's assistance."

"Perci mentioned Nate once, but you never have. Who is he?" inquired Kit.

"I'll tell you more about Nate on the way," Mythral replied. "I just want to use him as an advance warning system concerning MorKano's activities in Realm Three."

"Wouldn't that be dangerous for Nate?" asked Kit.

"No. Nate has no fear of dark wizards," Mythral continued, despite Kit's questions. "Again, we'll talk about Nate later.

"There are a few other good wizards I'd like you to meet. We'll see as many as we can on this trip."

Press as she might, Kit could get nothing further on Nate. For some mysterious reason, Mythral felt their meeting with Nate was essential. Mythral assured her after they met she'd understand. That sounded like something a parent or teacher would say when a better explanation eluded them.

"At least tell me more about Realm Three and our trip," Kit begged.

Mythral explained, "The real reason for our visit to Nate must be kept secret. Yet, our presence in Realm Three will be known to all. Entry to Realm Three is via a single gate, protected and controlled by wizards loyal to the

Council. However, I suspect spies have infiltrated those guarding the portal."

"Why not just truth-read those guards?" inquired Kit.

"Because a person under a spell may believe what they are saying. Therefore, the official story is that I'm taking my new protégé to see and understand Realm Three, on sort of a tour. Some risk is involved because MorKano is unlikely to pass on such a good opportunity to strike at me. However, I have taken precautions. We will be quite ready for such an attempt."

Finding Mythral in a talkative mood, Kit pressed further, "I have heard all sorts of stories about Realm Three. Yet, no one I have met, including Perci, ever has been there. What is it really like?"

Mythral's answers were unsatisfying. "Realm Three must be experienced to be understood and appreciated. Make no assumptions. Realm Three is not what anyone would expect based on the stories circulated in Realm Two.

"While Realm Three initially was designed as a 'safe' place to put the worst of the worst wizards, it is much more than that. More broadly, it's a place where any wizard or individual can go to escape society's norms and rules. Many good wizards have chosen to relocate to Realm Three and risk the obvious dangers simply to enjoy freedoms and privacy not available in Realm Two.

"In Realms Two and One, everyone lives under a social contract that imposes norms and laws. The formality and details vary from place to place, but everywhere people live together, some degree of a social contract exists among them, enforced by peer pressure, shunning, economic sanction, imprisonment and, even worse, mental and physical abuse.

"Realm Three has no social contract. While some individuals might band together and create one for themselves, behavior is not formally governed in Realm Three. As a result, those in Realm Three experience the extremes—good and bad, beautiful and ugly. The greatest beauty to be found in all three Realms is in Nate's valley.

"Certain attributes are required to survive and thrive in Realm Three: powerful magic, great mental prowess, or skill and cunning."

Circling back to her initial questions, Kit asked, "How does Nate survive in Realm Three? Which of those attributes does he possess?"

Mythral said, "Nate is the exception to the rule. His name is the answer to your question. His real name is unknown to me or anyone, although dark wizards often refer to him as 'the beginning and end of their worst nightmare.' Nate is something beyond anyone's imagination and experiences. While on very rare occasions a wizard is born with the ability to tap into nature's magic to some limited degree, Nate does so without thought or apparent effort. His power is 'innate.' Get it? 'In Nate.' Or 'Nate.' Obviously, he did not object too strongly to the nickname, since I am still here, so it stuck. Until he chose to emigrate to Realm Three, he must have been living quietly in some remote corner of the realm. I'm not sure anyone knew he existed before that.

"Nate can do literally anything, as far as I know. Nature seems to pull off a sort of balancing act. Nate got unlimited power and no interest in using such power for anything but his enjoyment of life, nature, and beauty. I often have wondered what music created by him would sound like, if he had any interest in music. Perhaps it would be too beautiful for anyone else to tolerate.

"Despite his unlimited power, you have no need to fear Nate, or indeed anything, once you enter his valley. That is, unless you find a way to irritate him. He will not suffer fools, nor anyone who seeks to use him or his powers. When he first arrived in Realm Three, many tried to enlist him and his power for their own purposes.

"Nate told them to get lost. Those who persisted and invaded his valley with their schemes and bad intentions did not leave. They remain, but no longer as irritants. Nate never would destroy any living thing. He would, however, transform it into another piece of nature. The extraordinary trees or bushes you see may once have been dark wizards."

Mythral explained it all as he and Kit walked to the center of Fairhaven and the portal into Realm Three. Once there, Mythral spoke briefly with the gatekeepers and then signaled Kit to step forward.

Mythral explained, "Our trip via this portal will be mostly like the trip between Realms One and Two. Here the spell is a two-part safety mechanism. Those wishing to be transferred say one part of the spell, and the gatekeepers must speak the other part." After a very short incantation, Kit saw the room in Realm Two disappear and found it immediately replaced by a much more spartan room, in Realm Three, she guessed.

Mythral spoke upon arrival, "To facilitate our tour of Realm Three, I have enlisted the assistance of two gryphons. Magical creatures all are sentient to some degree, but gryphons are more so than most. Even more than dragons. While such creatures do not practice magic, per se, they do possess natural defenses against magic."

"I must have skipped class the day they covered magical creatures, so I'll need more details," quipped Kit.

"Only a few magical creatures chose to immigrate to Realm Three, but gryphons always have loved to fly fast and furiously. Realm Three's enhancements offer more freedom for flying. As for the dangers of Realm Three, such magnificent creatures quickly found Nate and his valley to be a safe, welcoming haven from those dangers. Because of their association with Nate, no one dared harm these creatures. Many dragons chose to come as well, for the freedoms and less human interaction. However, dragons are rather dull-witted. Whereas the gryphons are curious about new things, and they like a bit of trouble."

This common friendship with Nate, and perhaps Mythral's hint of some potentially dangerous and exciting adventures, was how Mythral had convinced two of the gryphons to provide transport services.

Upon exiting the building, Kit was speechless, nearly, at the sight of the two gryphons. Horses always had impressed her with their size and graceful, powerful bodies. The gryphons' lion-like bodies were bigger and more powerful-looking than any horse she had seen. Their eagle-like heads and wings were rather disconcerting. The combination seemed unnatural, even a bit frightening. As Kit made eye contact with one of the gryphons, an immediate sense of trust and honor washed over her, displacing her concerns. She sensed an undercurrent of mischief—playful, not harmful. She immediately liked these two gryphons.

Mythral interrupted her thoughts. "The male's name is Fast, the female's Furious. Nate chose these names after getting to know them. It is unclear whether he used his magic consciously or unconsciously, but the gryphons now assume these always have been their names. Also, whether by nature or Nate's magic, these two gryphons are the fastest creatures in all the Realms."

While flying over Realm Three, Mythral suggested they practice the mental communications Perci had been teaching Kit. *Often the noise from the rushing air, especially when Fast and Furious are racing at full speed, is too much for normal conversation. As I explained earlier, Nate's valley is our only scheduled stop. If not already known to others, that visit to Nate would be guessed easily, so I have scheduled it last. By doing so, I hoped any dark wizard reception party would grow tired of waiting. Additionally, I want Nate to allow us to spend the night at his home.*

When Kit asked why, Mythral mentally replied, *All will be clear in the morning. However, there is one other stop to make before Nate's. You can see a great deal of Realm Three from the air, excluding, of course, the dangerous areas. What you cannot see from up here is what lies beneath. We are going to make a quick stop at Gemma's cavern.*

Time allowing, but probably not during this trip, I'll take you to see Salacia's water palace. Her unbelievably green and lush place is nestled in a mountainside with a lake in front and a forest surrounding it. But the real surprise is her home. You move from room to room by way of water tubes. She refers to them as 'aqua channels.'

If you ever get invited, definitely visit Realm Three, as long as you take a powerful wizard along to protect you. The enhanced flavors of my favorite meals are out-of-this-Realm. I always enjoy Nate's valley and Gemma's cavern, but you won't see me anywhere near those aqua channels. The idea of being trapped in a tube of water makes my fur stand on end.

CHAPTER 42

GEMMA'S CAVERN
[Realm Three]

As they made their approach to the cavern, Mythral explained a bit more about Gemma. *Even before the creation of Realm Three, Gemma was one of my favorite people. In my youth, her work with gemstones fascinated me. She cuts and facets them in the most wonderful shapes, and the stones have spectacular colors.*

Later, I came to appreciate her insights and intellect. Somehow faceting has given her a unique perspective on life. The task requires staring at rough stone for hours. Then she sits at a cutting and polishing device for even longer. Now I recognize that method is how we solve problems—by focusing upon them.

"She tried to explain it to me once—something about starting off with a very specific and detailed plan on where and how to cut each of the many dozens of facets on the stone. Once she begins working the stone, she must continually adjust her plan.

As Mythral paused, Kit interjected, *Well, isn't that exactly how life is? You have a plan, or a sort of plan. Then as you move forward with that plan in mind, you constantly have to adapt it to fit the circumstances. Of course, there always are some people who have no plan whatsoever, and life just takes them where it will.*

Maybe that's all it is, Mythral commented, *but it seemed like something more to me. Anyway, I can tell you she knows how to store magic in gemstones for later use, to enhance one's power. That is how she defends herself and her cavern from intruders in Realm Three.*

Her cavern and its side tunnels are full of uncut gemstones, which she seems to enjoy as much as the finished stones. When we land, do not enter her cavern until I have announced us. We must get permission.

After dismounting and approaching the cavern's entrance, Mythral sent a magical announcement into the cavern. Shortly, a stunning wizard dressed in robes of a myriad of sparkling jewel tones appeared just inside the entrance. Her bright topaz eyes were even more impressive against her bronze skin.

"Sorry to keep you waiting, Mythral," she greeted the visitors. "One cannot be too careful these days. And in case you are one of those nasty wizards in disguise, tell me what we ate on your last visit."

"That will test my memory, Gemma. Let me think. Ah, now I remember. I was in a hurry and had nothing to eat, but I did have a quick cup of tea."

"Well, then, as long as you can vouch for your friend there, come on in, and I'll make sure you don't leave hungry this time. I traded some finished gemstones for some delicious fairy cakes just yesterday."

"They're not made from actual fairies, are they?" asked Kit. "Or are they made *by* fairies?"

Chuckling and tossing a questioning look in Mythral's direction, Gemma replied, "No, my child, we call them fairy cakes for their light and airy texture. I am guessing you must be from Realm One."

After a few more steps into the cavern, Kit's questions came to a halt, even if her feet still were moving. All around her in the walls, the ceiling, and even the floor were embedded gemstones. *These would be worth a fortune back home,* she thought.

Noticing Kit's focus, Gemma said, "What you see here are just the stones that are not worth mining. The really good ones have been removed. If we have time, I'll show you one of the new tunnels and some really great rough gemstone material.

"In Realm Two, you never would find more than a few different types in the same area. However, something about Realm Three is very different, and we have many types, such as tourmaline, corundum, and beryl, in one place. I feel certain Mythral knows why, but he refuses to enlighten me on that subject."

As they entered what must have been Gemma's main living area, she invited them to sit while she prepared the tea. Before Kit could make it to a seat, she was entranced by the brilliant cut gemstones scattered loosely on a table. The top of the table was a slab of polished black obsidian. Against the ebony black surface, the gemstones were alive with every color of the rainbow.

As Kit stared at the wonders and resisted the temptation to touch and feel the gemstones, Mythral spoke behind her. This caused her to jump several inches off the ground. "If you find them impressive now, wait until you see them lighted." With that, Mythral created a light that was extremely bright and focused upon the table. All at once, the entire room was ablaze in colors being flung outward from every stone. And then Mythral caused the light to shift and pulsate just a bit. Now the colors were swirling around the room—on the walls, ceiling, and every surface.

As Gemma approached with the tea and fairy cakes, Mythral brought the light show to an end. "Mythral's been doing that with my gemstones ever since he was a young boy. I do wish he'd come up with something new that I might put to some practical uses for defense or power storage."

During their visit with Gemma, Kit was given the tour and shown the basics of gemstone cutting and polishing. Mythral confirmed, as Gemma already had guessed, that Kit was his protégé and was from Realm One.

Upon confirmation, Gemma's face brightened as she said, "If you two will be working magic together, let me offer you a gift. I have a very pure piece of emerald I will cut for the two of you to use. Such a stone, with its particular internal structure, allows for a vessel in which your individual magic can be joined safely, without the need to open yourselves completely to each other."

"Kind of you to offer," replied Mythral, "however, Kit and I are able to bond for magic without the need for such a vessel. Going forward, I can't think of any reason she'd ever need or want to perform combined magic with someone she did not trust."

"Well then, let me offer Kit a perfect ruby I have finished in a most unusual rectangular princess cut. She might use it for a ring or even a pendant. It, too, has special properties. You can store a great deal of magic, your own or others', inside the stone, and then tap into that magic as needed."

Kit accepted the ruby with awe at the deep red color, which somehow still allowed flashes of light to be emitted from the heart of the stone. She was lost in her study of the ruby. Only slowly did she realize Mythral was speaking her name. "If we are to complete our tour before nightfall, we must be off."

After the customary thank-yous and goodbyes, Mythral and Kit exited the cavern to find Fast and Furious ready and waiting. As they mounted up, Mythral told Kit the next stop was Nate's valley.

CHAPTER 43

FIRE IN THE SKY
[Realm Three]

While flying towards Nate's Valley, Mythral speculated on the answer to Gemma's question: Why were so many excellent and different types of rough gemstones in one place? He told Kit the Three Realms Spell added just a bit of general enhancement to natural features in Realm Three as compensation to those who chose to live there. It must have been this sub-spell that accounted for the quality of gemstones in Realm Three.

Of course, he could not explain that to Gemma. She had not been a part of the Council of WISDOM when the Spell was cast. As a rule, with exceptions only as necessary, those outside the casting of the Spell were not to be told about it.

As they approached Nate's valley, Mythral mentally reminded Kit not to be a nuisance or to ask too many questions. Fast and Furious tensed beneath them. Riders and gryphons sensed danger. A quick survey revealed three dark wizards approaching them from the front, at 10, 12 and 2 o'clock. These wizards were on dragons and could not catch up with the smaller, lighter gryphons in a chase. So, they had chosen to intercept them. They must have been waiting here all day, in hiding. The dragons' scales reflected an uneven mix of gold, deep red, orange, and green tones. Their external beauty, to Kit's perception, was tinged with an aura of malice, or maybe just corruption.

Mythral mentally warned Kit that more dark wizards were likely stationed on each side of Nate's valley. Lingering here for the other dark wizards to converge on this side of Nate's valley would not be wise. Just as

Mythral was assessing the situation, one dark wizard sent a flare of magic into the sky, no doubt to signal others their prey had been sighted.

The distance between the three approaching dark wizards and the gryphons was closing fast. Mythral was more than ready for a frontal assault. But being surrounded by a dozen dark wizards from potentially six different sides would present some danger. Mythral easily deflected the initial attacks with a simple Blocking Spell. Clearly, these dark wizards were not skilled at directing spells from the back of a fast-moving creature.

Knowing Nate's valley was but moments ahead and other dark wizards soon would be arriving at this party, Mythral ordered his group to push straight ahead quickly. He mentally told Kit to be ready with a Blocking Spell as they pushed past the three wizards ahead of them.

This head-on maneuver seemed to catch the wizards by surprise. They had expected, and hoped, to turn Mythral aside and thus delay Mythral's little group while their cohorts on the other three sides of Nate's valley raced to their location.

However, Mythral and Kit, riding the fastest creatures in the Realms, simply dashed through the three wizards and quickly left them behind. As these three turned to give chase, six more appeared, three on each side and slightly ahead of Mythral's group. Even at gryphon speed, they would be able to intercept Mythral, given their angle of approach. As a further complication, any delay for combat would allow the three behind to catch up.

While the dark wizards' trap was about to successfully snare their prey, Mythral, as always, knew something they had overlooked. "Onward!" Mythral shouted. The initial assault from a distance lacked focus and punch. Mythral and Kit had no difficulty in blocking the attack.

As the distance closed, Kit expected a more determined and forceful assault from both sides. She was preparing to defend her side as best she could from at least three powerful dark wizards. Now she really was about to be tested.

Then all six wizards disappeared. The dragons still were there and were beginning to turn for home, but their riders were gone. The three original dark wizards, witnessing this from well behind the group, immediately turned away.

Kit thought to herself, *Bullies in Realm Three are the same as anywhere—brave only when they believe they have you outnumbered or overpowered.*

CHAPTER 44

NATE

[Realm Three]

Mythral finally told the gryphons to slow down a bit. He turned to Kit. Surprise was evident upon her face. *That was some spell!* Kit exclaimed. *I never sensed you composing it or sending it towards them. How did you do it? I know 'unmaking' something is dangerous at best. I didn't think you could transport other people without being in physical contact.*

Mythral smiled that smug little smile of his and replied, *I did nothing. However, I can tell you we now are in Nate's valley. Further, I can assure you he knows it. As you just have witnessed, Nate permits nothing evil to enter his valley. More accurately, he does not permit it to stay evil. You'll no doubt find those six wizards adorning his valley as some extraordinary flowers, trees, or even just pretty rocks.*

Again, I urge you to pay very close attention to all that you see and feel while in Nate's valley. You'll never be closer to pure magic than when you are here. Your connection to magic and to sensing will be greatly enhanced. This experience with pure magic is the primary reason we came.

Much may be revealed to both of us. Even Cat seems impressed by Nate. Cat once said to me that if Nate put his mind to it, he could sense the whole Time-Space Continuum, present, past, and future. I have yet to figure out the connection between Cat and Nate, but it is no doubt a fascinating story.

Mythral explained that out of respect, if not caution, they would dismount some distance from the house and approach on foot. They dismounted the gryphons and let them return to their homes until they were needed for the return trip. Kit stopped and looked around her. Realm Three outside of Nate's valley was sharper and more vibrant than Realm

Two or Realm One. Nate's valley was a step beyond that. Sights, sounds, and smells were different in ways that were hard to explain. It wasn't just that they were sharper and more intense. They vibrated with extra energy and life. The air was somehow softer, too, as if just refreshed by a gentle rain.

Listening closely, Kit could hear the rushing water of nearby streams and waterfalls tumbling over stones polished smooth by the running water. Walking though the dense forest that surrounded the borders of the valley, their steps were muffled by the thick layer of fallen leaves and deep green moss underfoot. The world around them was alive with energy and magic.

When they finally left the woods and stepped into a clearing, Kit gasped in surprise. Brilliant flowers carpeted the valley before them in every color imaginable. Many she could not name. Strange, beautiful, exotic plants were everywhere. The gentle breezes carried intoxicating fragrances from the blossoms all around them.

Then she noticed something even more impossible and extraordinarily wonderful. All of these marvelous scents were isolated. They refused to blend or overlap. If she was enjoying one delightful scent, no other scents intruded. In the distance, a towering waterfall flowed from one of the mountains surrounding the valley. It morphed into a large stream that rushed across the valley's floor. Not far from the waterfall was what appeared to be an enormous house. Mythral led Kit across the valley to an intricate wooden bridge that crossed the stream. As they crossed the bridge, they were much closer to the waterfall. Kit experienced a sensation of buoyancy, a lightness of being, unlike anything she had felt before. Mythral explained that the sensation was caused by the magically enhanced negative ions from the waterfall.

After a few more moments of soaking in the negative ions, they stopped a short distance before the most fantastic structure Kit ever had seen. Two massive trees, each over 75 feet tall, framed the front door. The door itself, made of very thick, heavy wood and covered with carvings of strange creatures, reached up nearly to the floor of the second story of the home. Mythral told her the carvings portrayed inhabitants of the valley.

The door was surrounded above and on both sides by windows inset with colored glass cut into intricate images of the flowers and plants they had seen as they walked through Nate's valley. Kit stepped back, intrigued and stunned by the complex beauty of the house. Mythral stepped up to the door and pulled a heavy cord beside it. A haunting melody floated through the air.

The opening door revealed an unusually tall man with broad shoulders and muscular arms and legs. He radiated tremendous power and well-controlled strength and energy. He had thick, dense, curly hair the color of roasted chestnuts, and a short beard, both neatly trimmed. His thick woven shirt was a deep forest green that shimmered in shades Kit could not even name. These dark greens emphasized his green eyes, which hinted at warmth and kindness, but now the man was scowling disapprovingly at his uninvited guests. Nate highly valued his privacy, and he did not like intrusions. Mythral always was welcome, but not outsiders. Without any exception he could remember in decades, Nate always had found that anyone he did not know already was not worth knowing.

In a brief exchange, Nate accused Mythral of being responsible for the latest intrusion of six dark wizards into his valley. Mythral shrugged his shoulders and said to Nate, "I wanted to see you, and I want you to meet my new protégé. I issued no other invitations."

After a few moments of silence between them, Nate sighed and said to Mythral, "Since you generally prove yourself to be entertaining and trustworthy, I will give the girl a chance." And then, secretly winking to Mythral, he said, "However, if she proves herself a fool, I'll transform her into a book for my library." Turning to Kit, Nate asked, "What book would you like to be? I sense you love books."

Before Kit could consider her reply, Nate turned and led them into his home. Once inside, Kit's worries ceased. Neither for the first time nor the last, she stared in wonder at her surroundings. The front door opened into a large, comfortable room with an immense fieldstone fireplace at the far end, large enough to accommodate a man standing with outstretched arms.

In front of the fireplace, ablaze with sweet-scented fire, sat several comfortable chairs upholstered in warm shades of green, rusty red, and gold. The fabric colors seemed to pulsate with an extra vibrancy Kit could not put into words.

The room was filled with light from the many tall windows. Seats covered with thick, brightly colored cushions sat beneath most of the windows. A compact, efficient kitchen was located against the left wall of the room, and along the right wall of windows was a dining table long enough to seat dozens of guests. After Nate's attitude at the front door, Kit wondered whether the table or the house ever had seen more than three or four guests at one time.

Once they were fully inside with the door closed, Nate approached Kit and took her hand while he stared intently into her. She was apprehensive, considering her first hand holding experience with Mythral. However, Kit did not feel threatened. She felt her entire being was under examination, as if Nate were glimpsing or sensing pieces of herself from the past and the future.

After mere seconds, Nate's face changed from concentration to surprise, and then he broke into laughter. Soon Nate was doubled over. Mythral never had witnessed Nate so out of control during their long friendship. Finally, Nate recovered enough to turn to Mythral and ask, "Do you have any idea who this girl is?"

Mythral was dumbfounded by the question, but he managed to respond, "She is my new protégé."

Nate said to Mythral, "Oh no. She is so very much more! She is the end of who you were, Mythral. And she is the beginning of what will be." Then Nate erupted into laughter again. When he finally regained control, Nate asked Kit her name.

Kit responded, "Kit for short, but my full name is Cinta Kilme."

This time Nate's face went from mirth, to shock, and then to a look of understanding. Nate's next words sent a chill down Kit's spine, for reasons she could not yet comprehend. He said, "Cinta Kilme is a most appropriate name for your future self, but you have yet to earn that name. If Mythral does not know the story of the first Cinta Kilme, ask me at dinner, and I'll tell you about her."

Before Kit could say anything further, Nate announced he never had laughed harder in his life. "This calls for a real celebration!" he proclaimed. He then told Mythral to take Kit to the guest rooms to freshen up and to join him for dinner in one hour.

Mythral led Kit along the right wall of the room, through the door at the back of the room, then through an enormous library with floor-to-ceiling shelves filled with books, to a spiral staircase in a back corner of the house. He had to tug on Kit's sleeve a bit to get her to move through the well-stocked library without getting distracted.

They climbed to the second floor of the house. Although the stairs continued up to a third-floor tower, from which Nate could observe activity throughout his valley or just enjoy its beauty and tranquility, Mythral and Kit exited on the second floor. Mythral warned her that no one was permitted in Nate's tower or in his private quarters without very specific permission.

From the moment they left the library, Kit peppered Mythral with questions. "Do you know about this other Cinta Kilme? Why was Nate laughing at me? Am I in any danger from Nate?"

Mythral shook his head and responded, "I think he was laughing about you, not at you, but I don't get the joke. We'll let him explain in his own time and way. Meanwhile, Nate's valley contains the purest magic anywhere in the Three Realms. By spending time here, I often learn more about the Realms, magic, and myself. I have a strong feeling you need to do the same. Let's just keep an open mind and see what we learn."

Mythral was puzzled as he stopped in front of the guest suite door that mysteriously had his name on it. He had not told Nate of his plan to visit. He opened the door to find a set of rooms lavishly furnished with dark, heavy, medieval-looking carved furniture and richly colored tapestries.

Kit continued down the hall until she, too, came to a door with her name on it. When she stepped inside the set of rooms chosen for her, she felt as if she had walked into a dream. The rooms were bright, light, airy and filled with delicate furnishings that looked to be designed and created by fairies or some other happy magical creatures. As her practical nature slowly pushed through her amazement, Kit rushed out her door to Mythral's room and asked, "How do we know when an hour has passed?"

Mythral smiled and said, "Nate thinks of everything. You will hear bells ringing. That is my best attempt to describe the sound, anyway. When you do, simply proceed back downstairs. Again, I must warn you, go nowhere you have not been specifically invited, and do not ask too many questions at dinner."

Kit found a fully functional bathroom with hot running water in her rooms. After their long journey, she and Mythral set about cleaning and refreshing themselves. After a simple cleaning spell on their robes, they were ready for dinner. As they heard the chimes described by Mythral, the aromas of the magnificent feast awaiting them below reminded them they were hungry. Tea and cakes at Gemma's cavern had been their lunch this day.

During dinner, Nate put off Kit's questions about her name. "Storytelling is best done after a meal, while sitting around the fire. But

I'll say this much: Your name in elvish means 'small choice.'"

"Elvish? The *Remedial Spelling* book mentioned elves, but I got so distracted that day I forgot to ask Mythral about them. Please tell me about them."

Nate laughed again at Kit's enthusiastic questioning. "That, I suspect, is a very long story, of which I know very little. They say the elves grew tired of humans and their bickering and left the realm long before the Wizard Wars. All they left behind was their language and the wording of many spells. Rumor has it, a portal to their new world exists if you know where and how to look. That's all I know, but you might try dragging more from Cat on one of his rare good days."

She can try, but I promised the elves I would not reveal where they went. They, in gratitude, enabled the magic that lay dormant within me. As I said earlier.

Changing courses, Kit asked Nate why he didn't just do away with all dark magic, or at least all dark wizards. Even if it did not last forever, surely their absence would bring about many years of peace. To Kit, the answer to all the evil in the Realms seemed simple, given Nate's powers.

Nate began his reply by saying, "While 'simple' solutions often are good solutions, 'easy' fixes tend to backfire. If easy worked, we never would have any hard problems. Just look at the Three Realms solution to dealing with evil wizards. Ask Mythral if the problem has been solved or only grown while out of sight.

"Instead of fighting the good fight every day to keep evil in check, the Council of WISDOM chose to ignore evil by hiding it away here in Realm Three, where it has been ignored. Evil has managed to grow stronger without any opposition. Not even I could extract evil from the balancing forces at work in our Realms.

"If I were to try, who would be transformed? Just the worst wizards? Who would decide, and how? What about harmful insects, creatures, and diseases? If one starts down this path of weeding out all evil and bad things, where does it end? Should we make a world containing only a few truly good people, like our Mythral here, or should we allow for a few flawed individuals?

"Does great power alone make me wise enough to choose? Or give me the right? Be careful with your answer, Kit. Your liking or trusting me should not be a basis for answering that question." With the last comment, Nate lost his softness and became bigger and harder. His body radiated power and force, so much so that Kit actually began to fear him. Then suddenly Nate was himself again.

"Letting power or anything else rule you is dangerous; it changes who you are, and that takes you further away from discerning right from wrong. What if MorKano were the most powerful wizard in the Realms? Were Mythral and I not here, he might well be. Does might make right? The answer always has been no. But if good people do not actively oppose evil, then evil will win.

"No. I would rather turn myself into a mountain or a pebble and let fate take me where it will, than to become responsible for managing the Realms and everyone in them. I will *not* assume responsibility for the lives, choices, and mistakes of others. But enough of this discussion. Let us take our drinks in front of the fireplace, and I will tell you the story of a most insignificant little fairy named Cinta Kilme."

CHAPTER 45

WHAT'S IN A NAME?
[Realm Three]

As Nate had told Kit earlier, her name was an elvish one that translated as "small choice." But there was more. The name itself had a history, or at least a fairy tale, associated with it. So, Nate told them the Cinta Kilme fable.

"Long before Mythral's time, and mine, magic and magical creatures lived mostly in harmony with one another. Then the first real evil arose in the world. It was a wizard who sought more and more power with which to control more and more of the world around him. For reasons unknown, this wizard had lost all love for life and beauty. He sought only power and then more power. I will call this wizard 'Koorman,' even though he had no name in the original story."

"Why give him that name if he had none to start?" asked Mythral, whose mind could not stand an unsolved riddle or loose detail.

"The reason for the name lies in the future. You will have to wait for your answer. No more interruptions, please. Koorman started to gain power by stealing it, first from the weakest of the magical creatures.

"While the fairies were plentiful and possessed magic, that magic was not strong in them individually. Fairies were free spirits and rarely acted in groups or stayed focused for very long. They were an ideal target for this evil wizard. Koorman simply walked among the communities of fairies, casting spells to paralyze them. Then he tossed them, one by one, into his mouth, consuming them and their magic.

"Even when the fairies became aware of this, they were unable to organize or defend themselves in any effective way. Each fairy he consumed added only a tiny bit more to this wizard's total magic. However, these tiny amounts began to add up to a significant increase in his powers.

"Eventually, the evil wizard made his way to a community where one small, insignificant fairy lived. Seeing that her world was about to be ravaged by this evil wizard, the little fairy took it upon herself to make a difference.

"This tiny fairy was unusual in her ability to see consequences beyond the next moment. The easy path would have been to run far away, to let others deal with the threat, and to hope evil never showed up on her doorstep. But this little fairy was most unique in that the selfish course of action never even occurred to her. Instead, she assembled the most potent poisons she could find and set herself directly in the path of the evil Koorman.

"As he approached, she turned as if to run and then drank her poisons. His spell captured her and all the others nearby. They all were unable to move. Koorman swiftly consumed them each in turn. However, when he came to this one fairy, he stopped. There in her eyes was a look he had not seen before. Neither fear nor helplessness.

"It puzzled him, and perhaps he should have thought more about it. But she was one small, insignificant fairy, and he was now the most powerful wizard that had ever walked the realm. Soon he would be beyond challenge by even a group of strong wizards. With contempt for whatever this small fairy might be feeling or thinking, he snatched her up and consumed her.

"Fairies are light and flimsy, so in no time at all the poisons she had consumed just before being captured were released into his body. Within seconds, Koorman's death was unavoidable. In his greed and haste, he had taken no precautions, and now a counter-spell was impossible because he was paralyzed.

"So, this tiny choice by one small and insignificant fairy saved all the fairies, and likely the rest of the world, from this greatest of evils. In honor of her sacrifice, she was given the name *Cinta Kilme*, elvish for 'small choice.'"

As Nate finished his story, Kit immediately was full of tears and questions about how that name was or would become appropriate for her. Nate told her, "Too much knowledge of the future can be a potential paradox. It is best to leave nature alone to take you where it will and on its own path and in its own time. Foreknowledge only complicates matters."

Then Nate announced the hour was late and the time to sleep had come. On the way to their rooms, Mythral again reminded Kit that Nate's valley, and especially his home, was awash in pure magic. She should pay close attention to any dreams.

Elves, elves, elves. Yes, I know. They keep popping up in the story, but I haven't told you anything about them. They really don't play a role yet. Be patient. They just might appear much later on Kit and Mythral's Time-Path.

CHAPTER 46

ASSAULT PLANS
[Realm Three]

Earlier that same day, MorKano had been implementing Plan B. Having failed to intercept Mythral before he entered Nate's lands, MorKano was readying his unthinkable plan: a direct attack inside Nate's house. To succeed, the attack had to be totally unexpected.

"Go over it one more time, Valak," MorKano demanded of this mostly trusted but expendable dark wizard.

"I will fly to Nate's border late this evening and use the Power Removal Spell. Once I am without dark magic, I can safely gain entry and access to the house."

"Not until you have used that first yellow gemstone to shield your presence with neutral magic," said MorKano with obvious impatience.

"Yes, of course. Inside the house, I'll locate Mythral's bedroom. I'll use a green gemstone to restore my powers and using all the red gemstones for extra power, I'll immediately destroy Mythral before Nate knows I am there. Then I'll ..."

Agitated by his underling's omissions, MorKano interjected again, "Do not forget about the girl. If she is close enough, do her as well. Then use the Power Removal Spell and the second yellow gemstone to hide from Nate, and get out."

"Okay. Once off the property, I'll use the final green gemstone to restore my powers and return."

Dispatching Valak for his mission later that night, MorKano reflected on his good fortune. Mythral had foolishly remained in Realm Three long enough for him to execute this pre-planned attack. Once Mythral was dead, nothing could stand in his way. The Three Realms Spell would be undone, and he alone would rule over a single realm. So many facets of this plan had fallen into place—and just in time to catch Mythral by surprise.

The Power Removal Spell had long fallen out of use, and memory, but it was well documented. During the plagues of ages past, it was common practice for infected wizards to voluntarily remove their own powers to prevent serious injury to themselves and others during the periods of madness that often accompanied the plague. The spell to involuntarily remove another's magic also existed but was not easily or safely performed. It often backfired on the spellcaster. Restoration of power, once the madness passed, usually was performed by a family member easily enough.

Then there were those all-important gemstones of power. *If Gemma had not refused my simple request for them, her friend would still be alive. Gemma has but herself to blame. No one will find Ergotimos's body for a couple of days. Too late to alert Mythral or anyone else.*

CHAPTER 47

THE STUFF OF DREAMS AND NIGHTMARES
[Realm Three]

Kit's first dream was of her parents. She had no actual memory of them, but she sensed they were her parents. The love and caring naturally were there, but there also was a familiarity from years of being together.

In this dream she still was a young child, but her actual childhood in Realm One was without her parents. Then she realized the connection she sensed might be in the future and not in the past. Recalling her lessons on the continuity of the Time-Space Continuum, she wondered if she could have gone far enough into the future to return to the past.

Kit drifted into another dream. Only this one she found very disturbing. She saw herself working a powerful spell with a dark wizard whom she instinctively knew to be MorKano. So repulsed was she by the thought of working with MorKano, the worst of the dark wizards and Vivyen's murderer, that it shocked her out of the dream before it ended. She now was wide awake and filled with fear at the prospect of turning to dark magic.

However, the magic of Nate's home that surrounded her was too strong, and soon she was asleep again. While she dreamed no more dreams that night, she did hear a soft, almost motherly voice whispering to her, *Fear not your future, my child. Trust in yourself.*

Down the hall in his own rooms, Mythral dreamed of the future he and Vivyen should have had: marriage, children, less time dealing with evil, and more time appreciating and enjoying life. Somehow in this dream, evil had been defeated, at least for a while. The Council of WISDOM was dealing with the issues of the Two Realms without constant support from Mythral.

Mythral dealt with Realm One, and the Council of WISDOM handled the other Realm. It all seemed so impossibly wonderful that Mythral dismissed it as an actual dream, instead of a sensing of the future. After all, Vivyen was dead, and evil slowly was gaining the upper hand.

Then, still half asleep, he saw it. *Wait. In my dream, there were only two Realms. The Two Realms solution was what I initially had proposed. The Three Realms solution was something the Council of WISDOM had insisted upon. Could I be sensing an alternate Time-Space Continuum where the choice had been two Realms, not three, and where it had worked?*

Then reality struck Mythral through another inconsistency. Vivyen had been killed just prior to the Three Realms Spell. Even if the Council had chosen a Two Realms version, Vivyen still would have died before the casting of the Spell. This must have been just a normal dream in which Mythral, out of a desperate longing for his lost love, had altered some facts.

Later that night Kit, once again awake, faced a new dilemma with no good solution. A common occurrence in Mythral's world of magic, it seemed. Should she share the details of both dreams with Mythral? Should she tell Mythral she would work with MorKano in the future? How could Mythral ever trust her after that? Why should he? Then again, why should he trust her if she did not tell him the truth about her dreams?

In the end, she decided to postpone telling Mythral. She needed to better understand whether what she had sensed was predetermined to happen or merely one possibility. After all, wasn't Mythral's choosing an apprentice primarily motivated by his need to alter his sensed future demise? If Mythral could alter the future enough to avoid his future death, surely she could avoid working with MorKano. Maybe. Or, more likely, for the moment she was rationalizing her decision to take an easier, less confrontational path.

Kit suddenly was standing in front of Mythral's door. How and why was she there? Maybe she really wanted to confide in Mythral and her subconscious had made the choice for her. *Might as well get on with it,* she thought as her hand lifted to knock.

Then she sensed the magic. First neutral, then alarmingly evil. Dark, dangerous, and close. And it was inside Mythral's room!

Never one to freeze in a panic, she blew the doors off their hinges with a surprising force of magic. Valak was between her and Mythral's bed, poised to release a deadly spell. Kit's immediate action was what saved Mythral. Her explosive entrance caused him to spin around and attack her.

The next instant was a blur. Even with her powers already running on full steam, her instinctive Blocking Spell, *Tafnen Balan,* barely worked. Her attacker went stiff as a board and began a slow backwards fall. But before impact, he was transformed into a dull red rock with many fissures and imperfections that shattered into a thousand pieces as it slammed onto the floor.

The three-way discussion afterwards established the facts as follows. The assassin's successful entry was a mystery to Nate and Mythral. Nate instantly knew when any dark magic crossed his borders. Kit's report of the neutral magic immediately prior to sensing dark magic led Mythral to guess the means. Kit's timing and instinctive reaction had saved the day—or night, rather. As Kit was tossing up her Blocking Spell, Mythral was attacking from behind with a Stun Spell. Nate swooped in at the end and transformed Valak into a rock.

Mythral inquired about Kit's timely arrival at his door. Again, unable to decide the best course, Kit delayed by saying she must have been half asleep and something led her to Mythral's door.

"One of the many lessons to take away," said Mythral, "is to use a Deflection Spell when no one around you would be at risk. It requires much less energy than that Blocking Spell."

Nate closed out the review. "As dawn is near and more sleep unlikely, breakfast will be served in 30 minutes. Barring further distractions."

To tell or not to tell Mythral? As she returned to her room, Kit again wrestled with the question that had led her to Mythral's door.

CHAPTER 48

BRIGANTIA THE WEAVER
[Realm Three]

After another wonderful feast for breakfast, Nate asked Mythral to drop off a special bush at Brigantia's place on his way back to the Realm Three gate. Brigantia was a wizard whose talent lay in infusing fabric with magic. Her clothes and garments were highly prized for their extraordinary array of colors and patterns found nowhere else, not even in nature. Mythral knew of her, but he never had met her.

Even more unusual than Nate's request was the bush he asked them to deliver. It resembled Realm One's fall foliage at its peak but with a much greater range of colors, all of which appeared to move and flicker like a flame. But there was no heat when Kit put her hand near the bush. Nate told them the bush had no name because he rarely labeled his creations. He said with just a bit of magical encouragement the bush would grow into a hedge in weeks. It was a special gift to Brigantia in exchange for a favor she was to do for him.

The gryphons, Fast and Furious, were waiting outside Nate's home as if they had known the day and exact time of Mythral and Kit's departure. A certain anxiousness was obvious in their demeanor as Mythral and Kit mounted up.

Nate also noticed Fast and Furious seemed to be champing at the proverbial (nonexistent) bit. He told Mythral and Kit the gryphons always were excited to visit Brigantia. For some reason they had a special appreciation for her work. Nate suspected the gryphons could sense something about the fabrics others missed.

Moments after takeoff, Mythral and Kit were descending towards

Brigantia's place. On the way, Kit noticed sheep in a field and asked Mythral about them. Using mental communications during flight, Mythral explained, *Those animals are for sourcing the wool Brigantia uses. She brought them with her to Realm Three but quickly learned she could not protect them on her property. So Nate lets them graze on his lands.*

During the short trip, Kit asked Mythral about the danger of another attack here in Realm Three. Mythral replied, *Unlikely. MorKano had no idea which direction we might take when leaving Nate's valley, nor when. After losing six of his fellow conspiring dark wizards, MorKano is unlikely to risk any more too near to Nate's valley.*

Once on the ground, Kit noticed that the trees surrounding the cottage in front of them were full of enormous spiderwebs. "Silk for her fabrics," Mythral answered before she could ask. They were met by a woman of indeterminable age, though she moved and acted like a young woman. Her red hair glistened in the sun and resembled some of the colors in the bush from Nate. Her hazel eyes were kind and shone with deep understanding. She warmly greeted Fast and Furious with some gryphon treats in the palms of her hands. Then she turned to Mythral and Kit for introductions.

She admitted to knowing much about the two of them from Nate. Apparently, Nate had dropped by late yesterday probably just before dinner. Brigantia accepted Nate's gift and said it was even more beautiful and fascinating than he had described. She invited them into her cottage, telling them their gift was ready and waiting. Mythral and Kit looked at each other in bewilderment as they followed her into the cottage.

Upon entering the cottage, Brigantia handed Kit a set of traditional robes but made of material she never had seen before. The robes' sky-blue trim around the edges shimmering in the light, seemed to be almost alive. Kit's initials in the same sky-blue were embroidered on the breast just above her heart.

Mythral took some of the fabric in his hand. His face showed puzzlement, and he then dropped into a deeper focus upon the material. Mythral told Kit, "You are indeed fortunate to have made this trip. Brigantia has infused these robes with the strongest of her magic."

Brigantia explained to Kit, "These robes will protect you from ordinary wizards' spells and from any magical attempts to befuddle your mind or impact your memory. With these robes on, you always will remain clearheaded."

Brigantia invited them to join her for tea as she explained more fully. "The thread comes from a tree Nate created just for this purpose. The rest of the process of creating the fabric is done by hand. Magic is infused into each piece of the cloth. Nate did not give me much time, but I already had the fabric and needed only to cut and sew it. Nate had implied some important challenges lay ahead for Kit, and she would need every advantage she could get."

Mythral clearly was impressed by Brigantia's gift. After tea was served, Brigantia explained she and Nate had been friends for years. Her friendship with Nate, and her apparent lack of value to the dark wizards, most likely were the reasons no one bothered her here in Realm Three. Nate sent her plants and flowers, and she sent him clothes to wear and fabrics for his home. Brigantia said no one would notice her fabric on Nate because he always was surrounded by so much pure magic, but he said he never would wear anything but her textiles.

Brigantia had Kit change into her new robes in her back room. Then she mentioned one other handy feature: "These robes never need cleaning." That put a look of pleasant surprise upon Kit's face.

Just as they stepped outside to say goodbye, Fast and Furious showed up ready to go. On the way to the Realm Three gate, Mythral communicated mentally. *Don't assume that Brigantia's only source of protection is Nate. No one knows just how powerful she is. She never uses her magic in an obvious way. However, I have it on good authority that a couple of dark wizards who tried to take advantage of her special gifts never were heard from afterwards. I am sure her friendship with Nate keeps a lot of new trouble away from her doorstep, but among those who know the past, she has her own reputation.*

CHAPTER 49

POSTMORTEM
[Realm Three]

Valak's failure was confirmed later when Mythral and Kit were spotted departing from Nate's. Neither had been reported as dead or even damaged.

MorKano was in a foul mood thereafter. Even a lengthy visit to his torture cells in the bowels of his fortress provided no relief. *It was a long shot,* he reminded himself. Yet, questions nagged at MorKano. What went wrong? Had his agent slipped up? Was Mythral even greater than his reputation? Was Nate able to act faster than his assassin? Or, was it that girl Mythral had foolishly taken as an apprentice?

He really had not expected Valak to make it out alive. Stealing gemstones and murdering Gemma's friend had been a risk. If Nate ever connected him to those acts--perish the thought. What had he gained? Apparently nothing but the enjoyment of torturing the gems' prior owner for the spell to use them.

Pushing this mystery into the back of his mind, MorKano faced his present victim. Now the only question before him for this morning's diversion was physical or mental torture? Corrupting an old saying about the journey being more important than the destination, he opted for a bit of both.

CHAPTER 50
SAME OLD, SAME OLD: TRAINING
[Realm Two]

The return trip to and through the Realm Three portal and the stroll back to the Realm Two bookshop were uneventful. Mythral sent Kit home to Realm One for the rest of that day and the next day. He instructed her to rest and recover from her testing and travels. Despite her impending return to school in Realm One, her training needed to be accelerated. Apparently, the information that Mythral was getting from his sources indicated a dangerous plan was about to be implemented by MorKano.

Two days later after school, when Kit returned to the bookshop in Realm One, she walked in to find Mythral reading a newspaper. She was surprised, and Mythral appeared somewhat embarrassed to be caught reading the local Realm One paper. Mythral explained, a bit too hastily, that he always was fascinated by how normals perceived the Realm he and the Council of WISDOM had created for them. Despite Kit's having heard the story many times before, Mythral proceeded to remind her of the origin of the Three Realms and their purpose. Somehow, he seemed to think something in the newspaper connected with the Three Realms story.

Mythral called Kit's attention to a piece on the universe, dark matter, and dark energy. Kit skimmed the article. Mythral said, "I sometimes wonder if your scientists look for complex solutions even when a simpler explanation is best. Take this article. The new finding is that the universe is expanding at a rate greater than initially predicted. They want to create complex and unknown variables, dark matter, and dark energy, to explain the findings."

To which Kit injected, "And you know a simpler answer?"

"It's fairly straightforward logic when you think outside the box—or, in this case, outside the universe. According to current theory, the universe is an expanding sphere of energy and mass moving outward from a single point and restrained only by gravity. Instead of adding unknown but implied variables inside that universe to explain the outward acceleration, they could just write the equation for expansion with one straightforward variable on the outside. The universe is expanding into some Void. Just call it negative space-time. That negative space-time would pull the universe outward by a factor that increases over time because the spherical universe is enlarging over time. The more surface contact between the two, the greater the outward pull. Then you add that one factor to the mass, energy, and gravity components of the normal expansion equation."

"Very interesting," said Kit, without any real conviction in her voice.

Noting her tone, Mythral changed the subject and announced some new training. This time he, not Perci, would be the instructor. "First, there are some finer points of magic often overlooked by the mentor. Way too much emphasis is placed upon conducting magic at the expense of understanding magic. Only those who understand how and why magic works can add to the total knowledge and appreciation of magic. Those without an understanding merely perform magic at a deteriorating level of proficiency. After all, if something isn't moving forward, it is either moving backwards or standing still. Knowledge and skill are likely to deteriorate over time if not actively stimulated or enhanced.

"Therefore, you should understand the interaction between dense matter and magic. Dense matter, such as water, soil, and many metals, effectively can block or dampen magic, especially dark magic. Can you speculate as to why that is, based upon what you already have learned?"

Both the subject matter and the question caught Kit completely off guard, and she had to stop to think. Her first thought was this was yet another of Mythral's tests, and there was some hidden meaning or unexpected twist. While her mind looked for some obscure insight, Mythral broke into her thoughts as though he had guessed them. *There is no hidden purpose or meaning to this question. Can you propose a reason why dense matter would have a greater dampening effect upon dark magic?*

"Well, you have said there is a fundamental harmony or vibration to the universe, which allows us to sense when a person is lying or when dark magic is afoot. Dark magic is 'discordant,' if that is the right term, with the natural frequency. This disturbance enables us to recognize when dark magic is being used or about to be used. I also know from my Realm One classes that light and energy waves do not travel as well through water and soil as they do through air. Let's see. There is yet one more connecting piece. Yes, I have it! Magic is a form of energy."

"All well and good as far as you have gone," said Mythral. "But what differentiates dense matter's impacts on good and dark magic?"

After a very long pause for thought, in a very tentative voice, Kit put forth a theory about which she obviously was uncertain. "The only difference I can see is dark magic's discord with universal frequency. I seem to recall something in a class about incompatible energy waves canceling out or interfering with each other. So, dark magic energy is more incompatible with matter than good magic energy is. The greater the incompatibility, the greater the discord."

"Pretty close to top marks," said Mythral. "It takes a special case for energy waves to 'cancel' or neutralize one another, but in general the incompatible frequency of dark magic meets more resistance from matter than does good magic, which is vibrating at the fundamental frequency of the universe. Now let's move from theory to practice."

Mythral announced his intention to enhance Kit's ability to enter deep trance, primarily for sensing the future. Kit always had wanted to learn about sensing. Sensing, after all, was the primary reason she was chosen as Mythral's apprentice. Mythral's sensing of his own death was why Kit was needed to help Mythral alter that future event. She had easily sensed the future during her first physical contact with Mythral. During these training sessions, Mythral felt an easy connection with Kit that was encouraging. However, during the current joint trance, he steered their sensing forward to that critical day of Mythral's death in MorKano's fortress, to check whether anything had changed from his original vision.

When Mythral sensed the big battle scene this time, unlike the prior times, he sensed three overlapping endings, something that never had happened before. A number of alternate endings were possible based upon different choices, yes, but never had he sensed multiple concurrent endings on the same Time-Path. He and Kit seemed to prevail over MorKano in two of the three scenarios, one of which was not very clear, almost as if he, Mythral, were not really present when it happened. The third path forward appeared to lead to his and Kit's imprisonment, with death to follow shortly. As the vision slowly faded, the prophecy echoed forcefully: "Mythral's choice will doom or save the Realms."

As they both emerged from their trances, Kit was full of questions, for she had experienced the same sensing Mythral had. Mythral indicated the need for calm, to review the specifics of such visions, in order to capture the details for further analysis.

Later, when they compared their individual perceptions of the vision, Kit knew she saw clearly all three potential endings, because she was a participant in all three. The one that was blurry to Mythral was the one in which she was working a spell with MorKano. Was that vision at Nate's destined to come true?

That it was just one of three potential futures gave her some hope that it would not actually happen. Yet, deep inside, Kit sensed the collaboration with MorKano would, in fact, occur.

If Mythral suspected Kit was withholding anything, he did not show it. While she mentally debated the pros and cons of sharing with Mythral both her dream and her vision regarding MorKano, the opportunity passed. Mythral, obviously distracted by his own internal thoughts, announced that they would continue the lessons later.

CHAPTER 51

AN INVITATION TO THE FAIR
[Realm Two]

When Perci resumed Kit's training the next day, he had a few remaining questions about her visit to Realm Three. Mythral's briefing to Perci on the events of their trip satisfied most of Perci's curiosity. Perci's questions to Kit were about her perceptions of the people she had met and places she had seen. When she seemed at a loss for words, Perci told her to start with her greatest impressions. Again, she seemed to struggle to assign an order of importance to her experiences.

Finally, Kit said, "Certainly, being in Nate's valley, and inside his home, was like walking through magic. No, more like floating through magic, as if in a pool of water but with no resistance. Everything felt lighter and effortless. Words really fail to capture the feeling. Next, I'd say, were the strange textures and vibrant colors in Realm Three."

"Since I never have been to Realm Three, you have to be more descriptive!"

"I keep trying, but none of my words do justice to what I saw and felt. Our language is just too vague. All I can say is I saw every color we know to exist, and more. They shimmered and moved as if they were alive. Some were fairly constant, but others kept shifting in hue and intensity. Some even seemed three-dimensional. The look and feel of things were all jumbled up. A surface might appear rough but feel super soft. One fabric I thought was burlap tore like tissue paper when I picked it up."

"That's a start," said Perci, "but I'll want more details after you have had more time to process your experiences. Next time, you can show me mentally and I'll have the experience rather than the story. Now, back to training."

Being distracted by their conversation and the return to routine, Kit initially suppressed her guilt about the dream of MorKano and the sensing session with Mythral. But as the day wore on, the weight of the secret distracted her from training. Perci noticed the small mistakes Kit was making and suggested they call it a day. However, before Kit started for her room in the Realm Two bookstore, Perci had another suggestion. There was a harvest fair in town that night, and some of Perci's friends were planning to attend. Perci invited Kit to come meet some younger Fairhaven inhabitants who were closer to her age. Kit, being caught completely off-guard, said yes instinctively, followed by a momentary panic. "But I have nothing to wear!"

"Don't forget, this is Realm Two. Most of my friends will be in robes or casual clothes. Oh, you can add a bit of color or a piece of jewelry if you like, but no one pays attention to fashion in Realm Two. Those robes Brigantia gave you will be the fanciest garments there. They are all you need to make a good impression. That sky-blue piping and your initials add some of the flair you described this morning. The fair starts at sunset, so we will leave in about an hour."

Once again, the events of the moment distracted Kit from her internal conflict over the MorKano dream and vision. To tell or not to tell Mythral? That was the question. The right answer seemed obvious, but Kit just could not bring herself to commit to it. Without meaning to, she was using a common stalling tactic. She had convinced herself "now was not the time." *After the fair tonight, or maybe tomorrow,* she bargained, *I'll resolve this problem and end all of this stress.*

CHAPTER 52
THE HARVEST COLORS
[Realm Two]

On their way to the fair, Perci explained that each person, upon entering the hall, would create a light globe and send it to the ceiling. This was how the hall was illuminated, by a hundred or more globes of light drifting back and forth across the ceiling. The spell was a simple variation of the Light Globe Spell that Kit already had mastered. She learned the new variation quickly. "The building being used for the fair is something of a community hall," Perci explained. Perci, for some reason, was uncharacteristically talkative on the walk to the fair, and Kit began to wonder if he was nervous about something. Maybe about introducing her to his friends.

Just as Kit made this observation, Perci began explaining about the hall. "It may seem strange for such a large building in our snowy climate to have such a shallow pitch to the roof. Unlike in your Realm, here, magic is used in the construction to keep snow from piling up and adding too much weight. So, no need to worry about the roof caving in on us."

Yes, Kit thought, *he definitely is nervous about something.* Before she could speculate further, they had arrived.

Upon entering the hall, Perci created his globe first, and it was surprisingly similar to the sky-blue color in Kit's robes. He almost had captured the shimmer, as well. Afterwards, he said to Kit, "I hope you do not mind, but I never have seen anything quite like you—I mean, *that color*—before."

She pretended not to notice his verbal stumble.

As his globe floated to the ceiling, there were many impressed "ooh"s and "ah"s from the other fairgoers, some of whom approached Perci to ask about his color choice, leaving Kit momentarily alone to choose her own globe color.

This being a harvest fair, Kit got an inspiration. Reaching into her memory to retrieve the bush Nate had given Brigantia, Kit created her globe and sent it to the ceiling. This time there were no utterances of awe; the room went completely silent. There on the ceiling was a globe like nothing seen before by anyone in the room. Autumn reds, greens, yellows, and oranges swirled inside the globe, pulsating and shimmering, alive. Eventually, the globe maker became the focus of attention. Kit started to feel self-conscious. The entire room's attention was on her. Just as the tension reached a breaking point, Perci stepped in and said, "Everyone, this is my friend and Mythral's new protégé, of whom you may have heard. Her name is Kit and, as you can see, she is a very gifted wizard. She also is extremely friendly, so please come and meet her."

The next half-hour was a blur of names, faces, and unending questions. Her answer to "Where are you from?" drew surprised looks. Apparently, it was not well known that Kit was from Realm One. The second most popular question was about her globe's color. When she explained it was inspired by Realm Three, their curiosity turned to awe, mixed with a bit of intimidation. No other person in the hall ever had been to Realm Three. The mere thought of it gave them shivers. However, as they talked more with Kit, everyone became quite comfortable and at ease with her. She felt she must have met everyone in the room.

Then she noticed the pretty dark-haired girl on the opposite side of the room. Jasmine. Staring at her. Under the circumstances, staring was normal, but something else was off about this girl. As soon as their eyes met, the dark-haired girl turned and moved off into the crowd. Having gotten only the barebones story from Mythral and Cat, Kit made a mental note to ask Perci about Jasmine later.

The music was a welcome change from endless introductions and curious questions. Soon most of the crowd was out on the dance floor, and she noticed Perci had returned to her side. "You have won them all over," he said, "despite your strange globe, your even stranger mentor, and your being from Realm One. You have a natural way with people."

"People are fine. I just can't stand the bullies, and occasionally the really self-centered people. One question they asked me, I could not answer. I was asked if any other powerful wizards exist in Realm One besides me."

Perci thought for a moment and replied, "As far as I know, the only other possibility is Toro. But, now that you ask, I don't see why there could not be more. Perhaps if we understood why you were in Realm One, we would know the answer. I am not sure how Mythral even became aware of you and your brother in Realm One. Although experience tells me, when Mythral and I are unable to explain things going on around us, the answer usually is Cat. Now, how about a dance?"

"I don't really know how to dance. We do a bit of square dancing on occasion back home, and I have waltzed a couple of times with my foster father. However, I'm sure I'd make a fool of myself if I tried here in front of your friends."

"Nonsense. If you have done any dancing at all, you know you just follow my lead and move to the music. Dancing is something I quite enjoy, and people say I have a strong lead."

> I have always thought of you two-footed humans as clumsy. But when two skilled dancers move on the dance floor—as one, with four feet—they can approach cat-like grace.

CHAPTER 53

A FAIR NIGHT FOR DANCING
[Realm Two]

After a couple of tentative turns around the dance floor, Kit felt like she had done this all of her life. Perci was the perfect partner. While she had simply to follow where he led, which he did very well, she occasionally got distracted. When that happened, her footwork got tangled up. Amazingly, only she and Perci noticed. He could sense her missteps before they happened and adjust accordingly.

From the beginning of their dance, Perci communicated with Kit mentally. When he initiated a particular pattern, he named it, so she could recognize and distinguish them. Some terms were familiar, like pivot, spin, and closed and open turn. Other terms were familiar but put to a new meaning, like grapevines and lockstep. Towards the end of a dance, Perci confessed his deep secret mentally.

Long ago, I went to Realm One once a week for months to take lessons at a dance studio. I love dancing so much, I wanted to see if there were any steps or patterns in Realm One that I would enjoy doing here in Realm Two. So you'll find my style is a mix of both Realms, and a lot of what I brought from Realm One now is now well established in Realm Two. I haven't told anyone else. They just think I'm highly creative.

As the music finished and she was about to speak, one of Perci's friends, whose name she forgot, broke in and asked for a dance with Kit.

Once the floodgates opened, Kit had a nonstop line of waiting partners wanting to dance with this beautiful, powerful, friendly wizard from Realm One. Even though the others were not as good at leading as Perci, Kit now was in the moment and one with the music. Whether her partners were a bit daunted by her, or concentrating on their footwork, there was little talking, which was fine with Kit.

She could see why Perci loved dancing so. When you were moving with the music and a good partner, it was almost like floating through the air, not unlike the calm oneness she felt during meditation. With a rare break for drink and food, Kit danced the night away and barely noticed that the crowd was thinning.

As the music stopped, Kit realized that Perci had replaced her last dance partner and was speaking to her.

"The evening is ending soon, and I insist on having the final dance with you. After all, I brought you to the party."

The tale of Cinderella came to Kit's mind—a dance and an evening that all seemed too good to be true. But then the music started, and Kit once again was lost in its spell. A waltz, and a fast one at that. Before she knew it, she and Perci were flying around the nearly empty dance floor.

The globe lights began to fade once their respective creators left the dance, so the lighting was quite subdued at the moment. No mental communication was needed for this final dance. Their bodies in closed dance position were communicating movement and intentions better than words could. This waltz was especially powerful and rhythmic, almost as if the music itself was moving them around the dance floor in patterns as complex as the music.

It was only as the music came to an end that Perci and Kit returned to the reality of the hall. Only then did they notice why the few remaining guests were staring—not only at their dancing, which was truly inspired and magical, but at the orb of light surrounding them. Somehow, Kit subconsciously had generated an orb around them that was the same mix of shimmering autum colors as her orb on the ceiling. As her awareness of the present returned, the orb around them began to fade.

On the way back to the bookshop, very few words were exchanged, aloud or mentally. Each was lost in private thoughts. Not until they arrived at the bookshop door did they realize they had been holding hands.

They reached the spiral staircases at the back of the shop. While Perci prepared to ascend to his room upstairs and Kit to go downstairs to her room in the secret half of the cellar, they both sensed the awkwardness of the moment.

Kit still was caught up in the magic and mood of the evening, and as Perci leaned in to kiss her cheek, she turned her face towards him and their lips met. At first Perci began to pull her closer, then he suddenly held her away from him. "Kit, we cannot start down this path. It would complicate everything. You cannot afford to be distracted from your training, or from the battle to come."

Suddenly embarrassed that she might have felt a deeper connection than he did, Kit's face reddened as she started to apologize. "I'm sorry. I thought you felt ... " but then she trailed off. A few eternal seconds later she was in Perci's embrace, being kissed well and good.

Afterwards they agreed, for the time being, to keep these new feelings to themselves, at least until they could discuss them further. With one final passionate kiss, they were off to their respective rooms.

CHAPTER 54

CONFESSION IS GOOD FOR SPELLING.

[Realm Two]

In the weeks that followed, Mythral was away much more often. While this gave Kit and Perci more time to explore their feelings for each other, Perci made sure that Kit's training did not suffer. However, Mythral's extended absence had Kit wondering whether he was suspicious. Did he know she was harboring secrets concerning MorKano? Worse, was he waiting, disappointedly, for her to speak first? Added to her guilt over the MorKano secrets was this new secret relationship with Perci.

These doubts crept in to distract her. She was making more and more mistakes during her practice sessions with Perci. Because Perci was the target for much of her practice spellcasting, he found some of her mistakes quite uncomfortable. Her Flash Bang Spells were so powerful that he took to wearing Realm One sunglasses at their sessions. Noticing her concentration slipping, he threatened to make her work with the *Remedial Spelling* book if things did not improve.

While working on her Boomerang Spell, *Balan Tafnen*, she made an awful mistake due to her lack of focus. The Spell was meant to simply redirect the incoming Spell back at the Spellcaster—instant karma. However, she enhanced the Boomerang Spell, absentmindedly, with a Memory Loss Spell. Subconsciously, she wanted to forget all about her dream and vision of spell work with MorKano. While Perci was ready for his harmless Blinding Light Spell to come back at him, he never thought to defend against the additional Memory Loss Spell. Fortunately, in light of their prior experiences and Kit's mistakes with some spells, Mythral had taught Kit specifically how to restore Perci's memory. She quickly did so.

Kit confessed to Perci what had happened. Since she technically did not have to tell him about his temporary memory loss, she felt honesty should count in her favor. But Perci said, "This has gone on long enough. If our relationship is this distracting, we cannot continue. One or the other, either your training with me or our relationship, must end!"

"It is not our relationship that is distracting me," she said. "It is something I should have spoken of, to Mythral and to you, but I haven't."

"Confide in me, please, or I'll have no choice but to report to Mythral that you are not in the proper frame of mind for dangerous missions."

Though she was reluctant to admit it, even to herself, Kit had longed to share the burden of her dark dream and vision with Perci. As the repeated lessons on objectivity had taught her, she was just too close to this particular problem to think clearly about it. There really was not much to tell; it was just too horrible to believe. Even more horrible to speak about. Taking a deep breath to settle herself and focus upon her words, she shared with Perci her secret fear of committing a future betrayal by working with MorKano.

"In Nate's home, I had a dream, and later, in a sensing session with Mythral, I saw the same thing. I saw myself working a very powerful spell with MorKano." Ignoring the shocked expression upon Perci's face, she rushed on to finish before his accusations began. "In the dream, I was so upset by it that I awoke immediately, so I have no more details. In the vision, it was happening at about the time Mythral and I are meant to confront those two dark wizards, and perhaps MorKano, in his fortress. There was a strange overlapping of possible or actual scenarios on the Time-Path right at that moment. So maybe the worst of the three paths does not actually happen." However good rationalization might sound, Kit knew it rang false, and now was not the time to deceive Perci. "Yet, I can feel it actually will come to pass, which terrifies me. It scares me almost as much as my concealing all of this from Mythral."

With that brief pause in her narrative, Perci injected the obvious solution. "Why haven't you told Mythral all of this yet? You no doubt feel guilt and shame for a perceived betrayal. Mythral and I both know there must be some other explanation." Perci disregarded the brightening surprise on her face as his words of support, not accusation, penetrated her guilt and fears. "Do you really think Mythral or I could ever believe you would willingly betray us? No. Clearly, there is more to the story than you saw in your dream and vision. You need Mythral to help you investigate this further. Indeed, there may be something within that event you saw that Mythral can use to our advantage. Certainly, he must be made aware of that spell work with MorKano in order to be prepared. Please don't ask me to keep your secret from Mythral. The timing is up to you, but I advise a full confession, as soon as possible."

The discussion with Perci left Kit feeling better and ready to talk to Mythral. However, Mythral did not return that day, or the next. The more Kit dwelled upon her secrets and her failure to confess them sooner, the more doubt crept back into her reasoning. Her fears began to grow, as they so often do when hidden away in dark places.

What if Mythral already knows and has been testing me the whole time? Then, obviously, I will have failed him. Yet, if he did not know and I tell him now, he might assume I'm only telling him at Perci's request. How, then, could he ever trust me again? The more she dwelled on it, the darker her thoughts and fears became.

"Enough!" Kit mentally shook herself and spoke aloud resolutely, to no one. "There is a right choice and a wrong choice here. I need only to clear my mind and focus on finding the right one."

Upon Mythral's return later that day, and with Perci there supporting her, Kit confessed all to Mythral. Had it not been for the developing bond with Perci, she doubted she'd have had the confidence to confess.

The relationship with Perci had enabled her to share her fears and guilt. No reaction appeared upon Mythral's face while he was in deep thought, digesting Kit's disclosures. Finally, he stirred, looked at her, and pronounced his judgement.

Or so it appeared to Kit, sitting there in anticipation and fear of being rejected for her weaknesses, for working with MorKano, and for selfishly withholding crucial information from Mythral. She no longer deserved his trust. It was a lesson learned at great cost. In hindsight, she now saw many days of her and Perci's time had been wasted, thanks to her fears and distractions. What other opportunities for more training or deepening friendship with Perci had been lost? Mythral's throat clearing caused Kit to look up as he spoke.

"I am extremely disappointed in our relationship, Kit. If you understand me and trust me so little that you were too afraid to tell me about your vision and your dream, all our time together and our training has been a truly great failure. I sincerely apologize for having let you down so badly. I have been so preoccupied with my own efforts to uncover the plots from Realm Three, I took you and our relationship for granted. Perci's stepping up in my absence, such that you could confide in him, is indeed fortunate. Now, let me sleep on this new information. Kit, you and I must spend more time together, for the sake of ourselves and the Realms. Good night to both of you."

"Mythral, please, wait just a bit longer," Kit requested. "As long as I'm divulging all my secrets, there is one more." "Perci and I have feelings for each other. We won't let that interfere with my training, but I do not want any more secrets between us. Secrets are too distracting, and the worry and guilt wear me out."

"I wondered how long that would take. You and Perci, being who you are, and doing what you do together every day, were almost certain to become close. I cannot think of two people better suited in values and purposes. However, I'd hold off on labeling it as serious until time and tribulations have tested your ability to both accept and forgive each other's flaws. I know through your young eyes you see no flaws now, but we all have them. I've been told I might think a bit too highly of my abilities. Though I'm not quite sure how it could be possible," he said, winking, I'll admit to the possibility. Now, I'll say again, good night, and get some rest."

While Mythral may be my favorite human, he has his flaws. From my perspective, his head is in the clouds on a few topics. He was a bit slow to accept my unique—dare I say, superior—wisdom and humor. But, to lecture teenagers on young love shows surprisingly bad judgment.

CHAPTER 55

JUST ONE MORE THING
[Realm Two]

As Perci began to say goodnight to Kit with a close embrace and a kiss, as had become their habit when alone, she stopped him. Holding back on what she already knew about Jasmine, she asked the question.

"As long as we are disclosing everything to everyone, there is something that bothered me at the harvest fair—more like someone. This girl. Probably older than I am and certainly more attractive, with raven hair. She stood across the room and stared at me most of the evening. She never introduced herself or came near me. However, even from across the room I could sense she was out of balance. Not quite evil, like a dark wizard, but something between confused and dangerous. I've often seen her around town staring at me." The look on Perci's face and the long hesitation confirmed that he knew she was asking about Jasmine.

"Well, in the spirit of confessing all, that was Jasmine. Everyone calls her Jas. She and I dated awhile back. Her grandmother is the only female wizard currently on the Council of WISDOM. So, Jas is well trained in magic. I quickly decided our priorities and values differed too much, so I decided not to see her anymore. About a week later, she insisted on meeting up one last time 'to end it properly.' Naturally, I agreed, and we got together for one last drink and talk. I cannot remember what we discussed, but later that evening I was infatuated with her. She never had seemed so fascinating and alive before that night. Fortunately, Mythral immediately recognized the symptoms. She had used a spell upon me, possibly using a potion in my drink. Mythral reversed the spell and added a Permanent Protection Spell in case she tries again.

"In hindsight, she probably saw me as the perfect stepping stone to her objectives. She wants to be the youngest female wizard ever selected to the Council of WISDOM. I, being Mythral's friend and confidant, have access to power and knowledge she deeply envies. My being a less powerful wizard than she was an added benefit. She probably assumed she could impose her values and desires upon me. She is so messed up now, I actually feel sorry for her. We should avoid her whenever possible. In fact, Mythral reported her misuse of magic to the Council. Her grandmother spoke in her defense, and the Council agreed to just a warning this time. However, they did order her to stay away from me as a precaution. I saw her there, as well. I did not want to spoil your evening by bringing up my past."

Finally, Kit had processed Perci's disclosure and said, "How could she possibly have thought she would get away with it? Surely, Mythral or others would have noticed the change?"

"That is one of Jas's flaws. She is so focused upon her immediate objectives, she fails to recognize the complications and obstacles awaiting her down the road. Anyway, she did what she did, and now we are where we are. I'd rather forget all about it. I guess I should have warned you about her. Please do avoid her, and keep a constant level of sensing turned on when you are outside the bookshop. You and Mythral are lucky that you can sense someone beginning to cast a dark spell nearby."

"I will be careful. I want you to promise to be extra careful. She doesn't sound like someone who is going to change her plans simply on Council's orders. So, love potions do exist. What I have read so far seems to indicate you cannot use magic to instill true emotions like love and loyalty. So, does that mean you did have feelings for her all along?"

"Your education on such spells is incomplete at best. True, you cannot make someone love you against their will. However, a talented wizard can use a Befuddlement Spell to hide the negative aspects of a person's character and enhance the positive aspects. Jas's carefully constructed

Befuddlement Spell had me focused solely on her good side and blissfully oblivious to her darker nature. Initially, I was attracted to her when I learned she was training young girls to use magic to protect themselves. While her motives seemed decent, when I probed deeper, she said, 'If the means cannot pass your sense of propriety, Perci, then focus upon the result, and recognize my methods as necessary to achieve it.' To which I replied, that was just another way of saying the end justified the means. There may be a good heart inside of her, but her values and approach to life are all messed up."

CHAPTER 56

THE BETRAYAL
[Realm Two]

Antenor and his family lived far away from Fairhaven, in a smaller village. While not the strongest of wizards, he had long been a dependable member of the Council of WISDOM, and he was one of the wizards who had assisted in the casting of the Three Realms Spell. When his prior request to meet Mythral in an out-of-the-way tavern in Fairhaven went awry for several reasons, Antenor made a quick exit from the tavern.

His new request to meet with Mythral privately at Mythral's bookshop seemed somewhat unusual after his initial choice of the Black Cat Tavern. However, there was no reason for Mythral to decline, and so the meeting took place less than a week after Kit's confession.

Antenor arrived in a state of anxiety most unusual for the mild, not too terribly important wizard. Antenor insisted they talk in a backroom, out of sight, as he stared out the windows at the street.

Before Mythral could offer a seat or refreshments, Antenor confessed he had been spying for MorKano, because his family was being held hostage. He'd pieced events together after MorKano's agent failed to show up to debrief him and wipe his memory. Without the regular memory wipe, Antenor began to recall things. He feared his family never would be released by MorKano. He feared the worst for them. Mythral insisted Antenor sit down and start at the beginning. "Leave nothing out," Mythral demanded.

As Antenor's story unfolded, Mythral grew more and more certain he could delay no longer in confronting the dangers that lurked within MorKano's fortress. The time to challenge his vision of his own death was fast approaching. Antenor was spying for MorKano shortly before the Three Realms Spell, so MorKano had an inside track on the business of the Council of WISDOM. Antenor believed MorKano's impending plan was to break the Three Realms Spell. He said MorKano had found some power source sufficient to pull it off and was gathering his followers, along with anyone who could be bought or threatened, to support him in the effort.

Suspecting even more treachery, Mythral truth-read Antenor during the entire confession. Antenor's statements rang true, and Mythral suspected nothing was amiss. Antenor had little to add in the way of specifics. He never had been to Realm Three. His family disappeared about two weeks prior to the Three Realms Spell. He could not even identify who among MorKano's agents had delivered the blackmail ultimatum. His wife and two daughters would die a slow, agonizing death if he failed to do all that was asked of him. Antenor was forced to submit to a Memory Wiping Spell after each meeting. His memory had been slowly returning after the ritualistic wiping ceased.

Mythral considered how all of this was meticulously planned and that it had the feel of MorKano, whose intricate and devious planning had been legendary. After considering Antenor's story, Mythral summoned Kit and Perci for a meeting early the next morning. Events were moving too quickly, and most appeared to be beyond Mythral's influence or control.

Without any dissent from the other two, Mythral decided he and Kit finally must brave the dangers, thwart the plan, and prevent Mythral's potential death in Realm Three. If Mythral and Kit did not return after two days, Perci was instructed to inform the Council of WISDOM of the whole scheme. If Mythral and Kit had not returned, the Council should assume the worst and do what they thought best. Mythral suggested the Council strongly consider destroying the portal between Realm Three and Realm Two. While not permanent, that solution might buy them some time.

Mythral and Kit would sneak into Realm Three using the Translocation Spell. With Mythral's close supervision, translocation should be not too dangerous for Kit. Their secret entry at least would give them an element of surprise. MorKano's agents certainly would be watching the portal gate in Realm Three for Mythral in disguise. However, the fate of the Realms must be put on hold for one final rescue. After their trip to Realm Three, Mythral might not be able to help anyone ever again.

Mythral explained his plan to Kit and Perci. "I first will reverse the effects of the last Memory Wiping Spell used upon Antenor and attempt to determine who has taken his family and where they might be. If successful, Kit and I will rescue his family and bring them here temporarily for safety. We cannot alert or send members of the Council of WISDOM to do this. If anyone besides us knows what we are doing and why, our enemy in Realm Three might have advance warning. Once we have found Antenor's family and rescued them if possible, we must translocate immediately to Realm Three. Our visit today with Antenor, and certainly any attempt to free his family, will alert MorKano. We must arrive in Realm Three before word of our activities here in Realm Two reaches MorKano.

"As part of the misdirection, Kit and I will return to Realm One now. If anyone has found a way to track my movements, they will assume that, for the time being, I am safely away in Realm One. Early tomorrow, Kit and I will translocate back to Realm Two, avoiding any gate, and attempt to rescue Antenor's family. If that goes as planned, then we will translocate into Realm Three and initiate the second half of the plan. While any of us are in Realm Two and outside of this shop, no mention can be made concerning these plans."

CHAPTER 57

SAYING GOODBYES
[Realm One]

As Mythral and Kit arrived back in Realm One and made their way up the rotating spiral staircase, Mythral confessed he had another reason for returning to Realm One this evening.

"You really should talk to your brother and your foster parents this evening. I don't want to alarm you unnecessarily, but my survival tomorrow is a long shot. You, at least, have a better chance of returning from our trip to Realm Three intact. After all, the Law of Equilibrium assures me I will, in fact, die tomorrow. Your being at my side when I try to alter that fundamental event puts you in serious danger. Say your goodbyes to your family as best you can without the details."

With a note of nervousness in her voice, Kit responded, "How do I say goodbye without explaining why I am saying it?"

Mythral suggested this might be one of those times when a white lie for the benefit of others was justified. He suggested Kit tell them she was off to Portland with Mr. Hartly for a book show to do some buying and selling. She should say she would be gone only for the day but might be back late. With the basic story agreed upon, Kit then asked Mythral the obvious and most troubling question.

"What happens if I don't return? I mean, if we should not survive tomorrow, what will that do to my brother and my foster parents?" Mythral explained that he had arranged for that contingency as well. Should he and Kit not survive, then Perci would pay her family a visit.

"He will say we were in a car accident on the trip, and you died quickly and painlessly."

Because of this unavoidable discussion with Mythral, the real possibilities of what might happen tomorrow began to sink in. Kit started to realize how much her decision to assist Mythral might cause pain and suffering to her family. When deciding to become Mythral's apprentice, she had considered only how she might save her family from dark magic. She had not factored in their suffering if she failed to return.

A thought came to Kit, and she asked Mythral, "Could you wipe their memories of me with a spell? Then you could restore those memories if I survive. That way, they could avoid the pain of losing me. I cannot bear the thought of causing them such pain."

Mythral's reply was without hesitation. "Yes, I could do so. But I will not do it. I can tell you from my own personal experience of losing Vivyen, to have loved someone and dealt with the pain of losing them is better than never to have known them at all."

Kit said, "I understand you intellectually, but emotionally I cannot understand how it would be possible to live with the pain of losing someone you loved, like a brother or parents."

"The pain never will go away completely," said Mythral, "but time and distance provide perspective, such that you can choose how, and what, to remember. This will take some explaining, so I'll walk you home while we talk."

As they left the bookshop and headed through the woods to Kit's house, Mythral seemed to be wandering mentally as he reflected upon how much he liked Realm One. Just as Kit was about to remind him of their intended topic, she stumbled over a root crossing their path. "Strange," she said. "How many times have I walked this path without noticing that root?"

Mythral's words pulled her back to the present as she regained her balance and walked on. "That bit of trouble you just had with the tree root is a good lesson about pain and time. You might have fallen and broken a bone. Let's imagine for the moment you got a serious injury and could not accompany me tomorrow. There is no telling how serious the consequences of one small root might be for the Three Realms. Stop. Turn around and look at the root. What do you see? How big does it appear to you?"

Kit replied, "Well, I'd have sworn it wasn't there last time I came through here. Now it looks to be about three inches off the ground and about twenty inches long. I just cannot see how I missed it all this time."

They walked a bit further, and then Mythral said, "Forget about the past, and tell me, how big does the root look to you now that we are farther away?"

"I know that it has not changed in size, but from this distance it looks much smaller."

After a few more minutes of walking, Mythral said, "Now look at the root and tell me what you see."

"At this distance," Kit said, "I cannot see it at all."

Mythral smiled and said, "So this is the answer I learned with Vivyen's death. Time equals distance as we move along the Time-Path. Over time we travel away from an event. Time makes things seem smaller. Like the root, you know it still is back there, and if you ignore it, you do so at your peril. However, the more time and distance you put between yourself and the event, the broader the perspective. Your initial feelings and reactions to that event will soften over time. The event itself will not. How you feel about it and what you take from it moving forward are the things you can control.

"If your brother and foster parents were to lose you, their pain would be great. The hurt never would leave them, but with time and distance they can come to focus upon the good memories and occasions and, eventually, let go of most of the pain."

As she began to think she understood, they arrived at her home. She started towards the gate with a "goodbye" and "see you tomorrow" on her lips, when a thought occurred to her. She turned back and asked Mythral, "Did you put the root in my path?"

The corners of Mythral's mouth turned up, forming that smile that let you know you always would be two steps behind, and he said, "I'll see you at the shop early tomorrow. We have a lot to do."

CHAPTER 58

MYTHRAL'S DOUBTS
[Realm One]

As Kit entered her home, Mythral returned to the woods, the path, and eventually his shop. He really did not have anyone to bid farewell. Perci knew all about the plan for the next day. Kit would be going with him. Nobody ever knew if or when Cat would appear, and he certainly could not be summoned. Mythral would be staying this night in Realm One, pursuant to the plan. He and Kit would translocate to Realm Two in the morning to begin the attempted rescue of Antenor's family. By translocating, Mythral hoped to catch MorKano and his co-conspirators completely off their guard.

The next day, Mythral would face his death in some dingy corridor of MorKano's fortress. Mythral had no doubt that injecting Kit into the equation would change the battle he had sensed with those two powerful dark wizards. There was no reason he, with his advanced knowledge, or he and Kit together, could not easily overcome those two. The variable was the Law of Equilibrium. Very likely that law would find some way to neutralize Kit's impacts, and Mythral's life would end, on or close to schedule. He could wait no longer to confront his own demise that he had sensed so long ago in his cellar. What good would waiting do? MorKano had been getting stronger as time passed.

With the plans in place and the decision no longer in doubt, Mythral returned to his shop to attempt one final sensing of what the next day might bring. Even if he should not survive, perhaps he might sense something to ensure Kit's survival.

Mythral entered the shop and, contrary to his usual practice, took a moment to magically secure the door. There never had been a dark wizard in Realm One, but he needed to focus deeply tonight, and he wanted to be ensured that there would be no interruptions. After rotating the stairs 180 degrees, he made his way up the spiral staircase to the secret set of rooms. As he entered his private rooms, he again secured the door with a magic spell. He took time to prepare the room for this all-important session. He warmed it, so in his trance-like state he would not risk physical stress. He calmed his mind through a series of stillness exercises. Next, with a quick spell, the ceiling disappeared. From the outside it still was there, but from Mythral's point of view, only the stars were visible. Meditating under the night sky reminded him how small he was in the vast universe and allowed him to deepen his focus.

Continuing with mental calming and breathwork, Mythral settled himself into a comfortable reclining chair and stared upward. On this early September night, the Milky Way was a streak overhead, arching from northeast to the southwest with too many stars to count. Mythral had enhanced the already dark sky over this small town with a Light Blocking Spell, so the view could not be matched. His thoughts wandered. *There in the northern sky are the Big and Little Dippers and Polaris. Endless beauty. Makes the problems on this one little planet seem insignificant.*

After so many years of following this routine, Mythral quickly slipped into a deep state of meditation and was ready to use his gift of sensing. Near-term sensing usually was much clearer than efforts to sense far in the future. Mythral had great hope that this night's session would provide useful information for the next day's events. At first, all went well. He zeroed in on the rescue attempt first thing the next day, and the sense of it was quite positive. He was surprised by the seeming minimal effort and resistance. The details were not crystal clear, but this first half of the plan felt successful.

The second part began as smoothly as the first. He and Kit seemed to have made it to MorKano's fortress and successfully dealt with the two initial dark wizards in the corridor. Then things got murky. As Mythral had feared, the Law of Equilibrium was not letting Mythral live without a fight. In previous sensing sessions in tandem with Kit, Mythral had seen three overlapping Time-Paths surrounding the confrontation with MorKano, each unique yet all coming from a common event. Nothing in Mythral's experience could explain how this was possible. Mythral changed focus and tried to penetrate the fog around the actual confrontation with MorKano. However, no matter how hard he concentrated, he could not get clarity, nor even a sense of Kit's part in it, if any. Getting nowhere, Mythral returned his focus to the paths leading away from that event.

As before, he and Kit seemed to prevail over MorKano in two of the three overlapping endings, but one of those was unclear. The third led to his and Kit's imprisonment, with MorKano standing outside a cell door explaining some horrendously evil plan. It was disturbing how clear the details of the third dark path were, compared to the other two. Though the imagery was clear in Mythral's vision, the words MorKano spoke were not. The smug look of evil pleasure on MorKano's face could not be mistaken. Somehow, MorKano had won. He had outsmarted Mythral and was in control of the events to follow. Then, once again, the prophecy echoed in Mythral's mind as the sensing session faded: "Mythral's choice will doom or save the Realms."

CHAPTER 59

WHEN FORWARD PROGRESS STALLS, REVERSE.

[Realm One]

The lack of clarity was a surprise to Mythral. His quick mastery of sensing had amazed his mentor, who, upon realizing how clearly and far into the future Mythral was able to sense, proclaimed Mythral the most gifted wizard he had ever known. And yet, Mythral's best efforts to sense this relatively close future event produced only a confused jumble of uncertain paths. Never had his gift of sensing failed him so completely. The more he reflected upon his failure, the more his normally unshakable confidence eroded.

To risk his own life for the Realms was all well and good. He did that routinely. But what had he done to Kit? How could he justify taking her into a life-and-death battle when he could not clearly sense even a likely positive outcome? He always had been overly confident, even reckless, because of his great powers and fast reaction time. Had he gone too far this time? Had his desire to outmaneuver the Law of Equilibrium and avoid his fated death been so reckless that Kit might well lose her life in the bargain?

"Enough!" Mythral reined in his runaway doubts and did what he always was lecturing Perci and Kit to do. He calmed his mind again to focus upon the real problem. Mythral had made himself a bargain. If he could not sense an acceptable outcome for tomorrow's confrontation in MorKano's fortress, he would not take Kit with him. He might still go alone, but he would not endanger her.

Surely something in his past training or studies of texts from the forbidden Schools of Magic might help. Mythral instinctively knew he was missing something helpful, but he could not bring it to his conscious thought processes. His mentor had said something during Mythral's early training about a way to work around a problem when the future solution could not be readily sensed. As Mythral never had that particular problem, he totally forgot what his mentor had said.

Once again, Mythral went through his deep meditation routine, slowing his breathing and deepening his focus. This time not to sense but rather to recall Galapas's words. Mythral had been a particularly challenging apprentice that day, asking questions all morning, attempting to outmaneuver Galapas. The answer to his last question, about what to do when sensing fails, was the one he needed to recall. At last, the words were in focus. How could he have forgotten such strange advice?

What his mentor had suggested was the opposite of sensing. More along the lines of wishing. However, with morning only hours away, Mythral was ready to try anything. His mentor had said to visualize the desired outcome as realistically as possible, move along the Time-Path to that outcome, and then look backwards. From that vantage point, it just might be possible to detect the path necessary to reach the desired future.

Without much to lose but more sleep, Mythral gave it a try. He chose an outcome as simplistic as possible. At the end of the next day, he and Kit both would be alive and back in Realm Two. Mythral wanted to give this technique the best chance possible. The less he asked of the future, the more likely he might be to find a path to that future—at least, that was his hope. With his vision of the future firmly in place, Mythral deepened his focus.

As the envisioned future became Mythral's reality at a certain point forward along the Time-Path, Mythral turned, so to speak, and sensed back, in reverse. At first, all he saw was the same jumble of overlapping paths at the time surrounding the confrontation with MorKano. So, he tried backing away just a bit farther into the future--it worked. The three paths they had sensed before were not actually overlapping; they were separate and distinct, emanating from the one event.

One path led directly towards Mythral, the other two diverged—a distinction easily missed when too close to the event. But how could three Time-Paths lead away from one event, given the Law of Equilibrium? Mythral would figure out the anomaly later. In the now and here, he had his answer. A safe and positive outcome from the confrontation with MorKano was possible. It certainly was not guaranteed, but it was possible! Now what Mythral needed was some sleep before tackling the morning's agenda.

CHAPTER 60

GOOD DEEDS AND CONSEQUENCES

[Realm Two and Realm Three]

Things are about to move quickly to some sort of conclusion, so I'll stop inserting myself until it is over and done. And no, I won't give you any hints. Well, maybe just one. "Everything will be all right in the end, and if it is not all right now, then it is not the end."[2] You are about to find out what that really means.

Freeing Antenor's family turned out to be just as straight-forward as Mythral planned. Antenor's full memory was restored easily, and his refreshed memories told Mythral where Antenor had met MorKano's agent. With the location and a convenient piece of Antenor's wife's hair from her brush, Mythral and Kit translocated to the meeting site and cast a spell, *Tov-Noss Ned Antenor*, to scribe for the wife's location. *This is easy. Too easy*, Mythral thought. No spell had been cast to conceal the location. Perhaps MorKano's agent had been careless, or maybe MorKano just had assumed no one would be looking for the captives. Nonetheless, Mythral always got shivers down his spine when difficult situations resolved themselves this easily.

No one was guarding the family when Mythral and Kit arrived.

Perhaps those two taken by Perci and Kit had been the only dark wizards connected to the kidnapping. The family was confined by a spell around the house, and Mythral needed no time at all to dissolve it. However, finding them so quickly, and so far from Fairhaven, presented a new problem. *How do I get them safely back without giving MorKano a chance to react? This rescue, or the breaking of the spell, might have been detected. Once again, I face the old challenge to balance the welfare of a few versus the good of many. To delay any further risks our mission and even our lives. That, in turn, puts the Three Realms in grave danger. Yet, why save this family, only to abandon them so far away from safety?*

Mythral excused himself to step into another room and returned seconds later with Perci. The presence of three rescuing wizards instead of two should not raise any questions or imply a Translocation Spell. He told the family Perci would escort them to the safety of Mythral's bookshop. Mythral insisted they speak to no one for two days, not even to Antenor. To do so, he explained, would put all of them at risk. Having been fooled by Antenor as MorKano's spy under a Memory Wiping Spell for all these years, Mythral quickly but deeply truth-read the family and found their agreement with these conditions to be willing and honest.

Having sent Perci and Antenor's family on their way, Mythral said to Kit, "I always have had my suspicions and reservations about good deeds. I really wish I could avoid doing such deeds, because they often seem to lead to more trouble for the doer. But I just can't seem to stop."

Kit said freeing the family really was necessary to remain true to who she and Mythral were. Even if saving them was not too important in the big scheme, integrity was worth the consequences. She suggested Mythral cut back on the less important good deeds.

Mythral cryptically replied, "The 'less important' good deeds often are those that make the greatest difference."

Mythral's countenance turned severe as he asked Kit, "Are you ready to end MorKano's schemes, and possibly ourselves?" Kit merely nodded in agreement. She did not trust her voice to hold. Once again, they formed a mental link so Mythral could watch and guide Kit through the Translocation Spell. Inside her head, Mythral told her, *Translocating between Realm Two and Realm Three is a bit severe. Just like this morning's jump from Realm One to Two, when you come out, you will be temporarily discombobulated. Adrenaline usually compensates quickly. Just be ready. We will arrive outside MorKano's fortress. I have done some prior reconnaissance, in disguise, and I know a way in.*

As they made the jump to Realm Three, Kit's doubts, long buried under the excitement of training and learning, arose in her conscious mind. She had prepared for this moment for months. But was she ready? Would she let Mythral down? Such thoughts soon were banished by her focus upon the spell, *Pathu Athrada*, and then her complete disorientation. Obviously, they had arrived in Realm Three. Mythral's control over both their spells was so smooth, she did not even notice.

That was Mythral in a nutshell. Always in control. Even when others were involved, it was Mythral who acted, Mythral who chose what and when. Despite his caring and compassion, he rarely gave much consideration to what others thought and said. He simply had a very high opinion of himself and unshakable confidence in his own judgement.

As they collected themselves and headed towards the fortress wall rising in the distance, Mythral curiously began talking about good deeds again. *Probably to distract me from my fears*, Kit guessed.

"Truth be told, there are not many who understand this, but a good deed, no matter how small or big, can change the world around you. The ripple effect of even the smallest of good deeds can be especially powerful.

"As a practical example, a great practitioner in any area of expertise, be it magic, music, woodworking, or anything else, might inspire young novices to pursue the same. A few might have success. But the impact is limited to those who already possess the talent, the opportunity, and the determination to excel in that specialized area.

"Much greater is the impact a common man or woman has when they are seen doing the right thing, regardless of personal consequence or sacrifice. Everyone has the potential to emulate these simple good deeds. Anyone can be inspired by such examples. The greater the personal sacrifice made for such selfless acts, the greater the impact upon those who witness it or hear about it."

With that, MorKano's fortress came into view. From a distance, it looked like a massive black rock dropped into a burned, barren field. Kit never had seen anything so foreboding. As they got closer, a feeling of dread enveloped her. Mythral and Kit arrived at the fortress wall. "Now what?" Kit asked.

A smile briefly flickered across Mythral's lips as he replied, "MorKano isn't the only one who can lay plans well in advance. Shortly after I sensed my own death in this fortress, I arranged a diversion to ensure MorKano would not be home. In one part of my vision, which I have told no one, as I was dying, I could clearly hear MorKano's laughter. I believed as long as MorKano was not home, I would be safe. MorKano never allows anyone into his fortress when he is not there. His paranoia was my security. In his absence, I translocated here and entered his fortress and explored a bit. His defenses are quite good, but not good enough. After learning all I could, on my way out, I decided to prepare a secret entrance, should I ever have need to enter quietly. Would you like to guess just where that entrance lies?"

CHAPTER 61

ENTRAPMENT
[*Realm Three*]

*T*he wall of MorKano's fortress is old but solid. It radiates an energy barely perceptible, a Protection Spell, no doubt, thought Kit. *That would explain the lack of vegetation.*

With a short spell, Mythral's secret door revealed itself immediately in front of them. As she entered, the hair on the back of Kit's neck prickled. She was overwhelmed by a feeling of pure evil. Kit shook her head to clear her thoughts and focused on the task at hand. Mythral's thoughts arose through the fog of evil surrounding her. *One of MorKano's many defenses is a very powerful Befuddlement Spell. In addition to many traps, that makes an intruder easier to ensnare. However, Brigantia's robes should protect you while you're in the fortress.*

The passageway ahead of them was completely dark, because there were no windows on this level of the structure. As they turned the first corner, Kit wished they could use just enough magic for a little glimmer of light! As they stepped further around the corner into complete darkness, Kit asked, "Where to?"

Mythral sighed deeply and continued to communicate mentally, *We have two choices: Confront my demise head on, or try to avoid it and seek MorKano immediately. The second option is more appealing, but logic and the Law of Equilibrium tell me I must first face those two wizards waiting for us. Avoidance is not a choice with the Law of Equilibrium. We must change the outcome, and that means facing those two wizards first.*

With yet another choice made by Mythral, he whipped out a very small cylindrical object, and the damp dark passage suddenly was illuminated by a small, soft white light. "You brought a flashlight!" said Kit in an accusing tone. "You told me I never could bring any unfamiliar objects, especially science-based ones, out of Realm One."

Before Kit could continue accusing Mythral of violating his own rules, he explained, insistent upon mental communication, *When I first was here, I could not explore the entire fortress. MorKano had extra spells protecting the upper levels, where he likely lives, and the dungeons below. I had insufficient time to work around those spells without disturbing them. So, I explored the main floor and this level immediately below it. They contain the great hall, some common rooms, a dining room, a couple of guest quarters, and a kitchen. All were very spartan and without interest, showing little or no use. As I suspected, once I got past the main door on my first visit, I encountered many traps and spells waiting for intruders. Magic in any of these unlit lower areas would have set off MorKano's alarms. So, on that first trip, as on this visit, I brought this flashlight to avoid the use of magic inside of the fortress. After all, what good is it being the one who makes the rules, if you can't make exceptions as needed?*

Kit conceded, but then she raised another objection. *What about kitchen and housekeeping staff? How did you avoid them on your earlier visit, and how will we avoid them now?*

Mythral, as always, had an answer for everything. *I had discerned no one is permitted inside of the fortress in MorKano's absences. Today, however, MorKano is at home, and our confrontation with the two wizards is about to happen. Some staff may well be around, but not likely on this lower level. Enough questions for now. Now is the time to face and defeat my would-be killers. I could do so alone, with what I learned from my sensing vision, but the Law of Equilibrium would not let that stand. Something much more unexpected must occur this day, and I feel certain that, somehow, you are part of that something.*

Towards Mythral's envisioned death the two of them moved. Because

Mythral now knew where in the fortress he would find those wizards, getting there was easy. On the way, Mythral explained his plan. As soon as they entered the corridor from his vision, Kit rushed ahead to the nook into which Mythral shortly would fling himself. As she entered the nook and prepared for the next phase, the two dark wizards attacked Mythral from behind and in front. All went according to Mythral's vision, with one important alteration. Now when he flung himself into that nook to avoid the Killing Spell, beside him would be an unexpected Kit, one of the Realms' strongest wizards, even if as yet untested.

As Mythral jumped out to launch the Entanglement Spell, *Gonathra*, towards the wizard in front, Kit released a Blocking Spell, *Balan Tafnen*, to the rear. The rock walls of the corridor behind them were hot and singed by the rear wizard's Killing Spell that had failed to reach Mythral and his mysterious new companion. The rear wizard's moment of surprise was just the opening Kit needed, and she quickly immobilized him. Mythral, having dealt with the wizard ahead, was whirling about to help Kit with the one behind. But Kit needed no assistance. As they secured these two with additional spells to avoid any interference from them, an evil laugh rang in their ears. Mythral told Kit he had heard the laughter in his initial vision of this encounter.

Kit said continuing was too risky, given the magical commotion they just had made. Why not take their two wins—Antenor's family and Mythral's survival thus far—and come back at a later, less expected time? Mythral acknowledged the wisdom of her suggestion but insisted risk taking was necessary from time to time.

As they proceeded further into the fortress, Mythral explained his thinking. *The old Hippocratic oath, "Do no harm,"[3] certainly is a good principle but it is not always helpful in the most difficult situations, and it can be an easy way for weak people to avoid taking responsibility. Solving a problem sometimes requires doing some degree of damage. If certain options are precluded by the "do no harm" rule, failure is much more likely. A choice, or refusal to choose or act, that results in failure is easier to justify if one can argue no harm was done. But pain and evil may be left to grow by failing to take a better option. Panic and brain freeze are the body's defenses against intellectually or emotionally valid actions that might violate the "do no harm" maxim.*

If we retreat now, my secret entrance will be discovered. We never again will have this same element of surprise. Time is not on our side, and this may be our one opportunity to stop MorKano.

Kit was not quite ready to agree with Mythral's logic. She suggested they let fate decide their course of action. If what they had just accomplished was the Inherently Unbalancing Event they hoped for, then Mythral's life and the Realms' future were secured—for a while. If not, they would press on. Mythral, without necessarily agreeing with Kit's reasoning, consented to a quick sensing session. As they paused their progress and joined minds for a quick trip into the future, they both sensed an ever-darkening landscape of confusion, where Mythral's death was not clearly imminent but possible, and three apparently overlapping Time-Paths seemed to be the origin of the darkness. After exiting the session, Mythral looked inquiringly at Kit, and, receiving no further objections, they moved on to locate MorKano and to put a stop to his plans.

CHAPTER 62

THE SPIDER AND THE FLY
[Realm Three]

MorKano had expected Mythral to survive the initial trap and was ready for him and anyone he might have brought with him. MorKano had set a second and stronger trap, but not with magic. This new trap would neutralize the magic of Mythral and his companions when they confronted MorKano in the great hall where he now awaited them. MorKano long had considered Mythral the only wizard strong enough and smart enough to stand in his way. Therefore, MorKano had instructed his spy, Antenor, to report back anything Mythral said or did in the Council of WISDOM. Right away MorKano was skeptical about this subject of "science" that seemed to bear such significance to Mythral. Realm Two and Realm Three had some rudimentary "science," but its usefulness seemed limited to the old, mostly forgotten art of potion making.

Yet, the topic seemed to run as an undercurrent throughout much of what Mythral had to say, and even on occasion appeared to be something he feared. So MorKano had "encouraged" some lesser wizards to learn all they could of science, or explain their failure during a session of his favorite torture methods. The results were disappointing at first—especially for the wizards who failed. After much trial and error, MorKano finally found the right wizards with the right skill set for the job.

The smartest wizard set to the task actually found something quite useful from the limited knowledge in Realm Two: an odorless, colorless gas heavier than air that, in concentrated form, would render someone confused or incapacitated. The less smart but more devious wizard devised a method of using the heavy gas against Mythral. Pour the gas into a room with blocked access points and a heavy curtain across the entrance. Upon entering, a victim would be completely incapacitated in mere moments.

MorKano added his own twist by standing on a dais above the gas, to watch his would-be confronters. The real beauty of this plan was that a wizard's normal defenses would be useless against the non-magical gas. Unless Mythral had come prepared to find science being used against him in Realm Three, he soon was to be an ignorant fly caught in a spider's brilliantly laid web.

Once again, Mythral was suspicious of how easily he sensed MorKano's presence. From his earlier explorations of the fortress, he knew MorKano was in the great hall just ahead and to the right. However, he did not know that the hall had been reconfigured so it had just one entrance on the lower level. An entrance which Mythral was approaching now. Mythral also was unaware of the poison gas that filled that hall. And while he that suspected MorKano might be aware of his presence in the fortress, he did not know MorKano anxiously awaited his entry into the great hall. MorKano intended to greet Mythral from his position high up on the dais.

Mythral, expecting the obvious traps, fortified his defenses and readied his spell to divert any incoming magic harmlessly and instantaneously into another dimension. As his final preparation, he instructed Kit, with her minimally tested powers, to stay out of the line of fire. One on one with MorKano, he had no doubts as to the outcome. As he approached the great hall, Mythral could sense only MorKano, though perhaps others were concealed nearby. MorKano definitely was planning something, but Mythral had a few magic tricks for which MorKano was unprepared.

As Mythral parted the heavy curtains hanging over the entrance, he only briefly noticed they were new. Before he could consider why, Mythral had entered the great hall and was now face to face with MorKano, if not eye to eye. MorKano stood on a platform a dozen feet or more above the floor. Defenses at the ready, Mythral invited MorKano to join him on the floor only to find his voice unsteady. Mythral quickly realized something was amiss. His own magic was faltering. He no longer could focus or concentrate. His final act before succumbing to MorKano's evil and unnecessarily painful Entanglement Spell was to mentally tell Kit to get out, because her magic could not defend against this trap. Mythral quickly and easily was ensnared.

Because they had maintained their mental link, Kit sensed what was happening to Mythral. Her years of experience in Realm One enabled her to identify this non-magical attack. Unlike Mythral, and every other wizard in Realms Two and Three, Kit had no built-in biases that would keep her from considering Realm One-type solutions. She could sense the effects upon Mythral's mind. Since Mythral had not drunk or eaten anything in Realm Three, gas was the only answer. Ignoring Mythral's instruction to leave, Kit instead rushed to his aid.

As she pushed through the curtains to enter, she was ready. She used the Catapult Spell to push the gas in the room up and out of the openings around the top of the room. Her main objective was to clear the gas away from Mythral, in case it was lethal. Her maneuver had an unexpected benefit, because it sent the gas directly towards MorKano, who momentarily was distracted while protecting himself with a spell of his own.

Quickly, Kit determined Mythral was alive, but before she could rouse him, she found herself alone to defend against the worst of the dark wizards, with no Mythral, no Perci, not even Cat by her side. At first, Kit held her own, which surprised and worried MorKano. No one other than Mythral should pose such a challenge to his powers. Who was this mere girl? Kit's lack of real experience in magical combat was, however, her downfall. MorKano backed her towards his original position in the room, and her sightline included the image of Mythral lying helplessly on the floor. That distressing image, plus her lack of stamina, gave MorKano the opening he needed to penetrate her Blocking Spell. As she lost consciousness, Kit wondered if she should have tried Mythral's Siphoning Spell. She had yet to really practice it, and Mythral was dead set against MorKano learning about it—but now he might simply be dead.

Soon Kit and Mythral, surprised to be still alive, found themselves imprisoned in a specially designed cell. Many layers of spells were woven into the cell's six sides so no magic could enter or leave the cell. The only good Mythral could find in their present situation was, while they were alone in this cell without magic, MorKano and his followers could not torture them, except with words—which was just what was on MorKano's agenda.

Kit told Mythral he had walked into a room full of gas, which quickly had rendered him confused and then unconscious. She briefly described her battle against MorKano and her defeat. The shame at having failed against MorKano was in her voice and was all over her face. Mythral comforted her by saying, "At least you put up a good fight. I just lay down and went to sleep. If I should actually survive this, let's try to keep that part out of the history books."

Not long after their imprisonment, MorKano appeared at the cell door to gloat through the bars and to twist the proverbial knife into Mythral. "When the fly falls into the spider's web, that fly may as well abandon all hope," were his first words to Mythral.

His second foray was a scornful rebuke of Mythral for bringing only a mere girl to their confrontation. Despite the words, Mythral detected a hint of respect for Kit. MorKano's bragging about his clever use of Mythral's precious Realm One science to defeat him was somewhat deflated when he learned Kit already had explained it to Mythral.

MorKano had expected, hoped for, several strong wizards to fall into his trap. The more wizards he could sacrifice, the easier it would be. "Easier what would be?" asked Mythral. Hoping for some useful information, he encouraged MorKano to talk. MorKano ignored Mythral's question for the moment, to stay on course, continuing to emphasize Mythral's foolishness in going first into the trap.

"You should have sent the girl to spring the trap. By sacrificing her, you might have had a real confrontation with me. That's what I would have done in such a situation."

Mythral replied, "I have no doubt about your willingness to sacrifice others. What you call smart, I call despicable and wrong."

MorKano replied with an ugly and chilling laugh. "Then it looks like smart is better than right!"

After poking Mythral about Kit a bit more, MorKano decided to plunge the knife all the way in and watch Mythral suffer. Time to let Mythral know his Three Realms had been controlled and directed by MorKano every step of the way; his greatest achievements were nothing but a house of cards, allowed to stand only to suit MorKano's purposes.

MorKano took great pleasure in explaining his brilliant subterfuges and deceits. "My scheme began before the Three Realms Spell was cast. I have been manipulating things all along. The information leading you into Realm Three was planted. Knowing the Council was up to something, I blackmailed Antenor by holding his family hostage. I required him to keep my agents apprised of the Council's plans.

"I disliked the idea of two realms. The absence of access to easy non-magical victims meant I had to seek out weaker magical victims instead, which might draw attention to my activities within Realm Two's magical community. Such a threat to the magical community would create more resistance to my takeover. So I had my spy on the Council of WISDOM suggest three realms, by pointing out the added ease and comfort the extra realm would provide when dealing with us dark wizards.

Finally, MorKano came to his most cherished piece of the puzzle, by which he intended to destroy Mythral before killing him. MorKano continued telling his story with gleeful venom in his eyes.

"Before you and your Council of old men could cast the Spell, I arranged to lure Vivyen into a public venue and murder her. I wanted you to know who did it. Vivyen's death was a mere convenience to me, to ensure you would be too preoccupied and heartbroken to see the flaws and dangers in the Three Realms solution. Vivyen's death would have the added benefit of guaranteeing I'd be one of the few 'lucky' wizards who got sent to Realm Three as part of the initial Spell.

"Oh yes," he nearly shouted, "I wanted to be sent to Realm Three, and it was so easy to manipulate you into doing it for me. The freedom of Realm Three, without monitors or spying eyes, allowed me to strengthen my powers and develop my plans in secret. You fools on the Council thought you were so smart and so safe in Realm Two!"

Savoring the look of utter failure and pain upon Mythral's face, MorKano delivered the final insult. "You asked earlier what 'it' was. Well, I have some news that is good for me and bad for you. Your death, and your companion's here, and a few other wizard prisoners, will be used to break your Three Realms Spell. You, the great Mythral, will be remembered as the key figure not only in casting that Spell, but in dissolving it! The magic released upon your death will be extraordinary. I'll use that release of magic, in lieu of cooperating dark wizards, to overcome and break the Council of WISDOM's Spell that sustains the Three Realms."

MorKano's exhilaration was obvious as he turned to leave, but he had one last barb to drive home. "I go now to prepare for the undoing—of you and that Spell. Rest well for the next few hours; I'll need your strength."

CHAPTER 63

HOW DID THIS HAPPEN?
[Realm Three]

If ever there has been a time when self-recrimination is justified, this is it! Mythral despaired. The Law of Equilibrium would have its way after all. Mythral would die very near the time and place he had sensed so very long ago. He never should have deceived himself about the chances of creating an Inherently Unbalancing Event.

How vain and selfish I have been! This wasted time and effort, trying to preserve my life, at the expense of preparing the Council of WISDOM to function without me. And now Kit's life will be sacrificed as well. All because of my selfish attempts to change the Time-Path in ways the Law of Equilibrium never would allow. MorKano was right. I am a fool. I have allowed myself and the Council of WISDOM to be manipulated by MorKano.

He then rehashed his mistakes and failings aloud for Kit to judge and condemn him before their execution. "I should have sensed easily the now-obvious flaws in a Three Realms solution." MorKano had seen that in the beginning. Why did I miss it? Why did I never look more closely at Vivyen's death? Why did MorKano attack her? Why then? Sensing my future death, I abandoned scrutiny of that specific Time-Path and chose, instead, to spend my time and energy trying to alter the future.

"Somehow, I failed to read Antenor's falseness when receiving the information that sent you and me into Realm Three. But then again, Antenor most likely had been manipulated by MorKano to believe his information was true.

"You were right—we should have taken our initial wins in Realm

Three and left to fight another day. But not me, not the great Mythral! I believed I could deal with any situation. I think I know so much. I need never listen to what others, including you, have to say. Kit, I am so very sorry for what I have done to you and for what is about to be done to you in my name."

Having constantly surprised Mythral in the past, Kit did not disappoint him now. "Fine, apology accepted," she said. "You may be ready to give up, but I am not. This may be one of those impossible dilemmas you are so fond of creating for me. Let's see how you deal with it! On two separate occasions, in that dream at Nate's and our recent sensing session, I saw myself working a very complex and dangerous spell with MorKano. While working a spell with MorKano doesn't sound good, it does mean my story is not over. My life will not end the way MorKano expects. If that spell work with MorKano is in my future, there may yet be a future for you as well.

"Now it is your turn to solve the impossible dilemma. Magic cannot enter or leave this cell. So a Translocation Spell is useless. We are unlikely to have the chance when they remove us for the sacrifice. We likely will be gassed or stunned before leaving here. We cannot use physical force on the cell. I have been trying that while listening to your rant. No doubt we'll be outnumbered when they enter the cell to take us, so physical resistance is futile. So now you, the great and all-powerful Mythral, get to show your brilliance and solve this riddle. You get to think outside the bag, the box, this cell."

CHAPTER 64

DESPERATE TIMES
[*Realm Three*]

With Kit's final words, an idea began to form in Mythral's mind. An impossible idea no sane person would ever consider. But what choice did he have? The greatest wizard of all time sat here imprisoned with his teen protégé. The Three Realms were doomed to chaos. Evil now ruled most of Realm Three. If MorKano's plans worked, a flood of evil soon would be unleashed upon a unified realm with all the inhabitants of Realms One, Two, and Three at grave risk.

For all his foresight and knowledge, the only option Mythral had left was an unproven Time Inversion Spell. Its success never had been documented, but its failures were legendary. So difficult to control, the Spell took two extremely powerful wizards working in perfect harmony to balance enormous magic. And here he sat, contemplating its use with a novice wizard whose wielding and controlling of such power was untried.

Still, she was a novice of remarkable talent and potential. The Spell's alleged last attempt predated Mythral's training. His mentor had mentioned a time when a great Void had threatened the long-term future of the one realm. His mentor's teacher and another powerful wizard had attempted the Spell together as their best hope of altering the future Time-Path upon which the oncoming Void would consume all. The greatest wizards of that time with a talent for sensing all had confirmed the end of the universe was approaching.

Yet the Void had not come. Was the sensing of so many wrong? Had that Time Inversion Spell actually worked? The debate lasted many years with no resolution. One of the two spellcasting wizards had died from

240

powerful dark magic, and the other had gone completely mad. The impact of their efforts remained a mystery. Their fate after attempting the Spell was certain.

This was the Spell Mythral now contemplated. The Time Inversion Spell would send him and Kit back along the Time-Path. There in the past they could use their knowledge of the future to alter critical events. Perhaps he already had attempted to invert time and was now in a state of madness. Mad or sane, he had only this one remaining hope. While magic could neither enter nor leave their cell, time was not so constrained. Time had to flow.

As with the creation of the Three Realms, "Mythral's Choice" always was the determiner of how mistakes got fixed or problems got solved. But, really, was there a choice this time? Instead of failing at the Time Inversion Spell, he and Kit could choose to check out early.

The Death Spell did not require much from a cooperating party. The end would be painless for both of them. That way at least MorKano would lack their life energies for the reversal of the Three Realms Spell. A false victory, though, and a temporary one. MorKano would simply find and sacrifice others as needed. Certainly, other members of the Council of WISDOM could be abducted to replace Mythral.

No, an early exit from this universe was not the choice for Mythral. But could he really attempt a Time Inversion Spell under these conditions, and with Kit as his balancing partner? Attempting this Spell had two potential benefits. First, they most likely would die from the attempt. Denying MorKano their life energies might disrupt his impending attack on the Three Realms Spell--for a while. A delay would give Perci time to notify the Council of WISDOM. The other possibility is that they might succeed.

Even if he and Kit cast such a Spell, they still needed perfect timing in ending the Spell. Once ended, how would he know what change might bring about an Inherently Unbalancing Event? Reversing time to get a do-over wasn't enough. What if the Spell worked, but Mythral's chosen changes to the past failed to generate an Inherently Unbalancing Event? The Law of Equilibrium would still compel his death, and maybe that of Kit as well.

What if his choice did more harm? Might he unleash the all-consuming Void? If he did nothing, the universe would survive, and MorKano could be opposed by those who survived. But if Mythral acted and it all went wrong, there might be no universe left.

Mythral caught himself invoking the "do no harm" excuse and immediately abandoned that thought. Then he was seduced by another procrastination tactic: *Why do these choices always fall to me? Have I not chosen often enough, and well enough, to pass this final impossible choice on to someone else?* Alas, there was no one else in the now and here—no one but Kit. Nor would he place such a burden upon one so young and inexperienced. Then he caught himself worthlessly "ifinating." Time was quite limited. He must focus upon the choices available and do his best.

His thoughts returned to the Time Inversion Spell. When properly conjured by two powerful wizards, the flow of time would reverse. More than two would throw off the balance and harmony. The standard flow of time was thought of as linear: the past was behind you, the present was around you, and the future was in front of you. Understood this way, the past already had occurred, and the future was yet to be written. All false assumptions given the nonlinear nature of time.

As the Time Inversion Spell took hold, the casting wizards, and only they, would begin to sense time flowing backwards. To them, the future in that Time-Space Continuum would appear to be behind them and the past now in front of them, as if they had turned 180 degrees. As they approached the past, they could choose when to end the Spell and step back into their Time-Space Continuum. They would do so with retained knowledge of the future from which they had cast the Spell.

Those around them at the point on the Time-Space Continuum to which they had returned would be without knowledge of the future. They had yet to experience it. Having returned to the past with full knowledge of the future, the casting wizards could make a choice, sensed or calculated, as to how best to generate an Inherently Unbalancing Event. Hopefully, creating a better future via an alternate Time-Path. Knowing what choices or actions could produce a positive Inherently Unbalancing Event would be the really tricky part.

CHAPTER 65

WHY ME?

[Realm Three]

If the Time Inversion Spell worked—and that was a very big if—then Mythral's choice would be critical to the Realms' salvation. He and Kit must be careful not to make any unintentional changes. Focusing on the one critical change needed would leave no time for pondering or sensing the effects of any secondary changes.

If the Spell and the change created an Inherently Unbalancing Event, they would be on an alternate Time-Path. They would be unable to return to when and where the Spell began on their original Time-Path. If successful, the new future would be determined by the Inherently Unbalancing Event and the choices they made, intentionally or unintentionally.

Yet, even Mythral's best guess at this critical change was just that—-a guess. His ability to sense the future might not be available when exiting the Spell. So the consequences of his choice may be unknown and unknowable in the here and now. Creating an Inherently Unbalancing Event in the past and generating an entirely different and new alternate future, how could anyone know the rules for that?

What if my guess, my choice, unleashes the Void again, or some other disaster? What if I make evil stronger? Isn't it still possible that someone else could eventually defeat MorKano? But then Mythral remembered his vision of the future in which he and Kit died. In that possible reality, dark magic won.

And for the second time in the last few minutes, he caught himself ifinating. The seductive habit distracted the ifinator from his responsibility to choose or to act. When looking for an excuse, a way out, or a rationalization, asking "Why me?" was an easy place to start.

The Time Inversion Spell required confidence and absolute concentration, with no room for uncertainty. If he allowed himself to be distracted, or to create doubt in Kit's mind, they likely would end up dead, lost in time, or utterly mad.

I have always had clues about the correct choices at critical moments. Usually time permits a sensing session for confirmation. Now and here, I have but one clue to the correctness of choosing a Time Inversion Spell: The right choice almost always is the hardest. That makes the near-impossible Time Inversion Spell a frontrunner.

Easier paths and choices simply test the weak-willed and teach lessons to those who would avoid responsibility. The right path is the challenging choice my teachers and elders said builds character. Mythral certainly had built up plenty of character over the years.

Time was limited, at least in the now and here. He must clear his mind and search for wisdom to make this choice. It seemed that the prophecy was true and that the fate of the Realms depended upon Mythral's choice. He must be as certain as possible of that choice. He could do no more.

As Mythral cleared his mind, he went back to the beginning of the current disaster. He searched for answers. What key moment would he change? He thought of MorKano's use of science against him in their final confrontation. Mythral had been so caught off guard by the gas that MorKano had captured him without a fight.

Certainly, he and Kit could escape the gas knowing about it in advance. But overcoming MorKano's traps might not be enough to create an Inherently Unbalancing Event. Defeating yet another dark wizard's attempt on his life just did not seem to be a truly drastic change to a fundamental event. However, it was all he and Kit had. Defeat MorKano and go forward from there. Once they accomplished that, they would have to wait and see how the Law of Equilibrium responded. Maybe, just maybe, the Time Inversion Spell itself would be enough.

CHAPTER 66

LET THE SPELL BEGIN.
[*Realm Three*]

Finally, Mythral gave up seeking certainty and proceeded with the Spell based upon sheer hope. He explained it all to Kit. Mythral mentally conveyed to Kit the basics of the Spell into which they must pour an enormous amount of power. Despite their mutual uncertainty, they joined minds and proceeded with the Spell. Kit mostly was on the sidelines, providing supplemental power and balance.

Mythral's mind was mostly closed to her. Yet she could feel him grappling with the Spell's complexities. Before he began, he admitted to having only read about it in the Schools of Magic. He was so fascinated by the idea of time travel that he memorized the Spell. Kit tried not to let the thought disturb her. Their lives, and the fate of the Realms, hung upon Mythral's ability to recall one immensely complicated Spell.

She could feel Mythral straining to get certain mental images and details just right. Mythral, who routinely performed complicated tasks without thought, now was under pressure. Kit stayed in the mental background so as not to interfere.

What truly impressed and scared Kit was the amount of magic Mythral was exerting on his part and extracting from her. She hadn't known the depths of the magic within her. Should she survive this day, she comprehended Mythral's source of enormous power and now her own.

As the Spell began to gel around them, Mythral sent Kit a mental warning not to lose focus. If they failed to keep focus and balance the power between them, they would be forever lost in the nonphysical part of the Time-Space-Continuum. Their bodies would die. Just as his warning penetrated her wandering thoughts, Kit grasped its meaning. She barely maintained her balance and focus as the final pieces of the Spell coalesced around them. Never before had she felt such pressure during a Spell. Strangely, instead of pushing in or down upon her like gravity, the pressure pushed outward, as if her very soul was trying to exit her body. She felt—-no, she knew—-that were she to lose her focus and balance, some critical piece of her would be lost into whatever lies beyond. If she faltered, the same would happen to Mythral.

Surprising herself, and certainly Mythral, who was observing her mental state while dealing with his own focus, Kit took a deep calming breath and settled easily into a deeper state. Sensing Mythral's approval helped her go even further. She had reached a point in both the Spell and her life where she possessed the confidence to accept whatever was to be.

Her life, at fourteen years, had been quite short, but what a life she had lived! Only three months ago in Realm One time, she had sat in her room, wishing for adventure. *Girl, be careful what you wish for*, she thought. If her life were to end with this Spell, in this effort to save Mythral and the Realms, she would be satisfied. Settling even deeper, to a level she did not know was possible, Kit focused upon maintaining the balance of power in the present moment. Nothing existed for her but her support of Mythral and the now and here.

Kit reached out to him with her mind for the first time since the Spell began and said, *I have the power balanced. You do what is needed.* She got no reply but sensed an increased strain upon her as she continued to balance the energies flowing between them. Then Mythral's thoughts were open to her. He no longer was shielding his thoughts and worries from her. Instead, he had accepted her as an equal partner and allowed her to listen in on his internal debate.

CHAPTER 67

A SPELL TO UNDO THE FUTURE
[Realm Three]

Mythral's past now lay in front of him. The past was like the future had been--amenable to free will. Using the Time Inversion Spell, the past was alterable by actions taken when the flowing backwards stopped and the spellcasters reentered the Time-Path. Being inside of the Spell kept one from impacting events until the Spell was ended and you stepped out of it into a specific point on the Time-Path. Then the changes began!

The Spell is working! Kit has proven herself up to the task with unexpected skill. She remains firm and balanced. That special connection between us must have played a critical role. But for how long? I have seriously underestimated her. Yet another mistake. So many errors in judgement of late--can I really trust my choices? Yet, I must not delay in choosing when to step out of the Spell and what events to alter.

He was about to undo the past and remake the future. Even after finally committing to this desperate act, Mythral still had no idea of what specific change to make and at what point in time to make it.

Until just moments ago, he'd kept his doubts and uncertainties hidden from Kit. Initially, he could not afford to have her distracted by his own doubts. Now she had proven herself his equal.

He was Mythral, the greatest wizard of any age, a title given to him by others. A title he had not disputed too loudly. He had done everything possible to avoid this terrible "all or nothing" gamble with the fate of the Realms. He had performed the impossible Time Inversion Spell with the assistance of a novice wizard—and a girl, at that. And both had come through it with their lives and sanity intact, which is more than could be said for the last two wizards who had attempted it.

Still, he had no idea of how to proceed. He struggled to untangle the web of possibilities and to discern the Inherently Unbalancing Event he needed so desperately to create. Every second he struggled prolonged the Spell, increasing Kit's chances of getting overwhelmed and losing concentration.

He could stop the Spell just before he entered MorKano's hall, disperse the gas he now knew about, and confront MorKano. But what if MorKano had a backup trap?

He could go all the way back to the Three Realms Spell and insist upon two Realms instead of three. Although, that would leave MorKano and an ongoing battle with magic in Realm Two. The most tempting, and dangerous, option was to go further back and save Vivyen from MorKano's death-trap. It was a selfish risk he could not take. Make too many major changes to the past, and who knew what the combined impact would be? No. Mythral restrained himself. *I must change only enough to ensure a better future.*

Mythral tried one last time to sense the future based upon some of the choices he had been considering, but no one could understand sensing during a Time Inversion Spell. Would he be sensing the impacts along the present Time-Path, or an alternate Time-Path yet to be created by his Inherently Unbalancing Event? Using all the energy and concentration he dared to spare from the Time Inversion Spell, Mythral sought one last time to sense the future.

Very dimly it came to him. He explored all the potential Inherently Unbalancing Events and all corresponding future paths. Each one was even more dark and evil than the future they now knew. He sensed absolute chaos, imbalance, and a singular realm. One thing stood out about the potential dark and evil futures: Kit was not there. In some, Mythral survived for a while, but not for long. None of this was of any help. He knew not whether he was sensing the fallout from a failed Spell or the ripple effects of a successful one.

He could not risk everything by rushing his choice, but neither could he risk certain disaster by delaying too long. During all of this, there had been nothing but silence from Kit. Mythral had forgotten that they were linked and that his doubts and frustrations now were being shared with her. Her sudden mental intrusion into his reflections brought him back to the present and their imminent danger.

Kit spoke without words directly into his mind. *What you search for cannot be known by operation of the mind or by reason. You have told me this quite often. It must be felt or known instinctively. I had to shut out the past and the future to avoid losing my mind at the beginning of the Spell. In doing so, I found harmony with the universe, and I can feel what needs to be done. I know when we need to end the Spell and what to change. Mythral, give over control of the Spell to me. Our chance to act is nearly gone, and there is no time to explain. Let me make the choice now*!

The possibilities raced through Mythral's mind. *Had she already gone mad? Could this mere girl novice have gained the knowledge and insight that so eluded the great Mythral? Could the "choice" that would forever change the fate of the Realms be trusted to such an inexperienced young girl?* All reason and logic weighed against abdicating his responsibility for making this final choice.

Is this merely another "Why me?" test? Am I being offered another easy out? She described exactly how I expect to know the correct choice. I was taught, and I taught her, that when a choice is right, it resonates in harmony with the universe. I can feel that certainty in her now. But the insane could sound certain as well, could they not?

I am in control of the Spell. I am at its center. She merely balances the energies. She cannot act unless I release control and swap our roles. I wish I could believe in her clarity of vision, because I have none of my own.

Yet, the prophecy clearly said the fate of the realms rested upon Mythral's choice, none other. Could she really be right and the prophecy wrong? Surely not! He had made up his mind. He would end the Spell just prior to entering MorKano's hall. He would levitate the gas so it would reach and immobilize MorKano. If the gas could not be levitated, he could levitate himself and fight MorKano at his own elevation. With his ability to siphon off MorKano's firepower into another dimension, there would be no real contest.

Unless, Mythral hedged, *MorKano has yet another backup plan.* He knew he would leave Kit unprotected if he failed. *But she is a strong and competent wizard.* Then he would let the future take its course. *If the future isn't sufficiently altered, then two other wizards could try again,* he reasoned. He had reached this decision right before Kit's intrusion into his thought process.

CHAPTER 68

MYTHRAL'S CHOICE IS MADE

[Realm Three]

Mythral, let me control the Spell now, or all is lost, Kit's calm voice was saying. Yet again, Mythral was faced with another of life's confounding paradoxes which seemed to be noticed only by those who sought certainty in doing the right thing. The prophecy said that Mythral must choose, but for the first time since becoming a master wizard, he had no clear sense of what choice to make. Another whom he trusted claimed to know what choice needed to be made, but she was not Mythral.

He could delay no longer. Mythral cleared his mind one more time with the intention of acting on his prior choice, when it came to him. Clear and certain it was. Both the girl and the prophecy were right! Mythral made his choice, as declared by the prophecy. The Spell ended.

Yet, the universe would be forever altered, not by the actions to follow in the confrontation with MorKano, but by Mythral's choice immediately prior to ending the Spell. His choice created the Inherently Unbalancing Event.

Mythral chose, for the first time in his life, to surrender control to another. Mythral's decision to trust his young protégé, and to trust her certainty, was "Mythral's choice." Paradoxes rarely exist except in perception. Mythral chose to relinquish control to Kit, thus placing the fate of the Realms in her hands. Mythral's choice was to let Kit choose.

His choosing her, first as an apprentice, then as a protégé, and now as his partner in confronting MorKano, led to her being the second wizard in the Time Inversion Spell. She was present and ready to make the final choice because of all his choices concerning her. Such choices as when to end the Time Inversion Spell must be felt as correct and balanced. Kit had felt that about her choice. Mythral had not.

As soon as he decided to hand over control to Kit, he could feel the unmistakable shift to a balanced and better universe. Only the two of them would know what might have been. Now there would be a future with Kit and Mythral both in it.

Mythral's pride had held him back only briefly. As they came out of the Time Inversion Spell, he had to know why Kit had chosen this moment to end it. He had to know what he had missed. What had she sensed during the Spell that gave her such certainty? Kit almost laughed out loud as she recognized another role reversal happening. Mythral was seeking knowledge and enlightenment from her.

She answered his question in an unexpected manner. Once the Spell ended, the future was changed for the better. Events would happen to seal the deal, and the Law of Equilibrium would ensure it. They were predestined to have a good outcome, based on the future she and Mythral now could sense ahead of them. Mythral's ultimate choice had created an Inherently Unbalancing Event and changed the universe forever. What they chose to do next with MorKano was much less important.

CHAPTER 69

SECOND TIME AROUND
[Realm Three
and Realm Two]

Kit had chosen to end the Spell after their defeat of the two dark wizards who had been sent to give them a false sense of success and just prior to their entering MorKano's gas chamber.

Kit told Mythral she would enter first this time. Now they knew the trap awaiting them was not fatal. MorKano wanted his victims alive so he could use their energies to undo the Three Realms Spell. Before entering, Kit would attempt to neutralize the gas based upon something she learned at school.

If she succeeded, then Mythral could defeat MorKano. If she failed, Mythral could try his backup plans. As they learned from their first confrontation, MorKano was so confident in his trap that he had no backup wizards to support him. Perhaps he had been concerned that the presence of too many dark wizards in the fortress might spook Mythral and make him turn back. With this foreknowledge, Mythral easily could surprise and defeat MorKano after Kit had dealt with his non-lethal trap.

All went as planned. Kit remembered a downward-leading staircase just before the entrance to the great hall where the trap was set. By gently levitating the curtain a few inches, the heavier-than-air gas used by MorKano could escape slowly. As it exited the hall into the corridor, Kit created a draft to carry it to the staircase, where gravity took over and drew the gas down to a lower level.

Without any way to calculate the exact volume of the gas or how long it might take to escape, she knew there was risk in both stopping too soon and waiting too long, lest she raise MorKano's suspicions.

When she felt that she had diverted enough gas so it was below head level and MorKano was none the wiser, Kit took MorKano completely by surprise. Entering the room designed to trap Mythral, she asked, while slowly circling to her right, "Will you surrender quietly this time?" Her voice cracked just a bit on this last bit of bravado. She knew that her experience in magic duels was limited. She never had fully attempted to use Mythral's Siphoning Spell. Yet, with her deeper level of magic newly discovered during the Time Inversion Spell, perhaps she could defeat MorKano. Instinctively, MorKano attacked with a powerful and deadly bolt of magic. With her newfound reservoir of magic, Kit had no trouble deflecting his attack off to her right, away from where Mythral would enter. *If this is his best, I could take him myself,* Kit sent to Mythral.

Maybe, Mythral replied. *But let's not let over confidence ruin us again.*

So, Kit remained a distraction, to allow Mythral to maneuver into the room and off to the left side—an addition to the plan before they reached the hall, in case they encountered a second layer of traps. Mythral's height would give him sufficient warning, should Kit start to show any effects from the gas. Kit had volunteered to be the "canary" that alerted Mythral, instead of miners, of unsafe conditions. MorKano was so taken aback by this small, insignificant girl challenging him that Mythral's entrance went unnoticed. The girl's phrase "this time" was somehow unnerving.

"If you won't answer her, then hear me. Surrender, MorKano, because otherwise I will make you pay for what you did to Vivyen." Again, MorKano was surprised and startled when he heard Mythral's voice from the opposite side of the chamber.

MorKano, clearly rattled and unprepared for the turn of events, spun towards Mythral with his defenses fully activated and hurled his reply with a bit too much volume. "You should have attacked when I was not looking.

Now, here in my stronghold, I'll finally end the great Mythral's career as savior of the realms. You were a fool not to attack first." Even before the words were out, a deadly spell was hurled towards Mythral. His plan to capture Mythral alive was in ashes. MorKano's plan now was to survive this unexpected one-on-one battle. Or was it two-on-one?

Mythral easily deflected the first assault and replied, "Unlike you, I never would attack from behind, or without offering you a chance to surrender." Again, Mythral had to deflect an incoming attack. As he suspected, MorKano was far too strong to be defeated with any spell until his energies had been nearly exhausted. Mythral settled in for the predictable outcome.

Mythral attacked occasionally to keep the fight going, while MorKano's incessant attacks were diverted harmlessly into the old standby alternate universe. Within ten minutes, even Kit could tell MorKano's magic was seriously depleted. Obviously, Mythral knew as well. Mythral's next attack was a Stun Spell delivered at full volume, and it broke through MorKano's failing defenses.

The battle was over.

While MorKano was unconscious, Kit and Mythral translocated him to Realm Two and the safety of Mythral's bookshop. MorKano soon was sent, unconscious and under heavy security, to the most secure cell in Realm Two.

CHAPTER 70

WHAT REALLY HAPPENED BACK THERE?

[Realm Two]

Immediately after Kit and Mythral's return from Realm Three and MorKano's imprisonment in Realm Two, the Council of WISDOM demanded an explanation from Mythral. The rendering was brief, taking only three hours. However, the use of the Time Inversion Spell to manipulate the outcome of the battle with MorKano was omitted in the retelling. As Mythral was the one narrating and even he wasn't completely clear on all the details surrounding the Time Inversion Spell, he felt it prudent to skip that part of the story. Who would believe it anyway?

Once Kit and Mythral settled in at the bookshop after the Council briefing, Mythral could wait no longer to hear from Kit all the details of the Time Inversion Spell and how she knew what to do. As if cued by some offstage manager, Perci and Cat walked into the room as Kit was about to begin her explanation.

Initially reluctant to share his embarrassing failure with Cat and Perci, Mythral then thought better of it. These two, more than anyone else, needed to fully understand what had happened. Even more important, they needed to fully comprehend Kit's role and importance in saving the Realms. To speed up the process of getting to Kit's part of the story, Mythral gave Cat and Perci a very short summation, with the assurance that Kit could add the details later.

Almost without taking a breath, Mythral explained, "We had information from Antenor, whom I thought was a reliable source. We freed his family that had been held as leverage for his spying in Realm Two.

We then translocated to Realm Three and successfully defeated the two wizards who had killed me in my sensing session long ago. Then, against Kit's excellent advice, I chose to continue further into MorKano's fortress and seek him out.

"Everything was part of MorKano's long con game, from the Three Realms Spell, to restoring Antenor's memory, to rescuing Antenor's family, and even defeating those two dark wizards in MorKano's fortress. In the end, we were captured in MorKano's gas chamber because I failed to consider all possibilities, and I failed to treat Kit as an equal in our misadventure. We were about to be sacrificed by MorKano in his attempt to end the Three Realms Spell, but we managed to escape by using a Time Inversion Spell."

Disregarding Perci's gaping mouth, Mythral continued, "After the Spell took us back to the confrontation with MorKano, Kit volunteered to neutralize his gas trap. I approached safely from the side. Who could have guessed MorKano would use science against me? We defeated MorKano, and he now is safely imprisoned here in Realm Two.

"Before you crashed our little party, Kit was about to fill in the specifics concerning the Time Inversion Spell, which is no doubt the part about which you have the most questions. Kit will do the explaining because," and here Mythral blushed for the first time since he was a child, "I failed to understand what was needed during the critical timing of that Spell. I had to turn control over to her. Now, if the two of you will stifle all of your immediate questions, I want to hear from Kit just what happened during that Spell."

"Mythral was so focused upon the past and future, he overlooked the all-important present. He could not detect a potential Inherently Unbalancing Event for our situation in the past or in the future, because that necessary event was in the present, our present, inside the Time Inversion Spell. Since my focus had been solely on the present, so as to maintain my sanity, I could feel the one choice that resonated with the universe as true and best.

"Only one choice could undo the darkness that lay behind us—in our future—as the Time Inversion Spell hurled us into the past. I knew beyond a doubt Mythral's final choice had to be the hardest thing he ever had done. As Mythral always lectures, the hardest choices nearly always are the right choices.

"I wasn't sure if Mythral could bring himself to do it, to give up control. But I knew what would create an Inherently Unbalancing Event. For Mythral, the most all-knowing and utterly self-confident wizard of all time, to leave the most important decision the Realms ever had faced in the hands of someone else. Only that would knock the universe so far out of balance, it just might create an opportunity to change the future.

"Before the Time Inversion Spell, we successfully avoided Mythral's originally sensed death at the hands of those two dark wizards. However, we had succeeded only in shifting Mythral's death slightly in time and place. Adding me to the mix hadn't really changed the Law of Equilibrium. My presence alone was insufficient to generate an Inherently Unbalancing Event.

"However, when Mythral chose to let a young female wizard take the reins of the most significant and dangerous of all spells, the universe shifted, and the Law of Equilibrium could not adjust quickly enough. Mythral's surrender of control marked the end of an era. The Mythral who never shared his burdens, choices, responsibilities, or nightmares with anyone was no more. I suspect even Vivyen rarely was granted access to Mythral's inner world.

"I'd been convinced, towards the end of the Spell, that Mythral did not have it in him. His stubborn refusal would have doomed the Realms to the darkest of futures. I had sensed, as Mythral had, some evil even greater than MorKano's control of all three realms lay beyond.

"Had Mythral clung fast to his need for control, the Realms' fate was something so wholly devoid of light and energy that, rather than emanate evil, it just seemed to suck the life from everything. When Mythral summoned the courage and trust to relinquish the spellcasting to me, he made the choice that was prophesied. The choice that would save the Realms!"

As they continued to discuss the specifics and share more details with Cat and Perci, Kit thought back to something Perci had said to her. She wondered if he ever had discussed it with Mythral, because, in hindsight, it explained everything. Mythral had been at the center of his own story and the story of the Three Realms for so long, he failed to recognize the uniqueness and significance of others' stories. He couldn't see anyone's story but his own being the most critically impactful. Who knew, going forward, what role her story and Mythral's story would play in shaping the Realms' future?

CHAPTER 71

THE END
[Realm Two]

If you believe the above chapter heading, you haven't been paying attention. The Time-Path has no end.

Mythral's choosing Kit as an apprentice and protégé, and then choosing to relinquish control of the Time Inversion Spell, did seem to have saved the world—at least in the near-term. For the time being, life was good!

Good had defeated evil. We have our happy ending. So now and here is an appropriate stopping point in Kit and Mythral's story. There is more, so much more in their future, but I'll leave that for our next meeting.

For now, know this: Deep in the structure of the universe, something still is wrong. Very wrong. Kit and Mythral can sense it but cannot name it--yet.

ENDNOTES

1   Attributed to Edmund Burke, including by John F Kennedy in a speech in 1961. Burke didn't say it, and its earliest form was by John Stuart Mill, who said in 1867

2   John Lennon

3   "First do no harm" is incorrectly attributed the Hippocratic Oath. Its actual origin is unknown.